DEAD of AUTUMN

Sherry Knowlton

Mechanicsburg, Pennsylvania   USA

Published by Sunbury Press, Inc.
50 West Main Street, Suite A
Mechanicsburg, Pennsylvania 17055

www.sunburypress.com

For information about special discounts for bulk purchases, please contact Sunbury Press Orders Dept. at (855) 338-8359 or orders@sunburypress.com.

To request one of our authors for speaking engagements or book signings, please contact Sunbury Press Publicity Dept. at publicity@sunburypress.com.

ISBN: 978-1-62006-476-4 (Trade Paperback)
ISBN: 978-1-62006-477-1 (Mobipocket)
ISBN: 978-1-62006-478-8 (ePub)

FIRST SUNBURY PRESS EDITION: September 2014

Product of the United States of America
0 1 1 2 3 5 8 13 21 34 55

Set in Bookman Old Style
Designed by Lawrence Knorr
Cover by Tammi Knorr
Edited by Jennifer Melendrez

Continue the Enlightenment!

For Mike and Josh with love.

Evil is unspectacular and always human,
and shares our bed and eats at our own table ...
                    — W.H. Auden, *Herman Melville*

Do not think lightly of evil that not the least consequence
will come of it. A whole waterpot will fill up from dripping
drops of water. A fool fills himself with evil, just a little at a
time.
                                    — The Buddha

Chapter One

Russet leaves spiraled like crimson dervishes and soared past the battered Land Rover as Alexa traveled the winding forest road. She luxuriated in the solitude of this early morning drive. At this time on Sunday, most people were either in bed or at church. Later in the day, this mountain road would be overrun with leaf peepers trying to catch the autumn foliage at its peak.

Alexa thought of this forty-minute drive to the nursing home as a trade off. She loved the journey more than the destination. Ever since the stroke, these visits with Grandma Williams could be heartbreaking. One of the advantages of moving home to South Central Pennsylvania was seeing her failing grandmother.

As the Land Rover sliced through bars of sunlight angling through the trees, Alexa mused.

This is so much better than sitting in some church. It's like meditation on wheels.

Alexa glanced in the rearview mirror, her thoughts interrupted by the whining English mastiff behind her seat. "Scout. What's the problem, buddy?"

Hearing her voice, Scout whined louder and draped his huge head over Alexa's shoulder.

"OK, OK. Do you have to make a pit stop, little guy? There's a place we can pull over soon. You'll just have to wait a few minutes."

Nothing but uninhabited state forest land stretched for miles around them. Alexa planned to stop at a parking area ahead. The trailhead parking lot was filled with cars most days; hikers in the summer and snowmobilers in the winter. This morning, Alexa expected that she and Scout would have the place to themselves.

A shaft of sunlight tinted a maple blood red. "Check out that tree, Scout. The color is unreal."

Screeeech. Alexa jumped and jerked her eyes back to the road. A white van barreled around the curve ahead. The van's left wheel careened across the solid yellow line. Startled, Alexa gripped the wheel hard and edged the Land Rover toward the berm to avoid a collision. Scout scrambled to keep his balance when the Land Rover's big tire hit a pothole on the asphalt lining the edge of the road.

Finally, the oncoming driver took control and guided the van back into his own lane. Alexa glimpsed two men wearing camouflage in the front seat as the van blew by her, still speeding much too fast for the twisting mountain road.

"Assholes," Alexa yelled. "Scout, the morning has totally lost its Zen." She managed a shaky laugh. "That guy might drive like a bat out of hell, but he's never going to win the Indy 500 with a beat up old van like that. No. With that camo look, they probably have their sights on NASCAR, not the Indy."

Still shaking slightly, Alexa pulled into her favorite spot, grabbed a leash and a big red ball from the passenger seat, and let Scout out of the car. The dog bounded out looking for the nearest suitable tree.

Zipping her light fleece jacket, Alexa drank in the velvety scent of the autumn woods, rich with the powdery spice of dry leaves and the darker tannins of forest decay. She ambled into the trees with Scout close behind, wanting to put some distance between the dog and the road.

"OK, Scout. We can take a few minutes for fetch before we go see Grandma. Come here."

Scout levitated off the ground spinning circles in the air, excited to chase the ball, one of his favorite games. The fawn-colored dog dashed back and forth after the ball, crunching the fallen leaves. On the fifth throw, Alexa recognized the signs. Scout was tiring.

"Last one, Scout," Alexa warned as she arced the ball high into the air, but her throw went astray. The ball clipped a low-hanging branch, plummeted to the ground, and disappeared over a small hill. The mastiff chased after the ball as it hit the dirt and rolled down the far slope.

For a few seconds, Alexa lost sight of both Scout and the ball. She rushed in their direction, calling out to the dog. She stopped dead in her tracks then sprinted when she heard Scout barking furiously. When the pitch of his bark rose to a high keen, an icy tremor fluttered down Alexa's spine.

Frantic thoughts of bears, porcupines, and animal traps flew through Alexa's mind as she reached the top of the rise. She slowed as she caught sight of Scout about twenty yards away. Still yelping, the red ball forgotten at his feet, the mastiff seemed riveted by a bushy area near the small stream.

The dog didn't appear to be hurt, but she still worried that some wild animal was involved. This state forest saw several cases of rabies every year, and she didn't want to confront a rabid fox or other animal. She picked up a fallen branch.

Despite repeated calls, Scout would not come to her. Alexa continued to edge nearer, her heart thumping. She glimpsed a bright flash of pink at the far base of the mountain laurel and wondered why Scout would flip out over a pile of trash. Tensed to flee, Alexa tiptoed still closer to Scout and whatever had him behaving so strangely.

A slight, blonde girl lay completely still beneath the mountain laurel, a patch of her torn fuchsia blouse lifting on the breeze. Her legs, clad in trendy blue jeans, skewed at an impossible angle to her waist. Her back rested on a pile of scarlet leaves, right arm flung above her head; blue eyes staring sightless at the sky.

Alexa gasped and let the branch slip from her fingers. She reached out to grip Scout's collar, and the dog immediately stopped his keening. An abrupt silence fell over the forest. The sudden quiet unnerved Alexa. The small slope blocked any sounds of traffic from the road. She could hear nothing except the muted burble of the creek and the dry rustle of autumn leaves.

The murmur of the dying leaves seemed to whisper a warning. Alexa scanned the surrounding area, but she and Scout were alone.

Alone with a dead body.

"Don't lose it here, Alexa," she muttered and reluctantly forced her gaze back to the young woman. Struggling to maintain control, Alexa let out a shriek when a gust of wind tore through the forest, tangling a shriveled brown leaf in the girl's silky, white-blonde hair.

Alexa finally regained her composure and began to deal with the situation. "Sit," she commanded Scout and broke her desperate grasp on the dog's collar. She snapped on his leash and slipped the looped handle over her left wrist. Steeling herself, Alexa knelt and touched the girl's neck, searching for a pulse. From the utter stillness of the body and the sightless eyes, Alexa knew instinctively that the girl was dead. But, she had to check.

When she found no heartbeat, Alexa jerked her hand back in horror. The girl's taut flesh felt cool, as if it had absorbed the chilly morning air. Alexa scrambled to her feet, fingers burning as if they'd rested too long on ice. Then, she fled back to the car for her cell phone, dragging Scout on his leash behind her.

Chapter Two

More than an hour later, Alexa perched on the open tailgate of a state park SUV. State police cars and rescue vehicles filled the gravel parking area.

She watched local volunteer firemen in fluorescent vests stand in the middle of the two-lane road to direct the mounting volume of traffic. The leaf peepers were out in full force. The volunteers, likely farmers from the nearby township, had difficulty concentrating on their traffic duties and gawked at the novelty of this huge police investigation.

Despite the swirl of noise and activity, Alexa felt numb. Although she had seen a few dead bodies in her twenty-nine years, all of those had been carefully arranged in caskets at a funeral home. Her only experience with violent death had been seeing her old dog hit by a car when she was eight.

Rocking back and forth on the tailgate, Alexa took deep cleansing breaths. The girl had looked so young and vulnerable, her body just lying out under the bushes, exposed to the elements.

Alexa had already waited forty-five minutes for the state police to arrive, and she was still waiting for them to interview her. She couldn't help but feel a nagging sense of guilt for abandoning the girl in the woods.

Scout slept in the back of her Land Rover, calm in familiar territory and unfazed by the beehive of activity outside the vehicle. Wrapped in a blanket from one of the ambulance drivers, Alexa couldn't get warm, even with the midday sun shining directly on her upturned face. The family said that Alexa took after Grandma Williams, who had been pretty feisty in her day. Right now, Alexa was having trouble connecting with her feisty gene.

5

Alexa studied the two policemen who approached from the tree line, obviously headed in her direction. The men both clocked in at six feet or more. Maybe the state police had a height requirement for the job, Alexa speculated. The younger policeman had kind brown eyes and dishwater-blonde hair. Dressed in a brown corduroy sports coat and tan chinos, he looked like a third-year law student—too young for police work.

The other cop wore a serious expression on his weathered face. The gray sprinkled through his close-cropped brown hair denoted his seniority. On a Sunday morning in the forest, this one wore a suit and tie. Something about the aggressive way he moved suggested an athlete, maybe a former hockey player with that scar on his temple.

"Miss?" To Alexa's surprise, the baby-faced policeman spoke first.

"Williams. Alexa Williams." She slipped off the tailgate and stood to face the two cops.

"Miss Williams. I'm Trooper Taylor and this is Corporal Branche; we're with the State Police Crimes Investigation Unit. We have some questions for you."

"Sure. I'm not sure what I can tell you that will help." Alexa hesitated and then words tumbled out. "Was she murdered? She was so crumpled. She looked like she had just been thrown there. She can't be much older than nineteen or twenty. Maybe a college kid. How could this happen here in Michaux?"

A uniformed park ranger joined the group. The ranger, who towered over the two policemen, introduced himself. "Hello. I'm Reese Michaels from DCNR. I am acting as the liaison for this case from the state park side of things."

Taylor turned back to Alexa and said, "We still need to have the coroner rule on cause of death, Miss Williams. But clearly, this death is questionable, and it is possible that she did not die back there in the forest. We hope that we'll find answers to all of those questions as we investigate this young woman's death. Right now, we need to know how you came to find the body."

Alexa walked the three men through the entire tale of her stop at the parking area and Scout leading her to the girl's body. She didn't try to describe the panic that had seized her when Scout started his frenzied barking or the cold, shuddery way she felt even now.

"Did you see anyone else here when you arrived? Any cars in the parking area?"

"No. It was deserted ... not surprising for the time of day."

Ranger Michaels said, "It sounds like you are familiar with this area. You knew about the trail and the stream?"

"Yes. I've spent a lot of time hiking around here. In my high school years, this hike along Tumbling Run was a regular weekend outing."

"Tell us a little bit more about yourself, Ms. Williams. You said you were going to visit a nursing home. Is that right? Why did you come on this road? What sort of work do you do?" Trooper Taylor took over the questions again.

"I was on my way to visit my grandmother at the Three Pines Nursing Home over in Franklin County. This road is the most direct route from my home. I'm an attorney. I work at my family's firm, Williams, Williams, and O'Donnell in Carlisle."

"Your husband didn't come with you this morning?" the Ranger asked with a quick glance at her left hand.

"No husband. I live alone."

"So, tell us again. Why did you walk down to the stream where you discovered the deceased?" Trooper Taylor questioned.

"I was chasing after Scout. He's actually the one who found the body." Alexa shuddered. "I've never heard him howl like that. I thought he was hurt."

"Did the dog disturb the body?"

"I don't think so. He was alone with her for a few seconds before I got to the top of the hill. But, the whole time I saw him, he stayed a foot or so away from the body."

"What about you? Did you touch the body?"

"I am pretty sure that I told someone this already. Yes. I touched my fingers to her neck. I was trying to find a pulse. But, she felt so cold. On the cop shows, they always say like marble. But that's not right. Her skin felt cold, but it had texture." Alexa rubbed her fingers on the leg of her jeans as she rambled on.

"You said there were no cars in the parking area. Did you see anyone in the woods?"

"No. I looked around after we found her. But I didn't see anyone. It was really creepy to be out there alone with a dead body." Alexa remembered the eerie whispering in the trees and her panic as she stood over the dead girl's body. Tears started to stream down her cheeks.

"I'm sorry. This whole experience has been a little overwhelming. I thought I could keep it together, but this has been an awful morning." She wiped at her eyes with her sleeve.

"We understand that this must have been a difficult for you, Ms. Williams. As an attorney, you understand how important it is to get all the details in a case like this."

"I practice civil law. But, I understand that you need to ask me these questions. The girl looks so young. It seems so wrong that her body would be out here in the woods. How could that happen?"

"That is what we aim to discover through our investigation." Trooper Taylor finished by handing her his card. "Thank you, Miss Williams. That will be all for now. We may be contacting you again. Let us know if you think of anything else."

As Alexa turned toward her car, Corporal Branche broke his silence, "Did you know this girl?"

Alexa pictured the porcelain face framed by white-blonde curls and the wide, vacant blue eyes. "No. I have no idea who she is. I didn't know her." Then, almost as if someone else was speaking, Alexa heard herself say, "But something about her seems familiar. It's hard to tell, seeing her like that. I think I may have run across her somewhere before."

The park ranger ended up driving Alexa home in her Land Rover. Alexa insisted that she could drive but didn't protest too vigorously about the arrangement. In truth, she continued to feel a little shaky. She was embarrassed about crying during police questioning, but every time she thought of the girl under the mountain laurel, tears came to her eyes.

After assuring Alexa that he could handle a stick shift, the ranger said he'd take her home and then have someone from the park pick him up from Alexa's house.

"It's a fairly short drive," she told him. "My place sits on the border of the park over near Hunter's Ridge."

Alexa had not fully appreciated the ranger's size until he folded himself into the Land Rover. His curly brown hair almost brushed the roof of the car. His broad shoulders and lanky body completely filled the narrow seat as his tanned hand reached confidently for the gearshift. Given her morning's experience, Alexa found his presence surprisingly reassuring.

Ranger Michaels kept up a constant stream of chatter as he drove. "I'm fairly new to this area, so you'll have to direct me to your house. I started my assignment at Pine Grove Furnace State Park earlier this year, so I don't know all these rural roads yet."

"OK, there are only a few turns."

"I really enjoy Pine Grove and the state forest. It's beautiful here. My last assignment was in the northwestern part of the state."

They had driven a few miles before Scout roused himself to come forward and check out the stranger. "Hey, buddy." Alexa said to the mastiff. "You must be exhausted from this experience."

"Who's this?" the ranger asked.

"Scout, meet Ranger Michaels."

"I don't think I've ever seen a dog quite this big," the ranger marveled. "You are such a handsome fellow, Scout."

He continued to chatter. "We always had dogs at home. I thought my black lab, Blackie, was a big dog. He was a peanut compared to this guy."

"You had a black lab named Blackie?"

"Yeah. What can I say? When you're six years old, you keep the names pretty simple. He was a great dog. Loved to jump in the neighborhood pond and chase ducks. My dad tried to take him hunting once. That was a disaster. The dog didn't understand that he was supposed to wait until Dad shot the ducks before he retrieved them."

"My second dog was a chocolate lab," Ranger Michaels continued.

Alexa made an effort to respond. "Let me guess, his name was Cocoa?"

"No. My family had gotten much more sophisticated at the whole dog-naming thing by then. We called him Hershey."

Alexa groaned. She liked this guy's goofy humor. "The lane to my house is just around this bend. It's on the left." A few minutes later, she pointed to her house ahead.

Alexa's home sat between a grove of towering pines and the rise of the mountain behind. A small grassy area in front of the cabin provided enough open space for sunlight to reach the house.

Ranger Michaels parked in front of the house. "This is a great place."

Alexa was touched by his concern when he hopped out to open her door.

"This place belongs to my parents. Even though they live nearby in Carlisle, they've had this cabin for years. We spent most of our summers here when I was a kid. When I moved back home and needed a place of my own, they said I could stay here. They don't come here as often since my brother and I are grown. Luckily, Mom won't live without all the modern conveniences, so the place is outfitted for year-round living."

Alexa continued to talk as the ranger opened the back door and Scout jumped to the ground. "I really like it here. It's great for Scout; plenty of room for him to romp and no close neighbors. I appreciate the peace and quiet. I spent my college and law school years in New York City. After years of the city, I'm happy to be home."

As he listened, the ranger fished his cell phone from a pocket. When Alexa saw him begin to dial, she warned, "You probably won't get reception here. I can only get it on the deck, sometimes. If it doesn't work, you can use the phone inside."

She walked up the steps to the wide deck and the front door beyond, her tall, lanky driver following. Scout already stood at the door, panting to be let in the house. "Hey, boy. You've had a crazy morning, huh? Go in and get some food and water."

She opened the door, and the mastiff dashed through. "He'll sleep for hours this afternoon," she said to Ranger Michaels, who had taken a seat on one of the deck chairs.

He held his cell phone at arm's length, waving it in circles. "You're right. I can't get any reception; zero bars. I need to call back to the station and get someone to pick me up."

"Sure. I really appreciate you putting yourself out to bring me home. You'll need to use my landline. Follow me." She led the ranger into the cabin and pointed out the phone in the living room. "Help yourself. Can I get you something to drink? Water, Coke, coffee?"

"Water would be great."

Alexa filled two glasses with ice water and carried them back out onto the front deck. She lowered her body into a weathered teak deck chair. With the afternoon sun warming her face, Alexa listened to the wind sighing in the pines and realized that she felt a little better now that she was home. In a few minutes, the ranger joined her and sat at the nearby patio table companionably sipping his glass of water.

"Mr. Michaels, I can't thank you enough. It was a pretty traumatic morning for me, and you made it easier by driving Scout and me back here."

"Call me Reese, please. I think you've held up pretty well. Not too many people could have a random encounter with a dead body and not totally fall apart. You dealt with the cops; you didn't need sedation; you're back home on your own. I suspect you're going to be OK."

He ran a hand through his thick brown hair and grimaced. "I didn't stumble upon the body the way you did, but it hasn't been a run-of-the mill morning for me either. In my job, I've dealt with two people who drowned and a few hikers and campers with heart attacks or serious injuries. Nothing like this."

As Alexa listened to Reese talk, she realized that the attractive ranger wasn't much older than she. "Will the park investigate this situation? Do you have training in unexplained deaths and things like that?"

"One of the requirements for the job is municipal police training. But most of the crimes that we deal with are things like drunks fighting in the campgrounds or kids setting the woods on fire with firecrackers. Sometimes, we work with the state police on crimes that take place on state land, usually poaching or drug deals. On something this big, we won't take the lead. That's the state police role. I'll just help with logistics, like today, or assist them on issues that relate to the park."

When a white SUV with green markings approached down the lane, Reese stood up and reached into his jacket pocket. "Here's my card. If you think of anything that you forgot to tell us or if you just need to talk about this some more, call me. You had a rough day."

She stood at the top of the steps as he walked to the passenger side of the car. A fresh-faced young woman in a park uniform sat at the wheel.

The ranger paused before he opened the passenger door, and said, "Maybe you should call someone to come out here with you. Your mom and dad? A boyfriend?"

"I'll be fine. Thanks, again."

Alexa watched the SUV pass along the pines and disappear from sight. Her parents were on one of their trips to someplace exotic, a month in the Amazon and other stops in South America. Realistically, she couldn't call them. She didn't feel the need to disturb her brother, Graham, either. Sundays were one of the few days he got to spend with his young family.

"As to the boyfriend, would I say that Caleb fits that category?" Alexa mused. The answer to that question was not clear, but she certainly didn't need him to come babysit her. She and Scout would do just fine.

Alexa shivered as she walked into the house, chilled by an unbidden thought. The young blonde lying under the mountain laurel would never again be fine.

Chapter Three

"Finally." Alexa sat up in bed the minute the alarm rang. She pushed the dog snoring beside her. "Scout, we have to get up." She yawned. "At least one of us got some sleep last night."

She rolled out of bed and headed for the stairs. At the top of the staircase, Alexa jumped aside as the giant mastiff lumbered by, desperate for his morning run. Downstairs, she opened the front door wide. After Scout barreled past her, headed toward the pines, Alexa rushed back upstairs to dress. Although the cabin sat in the middle of hundreds of acres of forest, Scout never wandered very far. Alexa could let him run on his own without worry.

Alexa tried three times before she could corral her swirl of curls into a loose chignon. As always, strands of honey hair streaked with lighter blonde highlights immediately escaped to frame her face. Looking in the mirror, Alexa saw a medium person—medium height and weight, not willowy but certainly not fat; medium hair, not blonde but not brown; medium hazel eyes, neither green nor gray. Surprisingly, men seemed to think that all of these medium aspects combined quite nicely.

She straightened the jacket of her severely cut black pantsuit and slipped on her most comfortable black heels. Finally, Alexa arranged a raspberry silk scarf around her neck, her small defiance to the expected uniform of a junior attorney in the firm of Williams, Williams, and O'Donnell.

Throwing an old barn jacket over her suit, Alexa carried her breakfast of steel cut oatmeal and orange spice tea out to the front deck. She wanted to grab every last minute outdoors. In a few weeks, the mornings would be too cold for the luxury of an outdoor meal.

"Scout, come. I have to leave soon," Alexa called. The dog pretended not to hear and snuffled his nose along the ground.

"Scout, now."

The rambunctious dog plowed through a mound of leaves as he heeded Alexa's call. The scattering orange foliage transported her back to the previous morning. She couldn't escape the image of the blonde girl with wide blue eyes. Alexa pulled her jacket tighter to ward off a sudden nip in the morning air.

The minute Alexa passed through the office door, Sunday flooded back once more. The lead headline in the morning paper, placed neatly in the center of her desk, proclaimed: "Dead girl found in Michaux Forest."

The article contained little information. The authorities still had not identified the girl. They had not determined cause of death, but the circumstances were "under investigation." The article said that the body had been found by a hiker but didn't name Alexa. Trooper Taylor was quoted, urging anyone with relevant information to come forward.

Alexa shuddered. How horrible that this young woman was dead. Even sadder, no one had come forward to report her missing. Someone out there must have loved her. How awful to have no idea that your sister or daughter or girlfriend is in the morgue.

Later that day between meetings, Alexa hurried into the kitchen to make herself a cup of tea. Two paralegals stood at the coffee maker, embroiled in a discussion about the dead girl.

Becky proclaimed, "It must be murder. The article says that this girl was young. She's not just going to die from natural causes out in the middle of nowhere by herself."

"I think it was an overdose." Jennifer put forth a different theory. "I'll bet that she was out there in the forest, partying with a bunch of friends. She ODs and the friends panic and hightail it out of there."

Jennifer turned to Alexa. "What do you think happened?"

"I'm not even going to speculate." Alexa tried to keep her expression neutral. "I expect that the police will figure it out soon. Maybe someone will come forward with some information about what happened."

Alexa couldn't tell them that she had been the one to find the body. The whole experience was just too raw to treat as gossip in the office kitchen.

When she arrived back in her office, Alexa found a new pile of paper stacked in the center of her desk. "Melinda, in here please," she yelled to her assistant. "Where did this come from?" she complained. "I have to finish the McCarren brief today. I don't have time for anything else."

"It never rains but it pours," Melinda cracked. "Your buddy, Brian, dropped that file off on his way to court. Says Mr. and Mrs. Lyons are coming in for their will tomorrow, and he doesn't think his hearing will be finished until after five o'clock. Killian is the judge, and you know what that means."

"Yeah, with Killian he might still be there at midnight. But, damn. Brian knows that I am jammed today. He thinks I'm his personal dumping ground. Anything he doesn't finish or finds too boring—just give it to Alexa."

"Well, you know what rolls downhill," Melinda consoled her boss in her typical cockeyed way. "When you're the junior attorney, that means you sit at the bottom of that proverbial hill."

"But, Brian only came to the firm shortly before I started here. A few extra months on the job don't entitle him to special privileges, like wangling the best assignments and passing the grunt work off to me."

"You can always talk to your brother or Pat O'Donnell about Brian."

"No. I'm not going to play the family firm card. Anyway, Pat works from home half the time and Graham would just brush me off. I think my brother actually gets a kick out of this little rivalry between Brian and me. He even encourages it, just like the way he egged on his friends when they teased me at school. I swear, some days Graham still acts like he's ten and I'm six."

"Well, Ben Franklin said 'out of adversity comes opportunity.'" The ample redhead slowly backed toward the door.

"Enough with the lame quotes. Get out of here." Alexa's giggles trailed off into a deep sigh as she tackled the daunting stack of legal documents.

At the end of the day, Alexa drove home in a reflective state of mind. Despite her bitching to Melinda, Alexa liked her job. When she graduated from Columbia, she had rebelled against Dad's assumption that she would join the family practice. Instead, she found a job at one of the gargantuan New York City law firms.

During her glowing second year evaluation, Alexa's boss confided, "If you maintain this level of work, you have the potential to make partner some day. Dan Baylor already has his eye on you."

A month later, Alexa handed in her resignation. The words "partner track" terrified her—years of long, grueling workdays and cutthroat internal politics. "No way." Alexa decided. "I am going home before Baylor, Trego, Wilson, and Gold grinds me into dust. Daddy and Graham will hire me in a New York minute."

When she turned down her lane, Alexa ended her reverie. She had made the right decision, trading concrete and the constant din of traffic for the forest and the sound of wind in the trees. She had satisfying work, family, friends, and the best dog in the world. "Except for that whole dead body thing yesterday, everything is perfect."

The next morning, Graham had already arrived in his office when Alexa breezed into work. She made a quick stop at her own desk to glance at the newspaper for news on the mystery girl. A small article announced that the police had made no progress in identifying the young woman.

Alexa tossed the paper down and walked across the office to knock on Graham's door. "Do you have a few minutes?"

"Sure. Come on in. I don't have anything on the calendar until ten o'clock. Have you heard anything from Mom and Dad?"

Alexa slid into one of the brown leather chairs facing Graham's desk. "No. I think they were going to be out of cell phone range for most of the trip. I don't really expect to hear from them until they get back from the Amazon. It is the Amazon, right? Or is it Africa, or France, or India?" she laughed. "I can't keep track of their travels since Dad retired; make that semi-retired."

"Yeah. Norris and Susan Williams, Carlisle's answer to Indiana Jones. They are having a ball."

"Did they call you? Is there a problem?"

"No calls or emails," Graham laughed. "But, I told them I'd look out for you while they're away. They worry about you being alone out at the cabin."

"Give me a break. I managed on my own for years in New York City. Plus, I have my giant guard dog. You are busy with Kate and the kids. You don't need to worry about me," Alexa protested.

Graham snorted with laughter. "You call that giant wuss of a dog a guard dog? A burglar could walk through the door with a Milk Bone and Scout would help him carry out your brand new TV. He would lead the burglar to your jewelry box in exchange for a scratch on the ears."

Alexa grinned at Graham's apt description of Scout before her expression sobered. "I did want to tell you about something that involves Scout. I would have talked to you yesterday, but I knew you had a court appearance." She paused. "Have you seen the news about the young woman found dead in the state forest over the weekend?"

18

"Yes. I read the article in the paper. How does that involve Scout?"

"Well, really, Scout and me both. We found the body."

After Alexa peeled her brother off the ceiling, she told Graham the entire story. She felt better after sharing her experience with him. Talking about the incident helped put some distance between Alexa and the shock she was still feeling.

"I'm concerned that the police interviewed you without counsel," Graham said.

"Graham. I just knew this would be your reaction. First of all, I am counsel, duly admitted to the bar in both Pennsylvania and New York. Secondly, I think the police are pretty clear that my stumbling upon the body was pure happenstance. I'm not a witness. I'm just the person who found the body."

"Are you at risk?" Graham frowned.

"What do you mean? At risk for criminal prosecution?"

"No. Personal risk," her brother said. "The police don't seem to be treating this as a suicide. So, it is likely that this girl didn't kill herself in the forest. That means someone else either killed her or is covering up an accidental overdose or something along that line. These people could lash out at you since you're involved."

Graham's statement surprised Alexa. Wrapped up in her reaction to finding a dead body and concern about the girl's identity, Alexa had never imagined that she could be in danger.

"Graham, no one but you and the police knows that I found her. They didn't release that to the news. Although the police didn't give me any instructions, I haven't talked about this to anyone. But, we don't know how she died. Maybe she had an aneurysm or a heart problem."

Alexa visualized the crumpled body on the ground, partially hidden under the mountain laurel bush. She shuddered as she thought of those blue eyes staring, unseeing, at the autumn sky.

"Graham." Alexa's voice faltered. "The worst part of all —it was just like the Babes in the Woods. When I saw the body, I thought, 'this must have been how the Babes looked.' Remember the Babes story and our elaborate reenactments from when we were kids?"

Graham pushed back his chair and came around the desk to hug his baby sister. "I know it must have been tough, Lexie. But, don't let local history or our ridiculous childhood games complicate this situation. Nearly eighty years have passed since they found the Babes. You need to focus on the here and now."

"I've really been affected by this experience. Finding a dead body near my old apartment in Brooklyn would have been shocking but not all that surprising. In the city, I read about violence every day. I even knew a couple of people in the office who had been mugged or burglarized. But, this random encounter with death in Michaux came as a real shock. And, it happened fairly close to the cabin, as the crow flies. I feel like there's been a tear in the fabric of my peaceful little universe."

"I understand that this has been upsetting, Lexie. But, you're going to get over the shock. It's critical to keep your involvement in this situation quiet. Don't tell anyone else about finding the body."

Back at her desk, Alexa contemplated the idea that the young girl had been murdered. Alexa zeroed in on a major reason for her distress. Whoever had killed the delicate blonde had expressed their contempt in the careless way they abandoned the body. The killer had tossed the girl in the woods like yesterday's trash.

The ringing phone interrupted Alexa's thoughts. "Caleb is on the line," Melinda told her. "I'll transfer him in. Do you have a hot date coming up?"

"Yes, we do. But, today's only Tuesday, right? He usually doesn't call this early in the week."

Caleb kept the conversation short. "I have to go out of town tomorrow. A big outdoor show near Philadelphia.

So, I thought I'd check in with you today. Are we still on for Friday night?"

"Sure. I'm looking forward to having some fun. It has been a very crazy few days."

"OK. How about I pick you up around seven? Sorry, I've got to go. A customer wants to buy rifle."

By the time Alexa said, "See you Friday," Caleb had hung up the phone.

Chapter Four

After work, Alexa headed straight to yoga. Just walking into the familiar yoga studio calmed her. For almost an hour, Alexa concentrated on spinal twists, sun salutations, and warrior poses. Near the end of class, the instructor moved to half moon, always one of Alexa's favorites. Thoughts of the dead girl and Graham's warnings sapped Alexa's focus, and she lost her balance again and again.

During savasana at the end of the session, Alexa let the distractions recede and found her center. Then, she remembered that savasana is Sanskrit for Corpse Pose.

Following class, Alexa and her two best friends sat in the outer room to put on their shoes. "Om Café?" Haley asked.

"Yes. I can make it tonight," Alexa affirmed.

"Let's go. I haven't talked to either of you this week," Melissa said. "I've been so busy with the Friday's opening. You've seen Clem Bouder's work before, haven't you? The guy's a frigging genius."

The three women chatted as they strolled to the nearby Om Café. While they placed the order for three chai tea lattes, Alexa leaned back in her chair and gazed fondly at her friends. The two were as different as night and day.

A tall, slender brunette, Haley always dressed with style, although a bit on the conservative side. She could do a television interview at a moment's notice with only a touch-up to her lipstick and a pat to her sleek chin-level bob. Her husband's job as an investment broker helped fund her spectacular wardrobe.

In contrast, Melissa was a free spirit. Her hippie parents named her after one of their favorite Allman Brothers songs and raised their daughter to live in the moment. She flourished in that environment and often seemed like a throwback to the early seventies. She dressed with a bohemian flair and always wore her long auburn curls loose in a cascade down her back. Melissa made her living running a small art gallery in town and was, herself, an accomplished photographer.

"So, yet another Lululemon outfit tonight, Haley. Did you just go through the fall catalog and buy one of everything?" Alexa teased.

Haley ran her gaze over Alexa's frayed sweat pants and ratty tee and sniffed, "Perhaps, I could lend you something for next week? I think I remember that t-shirt from summer camp in eighth grade."

"Hey. I always liked that t-shirt," Melissa chimed in. "I nearly cried when mine finally ripped at the seams. But, I still use it as a rag when I stain picture frames."

The waitress interrupted the friends' banter when she arrived with the tea. "We've got cranberry-orange scones tonight. Want one?"

"Not tonight, Ariel," Alexa declined. "I can't stay very long. Scout's been alone all day.

Melissa shook her head in refusal, and Haley said, "Maybe next week. Thanks."

"Haley, what's the Chamber of Commerce position on dead bodies popping up in Cumberland County's beautiful forests?" Melissa asked.

"How can you talk like that about a tragic situation? You should be ashamed of yourself." Haley admonished her friend.

"I'm sorry. That came out a little wrong. I think the whole thing is terrible. Apparently, the girl was quite young. The police don't seem to have a clue what happened. I just wanted to know if you have any inside information."

"No. Public Relations at the Chamber is in the dark. Maybe I overreacted because my boss has been so worried about the bad publicity. We get a lot of tourists this time of year: campers, hikers, the fall festivals. What if people get scared and stay away? Local business could lose a lot of revenue."

Alexa longed to confide that she had found the body, but Graham's voice popped into her head, telling her to keep quiet.

Instead, she observed, "You two talk like some mad killer is on the loose. It's a little early to jump to conclusions. No one even knows how she died."

"Alexa, you've spent too many years in the city. One dead body is nothing to you. Hell, they pile them up in the streets in New York, right?"

"As usual, you exaggerate, Melissa."

"It's not just the city," Haley interrupted. "She's always been like this. Remember when Alexa punched out little Johnny Gayman on the playground? I think it was fifth grade."

"Yeah. Wasn't he picking on that new girl, Angie? I can't remember her last name. Haley's right, Alexa. You've always been fearless."

"So," Haley clarified, "you need to understand that neither Melissa nor I—or anyone else in this little burg— are used to having dead bodies appear in the forest. Or anywhere else for that matter. The whole thing makes me nervous."

"OK, OK." Alexa wished she could tell her friends how wrong they were, that this particular dead body haunted her dreams. Instead, she smiled, "I get your point. And, what happened to that girl is tragic, no matter how she died. I shudder every time I think of her, dead and alone, out there in the woods."

Leaving the Om Café parking lot, Alexa had to wait for an opening in the traffic. As she punched the preset button for National Public Radio, Alexa noticed a group of kids in soccer uniforms spilling out of a blue van. Alexa smiled in sympathy at the harried woman who was trying to steer the group of boys and girls into the pizza shop two doors down from the Om Café.

The sight jogged her memory. "The van," she said out loud. "I never thought to tell the police about the van."

Driving home, Alexa debated the importance of the speeding van.

Was it relevant? Yes, it was driving fast. Yes, it came from the same direction as the girl's body. But, thousands of guys in camouflage drive around the woods in hunting season. Hell, half the population of Cumberland County thinks camouflage is appropriate attire for even the most formal social occasion.

By the time Alexa reached home, she still had not decided whether to call the state police about the van. She let Scout out and went to change into jeans. A few minutes later, she stood on her deck, searching for the big dog. She finally spied him, lumbering under the pines where the carpet of fallen needles muffled the sounds of his feet.

Scout raised his head, alert to the sound of a car coming down the lane in the gathering dusk. Alexa smiled as Reese Michaels unfolded his long frame from the SUV. Scout loped over to greet the ranger.

"I thought I would check in to see how you're doing." He approached the steps. "I'm glad I caught you at home. Wasn't sure of your schedule."

"Come on up. I'm doing OK. But, your arrival is timely. I just remembered something that happened on Sunday. And now you can give me your opinion about whether I should mention it to the police. Would you like something to drink?"

They sat on the deck in the fading light, Alexa with a soft drink and Reese with a beer. She told him about the speeding van that had startled her on the road a few minutes before the trailhead parking lot.

"I'm not sure if I should call the cops. It might not be related," Alexa finished. Noticing her agitation, Scout scrunched his body closer until he was lying on her foot.

"Anything could be important," Reese leaned forward. "At this point, I don't think they have much to go on. The police still haven't identified the body. What do you remember about the van? Color?"

"Sort of a dirty white. Maybe gray or tan. I don't really know anything about cars, but it looked like a million other vans on the road. It was old and looked pretty beat up. It seemed like a workman's van, no windows on the side; not the soccer mom type."

"Anything on the roof?"

"You mean like ladders or kayaks or something? No. There was a roof rack, I think; the kind that contractors and painters use. Keep in mind; I just saw this van for an instant. They passed me really fast. I was a little pissed that they ran over into my lane on the curve. They nearly forced me off the road. But, I just thought it was two hunters in too much of a hurry."

"Why do you say hunters? It was Sunday. No hunting is allowed."

"I didn't think of that. But, I said hunters because both men wore camouflage, even the hats. Of course, lots of guys around here have more camouflage in their wardrobes than anything else."

"Why don't you call Trooper Taylor? I have his number here in my cell. I can stay while you make the call."

When the plainclothes investigator arrived, Alexa repeated the information she had shared with Reese.

Trooper Taylor asked, "Did the van have any markings?"

"I don't remember anything on the side, like a company name or anything. I didn't really see the back of the van."

"You said that they reminded you of hunters. Was there a gun rack? Did you see any orange?"

"Oh, that's right. If they were hunters, they should have had orange vests and stuff. No, I don't remember any orange. There may have been a gun rack, but I can't say for sure. I just caught a fleeting glimpse of all of this. They were going really fast, and they startled me coming around the curve. They blew by so quickly, I didn't really see much at all. Sorry that I can't be more specific. And I don't know that they had anything to do with the girl. I just thought it was worth mentioning when I remembered seeing the van."

"Don't apologize. Calling me was the right thing to do. The chance that these men were involved in this incident may be slim. But, they may have seen something that could help us with this case. So, we appreciate your information."

"In fact, I was going to contact you anyway. Can you tell us where you were on Saturday between two and midnight?

"What?" Alexa gulped. "Do you consider me a suspect?"

"This is just routine." Trooper Taylor sidestepped her question.

"On Saturday, my friend Haley and I went to a Yoga Day benefit in Harrisburg. We left Carlisle around noon and stayed until four-thirty or so I had dinner at her house. Left around ten and drove home. If you need to verify with my friend, her name is Haley Donahue. I can give you her phone number. At one yoga session, there was a photographer from the newspaper. He may even have some photos of Haley and me."

"Thanks for the information," Taylor said, jotting the details on a notepad. "Do you own a gun?"

"A pistol? No. When I lived in New York City, my dad wanted me to get one, but I just didn't feel comfortable with a handgun in the apartment. There is a shotgun in the cabin. It's been here as long as I can remember. Dad taught my brother, Graham, and me to shoot with it when we were kids."

"That's all the questions I have for now." Taylor glanced at his notebook again before he spoke. "I am the lead investigator on this case, so call me if you think of anything else."

As the trooper rose from his chair, Alexa stood and asked, "Do you know what happened to her yet? Or who she is? Did she die on Saturday?"

The trooper exchanged a quick look with Reese, and then he said, "We have not yet identified the victim. But, I can tell you this since we will release the information to the newspapers tomorrow. She was a victim of criminal homicide."

The policeman's words hit Alexa like a blow, and she felt faint. In an instant, she was back in the woods gazing down at the young girl with the delicate face and vacant blue eyes.

Reese jumped to his feet and grabbed Alexa's elbow as she swayed. "Sit down," he suggested. "Give yourself a minute to deal with this."

As Alexa sank back down onto the nearest chair, Reese shot a dark look at the trooper. Taylor apologized to Alexa, "Sorry. Maybe I shouldn't have dropped that on you so abruptly."

Alexa brushed off his concern. "Don't apologize. I think I've known ever since I found the body that someone killed her. Then, they just dumped her under the bush. Still, to hear the confirmation is sobering. I've never had direct experience with death like this. It's a lot to absorb."

In bed few hours later, Alexa tossed and turned but remained wide awake. While Scout snored beside her, Alexa played the events of Sunday morning through her mind like a movie on automatic replay.

The van zipping by as she rounded the curve. Scout's frenzied barking. The girl in fuchsia lying motionless under the mountain laurel.

She couldn't explain why, but she felt an obligation to this girl. Intellectually, she knew that didn't make sense. She had no connection to this young woman other than finding her body in the forest. But, she couldn't shake the feeling that she had a responsibility to find out why the girl was killed.

Maybe, Alexa mused, it's because of the Babes in the Woods.

In the 1930s, three young girls had been found dead in the woods near where Alexa's cabin now stood. As a child, the story of the young girls' murder captured Alexa's imagination, perhaps because they were close to her age. Now, this young woman she had found in the forest played on her mind just like the Babes had haunted her youth.

Alexa vowed to act as an advocate for the dead girl. Until they found her true family, Alexa would become her family. Reaching this conclusion brought Alexa some peace. Rolling onto her side, she wrapped her arms around Scout and slept.

Chapter Five

Tuesday, November 20, 1934.

Sleep tender blossoms ...

Dewilla's stomach rumbled. Hunger stalked her every waking hour. A hollow beast had crawled into her stomach and snaked out to the tips of her fingers and toes. Sometimes, the monster roared so loudly that she could barely think. Today was Tuesday. The last time she and her sisters had eaten a full meal was on Sunday in Philadelphia.

Norma and Dewilla had gone wild with excitement when they slid into the wide red seat in the bustling diner. The steamy warmth, the buzz of conversation, and the heady aroma of food all around them enveloped the girls in a pleasant cocoon.

Dewilla's spirits plummeted when Daddy opened the heavy paper menu and said, "Girls, you will have to share a meal." Her little sister, Cordelia, started to cry. Dewilla felt dizzy until Norma reached to clasp her hand. As usual, Cousin Winifred just sat there looking adoringly at Daddy, oblivious to the distress of the three younger girls.

"I don't want any sass from you three," Daddy admonished. His voice lowered, "We have to make the money last until I can find a job."

Then, an angel spoke, "Why don't you join me and my boy? I would be happy to have you as my guests."

It took a minute before Dewilla realized that the dulcet tones came not from an angel but from the elegant-looking lady seated in the booth next to the Noakes family. Dewilla held her breath until Daddy answered, "Thank you, ma'am. I will accept your offer for my daughters. I am in your debt."

The girls wolfed down the food. Meatloaf, mashed potatoes, peas, and little square Parker rolls. The gracious woman even insisted that they order apple pie for dessert.

While they waited for the waitress to bring dessert, Daddy said, "Girls, where are your manners? Your mama brought you up better than this."

Little Cordelia piped up and told the kind lady, "Our daddy is looking for work. I was so hungry, and this food tastes awfully good. Thank you, ma'am, for me and my sisters."

"Yes, ma'am. You are very kind. We have fallen on some hard times, but I hope to find a job soon."

The lady replied, "Times are indeed hard. I wish you success in your search for work." The bell on the door tinkled as the stylish woman and her well-behaved son vanished into the night. A tendril of cold air slithered through the closing door encircling the Noakes as they tackled the apple pie.

Today, that Sunday dinner already seemed a distant memory. Dewilla had to stop thinking about that wonderful meal because it only made her hungrier. Leaning her head against the car window, she closed her eyes and thought instead about the good times with Mama.

Chapter Six

Alexa tapped her foot beneath the wide oak table and took a quick glance at the iPhone resting on her notebook. Eleven fifteen. Beside her, Patrice Collins, swathed in bandages, looked like she had fallen asleep in her wheelchair. Or maybe the meds had knocked her out?

Across the aisle Don Mead droned on and on.

Alexa chafed at each new remark. Would he never finish? How could the attorney find so much to say about a simple continuance?

Finally, silence.

Alexa jumped to her feet, "Your Honor. Once again, we ask that this matter be postponed until January. Mrs. Collins' doctors say she should be recovered enough by then to fully participate in the trial."

"Very well, Ms. Williams, I will grant the continuance," the judge ruled. "Mr. Mead, you and your client should be prepared for a January court date. Court dismissed."

After a brief conversation with Mr. and Mrs. Collins, Alexa turned her client over to her husband and hurried to the Land Rover as fast as her high heels would allow.

Next Wednesday, Alexa thought, I swear I'm going to wear flats. I always run late for the clinic and someday I'm going to break my neck in these heels. Besides, I always feel ridiculous climbing into this beast of a car wearing Christian Louboutins.

Alexa peeled out of the court house parking lot and headed toward the local family planning clinic. When she joined the family law firm, Alexa made a deal with her father to have Wednesday afternoons free to volunteer. She pitched the idea to her dad by playing on his ill-disguised contempt for Alexa's former employer.

"Dad. When I worked at the firm in New York City, I barely had time for sleep or a social life, let alone time for volunteering. That's if you don't count the day that all the junior attorneys had to spend picking up trash in Central Park. The partners needed to kiss up to one of their big deal clients who got an award from the mayor for his work with the city parks. So, the word came down that the junior staff had 'permission' to forgo billable hours for an afternoon and volunteer for park clean up."

"Exactly what I would expect from those leeches. Always looking at the bottom line," Norris Williams fumed.

"One of the reasons that I came home was to have a life. And, I would like that new life to include volunteering for some of my favorite causes. Real volunteering ... not something done just to please a law firm client. Frank says they could use me at the clinic one day a week."

"OK, OK. We'll give it a try. If you can't handle your workload here in the office, though, Graham will be all over you, Alexa."

Rushing through the clinic door, Alexa wobbled a bit on her high heels. Then she caught a heel in the cracked linoleum and nearly walked out of the shoe. As Alexa slipped it back on, she noticed two twenty-something girls staring at her red soles and whispering.

"That does it. Next week, I am going to wear flats." Alexa muttered under her breath.

"Hey, ladies." Alexa greeted the two women behind the reception counter. Barb and Tanisha had their hands full today. She checked out the waiting area. The clinic was packed. Women of all ages and one lone man occupied every dilapidated bench and chair.

When a very pregnant Latina teenager walked into the small room, a weary-looking brunette scooped a toddler into her lap and pointed to the now-empty seat. The pregnant girl waddled to the bench, pulled out her phone, and began texting.

"Boy, am I glad to see you," Tanisha exclaimed. "You can see that we are backed up today, and I have a report that I need to finish for Medicaid. Can you help Barb with intake?"

"Will do."

Barb stood at the counter helping a middle-aged redhead fill out a history form. Apparently the woman had literacy issues. In a soft voice, Barb read her each question and recorded her response.

Alexa picked up the sign-in sheet and called out the next name, "Roxanne Souders."

"Yes, Miss Alexa." A young woman dressed in a fast food uniform came to the desk.

"How are you doing, Roxanne? It's been a while."

"It surely has been, Miss Alexa. I came in today for my annual."

"The doctor will be pleased that you are coming in for preventive care. Here's a form to fill out about your health; any medical issues, any prescriptions that you're taking. You can fill this out while you wait for the doctor. Do you have insurance or Medicaid?"

"No, ma'am." She looked down at the counter. "Arly and me, our jobs don't give insurance, and we ain't got Medicaid neither."

"No worries," Alexa reassured her. "You'll qualify for the sliding fee scale. Did you bring all the forms so I can calculate what you need to pay?"

Alexa registered one person after another over the next few hours. For some, she took their insurance or Medicaid cards; for others, she collected their subsidized co-pays. Finally, Tanisha finished the report and sent Alexa to the phones. Alexa answered incoming calls and, in between, made reminder calls about the next day's appointments.

By four o'clock, the waiting room crowd had thinned, and Alexa offered to make a coffee run. Legal Grounds, the nearby coffee shop, had a reputation as a real hangout for college kids, but they only packed the tiny space in the evening.

Waiting in the empty shop for the eight elaborate specialty coffees, Alexa glanced at the newspaper on a nearby table, left behind by an earlier customer. She caught her breath at the face of a young girl with wide eyes staring from the page. In black and white, the pen and ink drawing rendered a fairly good likeness of the dead girl. But, the drawing's static quality hinted at the fact that the subject was a corpse. The headline screamed "Murder victim still not identified."

Alexa sat at the table to read the story. Mostly, the piece rehashed all the earlier newspaper and television coverage. The only real news appeared in the first paragraph. The police were calling the girl's death criminal homicide. Corporal Branche was quoted, saying, "We are actively investigating. Based on the coroner's findings, we have determined that this young woman's death is a homicide. We still have been unable to identify the victim and are asking anyone who recognizes the woman in this drawing to contact us."

"Miss, your order is ready. Miss. Miss?"

The barista's words finally caught Alexa's attention. She grabbed the paper off the table and stuffed it in her purse before stepping up to the counter to collect the cardboard box filled with cups. "Sorry. I was so engrossed in this article ..."

"No biggie," replied the guy behind the register. The girl chimed in, "Everyone's talking about this murder. You think that Carlisle is a safe place to live, and then something like this happens." The girl seemed to shrink into herself and even the male cashier looked slightly uneasy.

Alexa murmured in agreement. She saw that the violent death of someone their own age had really shaken these two college students.

Balancing the box of cups in front of her and preoccupied with thoughts of the murder, Alexa drifted down the block toward the clinic.

Maybe, she thought, someone will recognize this picture and come forward to identify her. But, how terrible would it be for her mother and father to find out about their daughter's death by seeing this picture in the paper.

When Alexa turned the corner, she stopped so abruptly that the box in her hands wobbled. A small group of people paraded back and forth in front of the clinic, carrying signs. Alexa sighed, in no mood to run the gauntlet today.

Her approach energized the protesters, who chanted:

"Baby killer."

"Save the innocents."

The group pumped their signs into the air. Two signs displayed pictures of bloody fetuses. Another featured a large cross with the words: Blessed are the Unborn.

No one tried to stop her from entering the clinic. Today, as always, the group adhered carefully to the borough rules: stay at least fifteen feet away from the clinic and never try to stop anyone from entering the facility. Of course, those rules didn't make it any easier for the patients who had to endure the chanting and graphic posters. Most of the women simply ignored the protesters. A few shouted back. Unfortunately, Alexa had seen some women turn away, daunted by the prospect of an angry audience to what should be a private visit to her doctor. Many of those women might have already been apprehensive about seeing a gynecologist. Alexa always hoped that the ones who left would come back when the protestors had gone.

The protestors didn't come every day. They seemed to favor Wednesdays. Alexa had checked the records at Borough Hall and learned that a group called Soldiers of Judah obtained the permit. The application listed the address as a Post Office box number. Dr. Kearns thought the group might be associated with a fundamentalist Christian church, but no one knew for sure.

"I see our friends are here again," Alexa observed to Barb and Tanisha as she walked through the door.

"Friends," Barb snorted. "They aren't my friends. None of my friends would walk around in a circle shouting at women coming in for medical care. Those pea-brains actually believe that God herself told them to come here and harass us. I think they got the message wrong but are too stupid to know it."

Alexa and Barb laughed, but the two women sitting in the waiting room just gazed at the floor. Alexa told them, "Don't worry. We can let you leave by the back door after your visit with the doctor."

Alexa turned to Tanisha, "What makes me mad is that these people harass everyone who comes in here, and most of these women are just coming for their annual checkups or for family planning. But, because we perform a small number of abortions, they scream at everyone."

Alexa stomped to the front window and peered out. The six women and two men now gathered in a circle, hands clasped in prayer. The women and one of the men were regulars on the picket line. She studied the second man, who was new to her. He seemed much younger than the others and dressed much less conservatively. The women all wore plain dresses that fell below their knees. The older man had dressed for the occasion in a suit with a string bolo tie and black-rimmed hat that shadowed his face. In contrast, the younger man wore frayed jeans with ripped knees, a plaid flannel shirt, and a baseball cap.

As if he felt her gaze, the younger protestor raised his bowed head and stared directly at Alexa. She felt a vague sense of unease at being singled out. The young man sauntered toward the curb, almost as if he planned to walk across the street and approach Alexa. Forgetting the pane of glass that divided them, she took an involuntary step back from the window. At that moment, the phone rang, and she turned away to answer, shrugging off the disquieting episode.

At home that evening, Alexa fished the newspaper out of her purse and reread the article about the young girl's death. Her emotional reaction to the story mirrored her response to the trooper's revelation the night before. Theoretically, the article should have been old news since the police had already given her an inside scoop on the homicide ruling. However, each new event related to this girl's death hit Alexa hard. Finding the girl felt like the first punch. Hearing the word "homicide" was the second blow. Reading it in black and white nearly delivered the knockout round.

Alexa vowed not to let any of the punches knock her down.

Get over it, Alexa chided. You're just the person who found the body. Be concerned about justice for that young girl and her family.

Once again, Alexa resolved to follow the case closely and act as an advocate for the girl.

Frowning at the paper, Alexa studied the sketch again. The black and white drawing did look like the girl she had seen lying dead on the ground. But, something bothered her about the likeness. Alexa couldn't put her finger on exactly what seemed wrong. The drawing just felt off in some way.

Alexa slammed the page, face down, on the counter. "Scout, let's go out for a walk. I need to get away from this for a few minutes." Alexa grabbed a warm jacket as the dog bounced to the door.

Chapter Seven

After work on Friday, Alexa rushed home to change. She was so ready to forget about everything for a night and just have fun. When Caleb picked her up for dinner, she skipped down the deck steps and climbed into his Ford Explorer.

"Hey," he smiled. "It's good to see you."

"Likewise," Alexa laughed. Who wouldn't want to see this guy? He was pretty gorgeous: one of those tall, dark, and handsome types with thick black hair. Even more striking were Caleb's unusual silver-gray eyes. Alexa teased Caleb that he must be part Siberian husky. But, at times, the transparent quality of his eyes made Alexa think more of stormy skies and Arctic ice.

Caleb was a lot of fun. They started dating a few months ago and fell into an easy routine; dinner on either Friday or Saturday when Caleb was in town. He owned a small sporting goods company and traveled quite a bit, buying for his business.

Alexa was happy with the casual relationship. She had made a huge change in her life, returning home to join the family firm. She had no interest in any more changes, like a big romance, right now.

A few years back, Alexa had fallen hard for another law student; they had been inseparable during their last two years at Columbia. But, just days before graduation, Trent had broken her heart. Her love had accepted a great offer from a firm in Los Angeles, and he made it clear that he planned to start this chapter of his life alone.

Alexa anguished over Trent's reasons for breaking up. Was he drawn to L.A. by the prestige of a big glitzy law practice? Or was it all those beautiful Hollywood women? Either way, the man she had loved and thought of as her best friend had walked out of her life in a heartbeat. It had taken Alexa almost a year to feel that her heart could continue to beat without Trent in her life. Luckily, a junior attorney at Baylor, Trego, Wilson, and Gold had little time to do anything but work and fall into bed from exhaustion.

Alexa was still gun-shy about another relationship when she came back home. Dating Caleb offered a nice distraction. She wanted to keep things light, and Caleb seemed to be looking for a good time, not a life partner.

"Where are we going tonight? I forgot to ask when we talked. I guess you would have sent me back in the house to change if we were going formal?" She glanced down at her slacks and light sweater. "And, of course, you're not wearing a tux."

"How about Cobb's Inn? I think the deck is still open. It's fairly warm this evening. Is that jacket heavy enough?"

Alexa lifted her jacket from her lap. "This coat's perfect. Do they have a band scheduled?" Cobb's Inn was just the ticket. They could have dinner, dance to the local country rock band, and chase any thoughts about dead girls right out of her mind.

Alexa enjoyed her evening with Caleb. As always, they kept the conversation light.

"You wouldn't believe the battle that is raging at the law firm. Half of the firm wants us to stock Hawaiian Gold coffee. The other half is pushing for the brand they sell at Legal Grounds. I forget what it's called."

"Jury Roast?"

"That's it, Jury Roast. Graham sent out a survey about coffee choices and we spent more time talking about the survey at the weekly attorney's meeting than we did about cases."

"What did they decide? I would vote for Jury Roast. I send someone out almost every morning to get me a Jury Roast with an extra shot of coffee."

"Whoa, a manly drink. What size, extra large?"

"What else?"

"Well, I could care less about which coffee wins out. I drink tea. But, you'll have to wait to hear the final choice. Graham tabled it until next week. You can't make such a crucial decision without due deliberation."

Although he was reserved about his private life, Caleb kept Alexa laughing with stories about some of the people he did business with in Atlanta. He launched into a long tale about two business associates who wanted to go to the Southern Belles lounge following a business dinner.

"I told the guys that I had a Northern belle at home who would put any girl at their gentlemen's club to shame. They still had a hard time believing that I would turn down a chance to see Southern womanhood at its finest." Caleb smiled.

"I'm glad to see that you put in a plug for the women who live north of the Mason-Dixon Line. But, I'm thinking that the ladies at Southern Belles don't quite fall into the Scarlett O'Hara/Melanie Wilkes category. No crinolines and hoop skirts there."

Caleb had a blank look on his face, clearly not catching her reference.

"You don't know who Scarlett O'Hara and Melanie Wilkes are, right?"

As Caleb shook his head, she continued, "*Gone with the Wind.* You might not have read the book, but surely you saw the movie? The Civil War? The fall of Atlanta? Clark Gable and Vivien Leigh? 'Frankly, Scarlett, I don't give a damn'?"

"Nope, I don't have a clue what you're talking about. I'm not that big on movies and definitely didn't read the book. It wasn't on the business major curriculum."

"Well, my point is simple. I expect that the ladies at a gentleman's lounge wear considerably less than the image that comes to mind of a real Southern belle. I've always felt a little sorry for women who dance in men's clubs to earn their living. It's gotta be a hard life."

Caleb surprised Alexa with his response. "I don't feel sorry for those women. There are a thousand jobs that they could take. Instead, they choose to parade around virtually naked in front of a room full of strange men every night. I would never go to a place like that. I don't need to compound their sins by watching the women degrade themselves." Caleb's eyes became storm clouds in the half-light of the deck. "I was raised pretty strict. Even today, my father would beat my ass if he found out I went to a strip club."

"It's hard to put yourself in someone else's shoes and question their life choices. I'm just glad that I've never been in a situation where I had to consider dancing in a gentleman's lounge." Alexa drew out the word gentleman in a droll way. "Plus, the only pole I've had any experience with is hiking up Pole Steeple. I don't think they would hire me."

When the band played the first bars of "Redneck Woman," Caleb jumped up. "This is one of my favorites. Let's dance."

Rolling her eyes, Alexa joined him as the female vocalist belted out the song. "Seriously, 'Redneck Woman' is one of your favorites?" she exclaimed, and then stopped talking because she needed her breath for the fast dance.

They spent most of the next hour on the dance floor. When the band played its version of a slow dance, the Eagles' "Desperado," Caleb swept her into his arms and whispered, "Do you want to leave?"

Caleb held Alexa close as they walked to the car. She leaned into his embrace, and he drew her into a long kiss. When they reached her house, Alexa and Caleb rushed in the door as Scout passed them in a hurry to go outside.

Shedding their coats, they hastened into the living room. Before she could sit down, Caleb slid Alexa's sweater from her shoulders and cupped her head in a long, slow kiss. She took his hand and led him up the stairs to her bedroom.

When she reached for the light switch, Caleb caught her hand. "It's more mysterious in the dark." Then, he stripped away her clothes, tossing them on the floor in haste. Alexa started to unbutton his shirt, but Caleb clasped his hand over hers. "Let me do it. It's faster."

Alexa ceded to his wish. Her entire body vibrated in anticipation. The sooner she had this man in her bed, the better. Their lovemaking was sweet and sexy at the same time. Caleb took his time, letting his mouth explore Alexa's body until she was ready to scream.

Alexa couldn't stand it any longer. She had to have Caleb inside her, but she had just enough grasp on reality to ask, "Condom?"

"You do it."

Sliding the condom over his erect penis heightened Alexa's desire. When Caleb entered her, Alexa succumbed to a whirlwind of passion, which ended only after they both reached a frenzied release.

"Do you have any idea how hot you are?" Caleb asked, head on the pillow.

"Back at you."

Alexa heard Scout woofing at the door. The mastiff could have been barking for the past half hour, but she hadn't heard a sound. "Luckily, I have no neighbors nearby to complain about the noise. Wouldn't that be some explanation? I have to go let him in," she said, letting her eyes linger on the curve of Caleb's waist where it joined his hip. In the dim light filtering from the hallway, the smooth sweep of tan flesh melted into shade and beckoned Alexa to stay. She wanted to spend more time exploring that tantalizing shadow but forced herself leave the bed.

"That's OK. I've got to go anyway. I need to get to bed at a decent hour. I'm meeting some friends to go grouse hunting tomorrow."

"My God. You will hunt anything, won't you? I didn't know you were allowed to hunt our state bird. That seems almost sacrilegious."

"But, just think of the skill involved in stalking such a wily creature."

Caleb's departure didn't surprise Alexa. Since the first time, their routine had never varied. They always did the deed at Alexa's place. Caleb left soon after. He never spent the night.

Since they'd met through Graham, Alexa knew for a fact that Caleb wasn't married. Otherwise, his behavior might have given her pause. In truth, Alexa liked the routine just fine because she wanted to keep things simple with Caleb. She liked Caleb. She liked sex with Caleb. But, she didn't want anything more from the relationship. Sometimes, Alexa wondered if she was dating Caleb to hide from a real romance. But, she always managed to shrug that thought away. Right now, Caleb was just what she needed.

Alexa pulled on a pair of sweats and a well-worn sweater before she went downstairs to check on her dog. "I'm so sorry, baby," she consoled Scout. "At least it's not cold out tonight."

Caleb shook his head as he bounced downstairs from the bedroom, fully dressed. "You treat that dog like a person."

Scout lifted his head and eyed Caleb but didn't approach. There was no love lost between her beloved dog and her casual boyfriend. She chalked Scout's disdain for Caleb up to a little bit of doggie jealousy. She wasn't sure why Caleb didn't warm to Scout. Perhaps he didn't like dogs. Maybe he just wasn't a fan of giant dogs that were treated like people. At least the two tolerated each other politely on these occasions when they met in passing.

As he opened the door, Caleb asked, "Are you free next Saturday? My lodge is having their annual fall picnic and get together. Hopefully, the leaves will still be good. Would you like to spend the day out there with me?"

"Next Saturday? I think that would work. What kind of lodge? The Elks or the Eagles? I don't remember you ever mentioning a lodge before."

"No. This is a private lodge that my family and a number of others bought in the early 1900s over in Perry

County. Membership is passed down from generation to generation. I guess you'd call it a social club/hunting camp hybrid."

"Sounds like fun. Call me sometime this week and let me know the details."

"OK. I'll be out of town, but I'll give you a call."

Alexa closed the door behind Caleb and sat down on the couch, running her fingers through Scout's smooth fur. The invite to this picnic puzzled Alexa. She had never met Caleb's family. They had bumped into a few of Caleb's friends over the months when they were out to dinner. But, Caleb rarely talked about anyone in his personal life. A few of his hunting buddies. His sister, Rebecca.

Alexa admitted that she played her cards pretty close to the vest as well. She talked to Caleb about her parents and their travels. Of course, Caleb knew Graham, who had introduced the two at a Chamber of Commerce luncheon.

When she thought about it, she and Caleb always stuck to the surface stuff.

Case in point: I spent an entire evening with Caleb and never mentioned finding the dead girl.

Perhaps this invitation to visit the family lodge just meant that he needed a date for the party. Still, Alexa was wary. Could this be a signal that Caleb wanted things to move beyond casual?

Caleb is gorgeous and oh so hot, but I could never get serious about him, she realized.

Even when it came to the surface stuff, they were much too different.

Chapter Eight

At nine o'clock on Saturday morning, Alexa was still burrowed under the covers. Scout snuggled beside her. Awake for more than a half hour, she had been watching the golden leaves outside the window waft back and forth in the breeze.

"I love my little tree house," she exclaimed in delight. Built in the old style with real logs and chinking, the cabin had stood for more than a century. The bedrooms, built as an addition to the original structure, stood at a higher level. In her front-facing bedroom, Alexa's windows looked right out into the treetops.

Alexa finally tore herself away from the view and her meditation on the fall leaves. "Scout, time to get up. It looks like a beautiful day and we need to spend some of it outdoors. In a month or so it will be cold and gray. Let's enjoy it while we can."

As Alexa's feet hit the floor, the bedside phone rang. She was surprised to hear Reese Michaels on the line.

"It's a great day, and I remembered that you're an expert on the local hiking trails. If you don't have any plans, would you and Scout like to go on a hike?"

Alexa didn't hesitate, "Sure. Sounds great. Can you give me an hour?"

Hanging up the phone, Alexa let Scout out the door for a quick run and then jumped into the shower. She needed to hurry so that she would have time for breakfast.

Alexa took Reese across the valley to a trail on North Mountain. She and Reese fell into a companionable pace, chatting as they hiked. Excited at the new smells, Scout trotted a few yards ahead.

"Scout doesn't have the stamina for a full-day hike. But he can do these five miles with no problem," Alexa said.

"He's certainly full of energy today," Reese agreed. "But, I'm not going to carry him back to the car if he gets tired. How much does this dog weigh?"

"Last time the vet put him on the scale, he weighed just shy of 200 pounds. She says that he'll probably bulk up a few pounds as he matures. He's a giant, isn't he?"

Alexa and Reese continued to joke and chat as they walked upward. Before the final segment of the trail, Alexa suggested, "How about we stop for a while?"

"Fine with me."

They stopped and drank from their water bottles. Alexa gave Scout a drink from his doggie canteen before he settled down at their feet.

From his seat on a fallen log, Reese scratched the dog's ears. He told Alexa, "This is great. I can't believe I haven't been over here before now. But, I haven't had much time to explore the area. The summer season keeps us pretty busy."

After a short, steep incline, they reached the summit of the mountain. Alexa led Reese out onto an expanse of huge granite—"Flat Rock"—for which the trail was named. Scout flopped down under the trees to watch.

"This view is amazing," said Reese. "You can see the whole valley from here."

"It's clear today. On humid days visibility can be limited."

Alexa pointed out some local landmarks and then sat on a rock. "I'm glad you suggested a hike. What a wonderful day. Sunny, a slight breeze, but cool enough for a jacket; a perfect day for a hike. Fall has always been my favorite season."

"I wish I had remembered my camera so I could take a picture of the valley. A friend and I exchange pictures of new places."

Alexa reached into her jacket pocket and took out her cell phone. "Stand up there on the rocks and pose. I'll take a picture to send your friend or post on your Facebook page. You can get a picture of the valley the next time."

Reese grinned, "I don't really do Facebook, but a camera phone photo is great." He called to the dog. "Come on, Scout. I want you in the picture, too."

Alexa was surprised to see the mastiff rise and lumber over to Reese. The dog really seemed to like this guy.

Reese stood in front of the boulders with Scout sitting at his feet. "Smile," she chirped and snapped a series of pictures.

Reese peered over Alexa's shoulder as they reviewed the photos. "Pretty good, actually. Thanks. I'll give you my email address so you can send them to me. Do you want one of you and Scout?"

"No, thanks. I've been here a zillion times."

On the way back, Alexa and Reese slowed their pace. Scout ambled along beside them on the descent. After twenty minutes or so, they passed the first hikers trekking upward.

"I'm glad we beat the crowd," Reese said. "It was great to have the trail to ourselves. One of the things I like best about my job is the peace and the quiet of the forest. A lot of my job involves working with people, and that's fine. It goes with the territory. But I really like to be out in the park on my own. When it's really quiet, the birds and the animals come out in full force. I saw a bear last week. It was just off Ridge Road in an open patch of scrub pines and grass."

"I've seen lots of deer at my cabin but never a bear. Every once in a while I hear a bobcat late at night. Scout goes nuts when he hears one of them scream."

Soon, the trio reached the parking area. After a drink for all, they loaded the mastiff into the back of Reese's Jeep and headed back across the valley.

"It's long past lunchtime," Reese said with a look at his watch. "Do you want to stop to get something to eat?"

"Do you like hamburgers?"

"Of course I like hamburgers."

"Then let's go back to my cabin and cook some burgers on the grill. I've got some in the fridge. That way we can sit out on the deck and enjoy some more of this great day."

During their belated lunch, Alexa and Reese got to know each other a little better. She told him about her years in the Big Apple and her decision to return home. "So, what's your story?" she inquired.

"I am a man of many facets, so it could take literally weeks to tell you my story."

Alexa laughed. She liked Reese's sense of humor.

"But, here's the short version. I went to college at Middlebury in Vermont. I majored in environmental studies. After graduation, I wanted to see some of the world. I got a job with a wildlife conservation organization in Africa. It was one of those jobs that paid next to nothing but gives you a great experience."

"I'm so envious. I've always wanted to go on safari in Africa. Where were you located?"

"I was lucky to be assigned to two separate projects. One tracked elephant populations in Kenya. The other involved big cats in Tanzania."

"That sounds amazing. How long were you there?"

"Two years. I loved it. Someday, I'll go back. I still have friends there. That picture that you took for me today. The guy I exchange photos with is John Lucas, who works with the Kenya project. We email back and forth all the time."

"Why did you leave Africa?"

"It was time. When I returned to the States, I went to Princeton for my master's. I used my field experience from the big cat study as the jumping off point for my thesis. After Princeton, I decided to move closer to home. My family lives in Western Pennsylvania, and I had been away long enough to miss them."

"And your chocolate lab named Hershey?"

Reese whooped. "So, you were listening that day. Actually, Hershey had gone to Labrador heaven by the time I came home from Africa. My parents downsized to a Jack Russell terrier. His name is Stover. My mom really likes Russell Stover candy, so it seemed appropriate."

"Is that when you started with the Department of Conservation and Natural Resources?"

"Yeah. I applied for a position as a park ranger at Roaring Falls State Park. I transferred here to Pine Grove in the spring."

"Middlebury, Africa, and Princeton? It sounds to me like you're a bit overqualified for Pine Grove Furnace State Park," Alexa commented.

"Says the Columbia Law School grad who is practicing at a small family firm in Carlisle, PA," Reese replied.

"Point taken," Alexa acknowledged. "I'm sure you get this question all the time, but your name is pretty unusual. I almost hesitate to ask after all the dog name stories—but where did your parents get the name Reese?"

He laughed. "I wish I had a dollar for every time I've been asked about my name. Most of the time I get jokes about Reese's Pieces. But, I'm not really that sweet. The explanation is much more mundane. It's a family name; the last name of my mother's favorite grandfather."

"I like it. It's nice to have a name that doesn't belong to six other people you know."

As they finished the burgers and a salad that Alexa had thrown together, Alexa looked at Reese and broached the topic they had avoided all day. "Anything new on the investigation that you can tell me about?"

"From what I understand, they've made very little progress in the case. The state police received a lot of calls about the drawing in the newspapers. But, none of the tips checked out.

"Apparently, this often happens when the police ask for help. They get calls from mothers whose daughters are missing, hoping desperately that this girl is not their child. They get calls from crackpots who are just into the excitement of calling the cops. And, they get some legitimate leads. But, from what I've heard, none of those leads have panned out. They still don't know who this girl is."

"Why haven't family or friends reported her missing? I guess the police have looked at missing persons reports?"

Reese's reply was thoughtful. "I only know a little about this, but we've dealt with a few runaways. We had a kid up at Camp Thompson last summer run away on his second day at Wilderness Camp. From that experience I learned that there are a lot of runaway kids in this country. Some are reported as missing. Some are running away from bad situations at home and maybe the parent never even tells the police that the kid is gone.

"With this girl, it's even more complicated because of her age. The coroner says she was in her late teens, at most twenty, legally an adult. Maybe Carlisle is not her hometown; maybe she wasn't in regular contact with her parents; maybe she was a drifter ... there are lots of reasons that she might not be missed."

"But they have to find out who she is. If the police don't identify her, they'll never figure out who killed her. She needs to have justice. It's just not right that someone killed her and then just dumped her under a bush."

"She was strangled," Reese revealed. "The state police aren't releasing that information, so don't tell anyone."

"I did notice that her neck was a little bruised when I felt for a pulse. But, otherwise, she looked unblemished. Wouldn't her face have been purple or something if she was strangled?" Alexa frowned at the memory.

Reese replied, "Apparently, it varies. I don't really know much about this. But the police told me that strangulation can be determined from these burst blood vessels called petechiae. If you watch any of the cop shows, you've probably heard them cite petechial hemorrhaging as cause of death. You can look it up online, too.

"Anyway, sometimes these damaged blood vessels are quite evident. Other times, like this, they are so small that they can only be detected in an autopsy. The autopsy also revealed a broken hyoid bone in her throat, which is an even more definitive indicator of strangulation.

"The police think that she was killed somewhere else and probably wasn't moved to that spot in Michaux until a few hours later."

Alexa had a fleeting vision of that jagged scrap of the girl's fuchsia blouse rippling in the wind. She shuddered to think of the fatal injury that the blouse covered. Perhaps the killer tore the blouse when he choked the life out of the girl's fragile body.

The sun had started to dip below the trees when Reese finally got up from his deck chair. "If I don't get out of here, you're going to have to feed me dinner, too."

"Thanks for a nice day," Alexa said as she jumped to her feet. "I'm not sure if your plan was to distract me from obsessing about the murder or if you really wanted to go hiking. Either way, I'm glad you called. It was a great day for Flat Rock."

Scout roused himself from a mat and walked over to say goodbye to Reese.

Reese obliged the dog with a vigorous scratch behind both ears while he replied to Alexa. "Perhaps it was a little of both, distraction and hiking. But, I had fun. Would you be willing to introduce me to a few more of your favorite local hikes?"

"Sure. Are you always off on the weekends?"

"It depends. There aren't that many of us, so the rangers rotate shifts."

"Well, I've got plans for next Saturday, but I could do something on Sunday. Have you been over to Three Square Hollow yet? There are one or two trails I like over there."

"I won't know if I am free Sunday until later in the week. By then we'll also know if the weather will be good. How about I give you a call by Thursday or stop by? I'm living in a farmhouse just east of the state park. I'm not far away."

As Alexa watched Reese's Jeep drive away, she smiled. "He's a nice guy, isn't he, Scout? You sure seem to like him. He's pretty easy on the eyes, too."

I feel comfortable with Reese, she thought. I think we could become good friends.

Chapter Nine

Accustomed to the protestors milling and chanting across the street from the clinic, Alexa mostly regarded them as background noise. As she approached the entrance on Wednesday, however, the group seemed unusually subdued. The reason for their uncharacteristic restraint became clear when she noticed the Carlisle police car parked in front of the door.

"What's going on?" she asked Tanisha when she breezed through the clinic door. "Are the police here?"

A patient, little more than a teenager, with a small child clinging to her hand walked up to the reception desk. "Miss," she said. "How much longer am I going to have to wait? I need to get to work for my three o'clock shift, and I'm starting to worry that I'm going to run late."

Tanisha rescheduled the young mother's appointment for later in the week, apologizing profusely for the delay. "Dr. Kearns is tied up unexpectedly. I'm so sorry that everything is backed up."

Shaking her head as she turned to Alexa, Tanisha said, "What a screw up. The police are back there with Barb, Dr. Kearns, and the other clinical staff. The doctor got a death threat this morning." Tanisha's gray-flecked cornrows jiggled back and forth punctuating her agitation with the situation. "Barb opened the letter. It looked like a joke, this piece of paper with letters cut out of a magazine to form words. In fact, that's what Barb first said when she opened it. She said, 'Look at this. Someone watches way too much TV.'

"But, when we read what it said, it wasn't so funny anymore. We showed it to Dr. Kearns, who mentioned that she's been getting this spooky feeling lately like someone is watching her. She hadn't said anything before because she thought she could be imagining things. But this letter put things in a different light."

"What did the letter say?" Alexa asked.

"I wrote it down." She pushed a piece of paper across the desk. Scribbled on it were the words, "RETRIBUTION IS MINE SAYETH THE LORD. YOU WILL BE THE THIRD TO DIE."

Alexa's glance out the window was involuntary. "Do you think it was one of them? I've always thought of them as misguided, not to mention a real pain in the ass. But, I never thought they were dangerous."

"Yes, honey. They look harmless enough. There's a whole world of harmless looking people out there, but all it takes is one. Look at that Roeder man who killed Dr. George Tiller in Kansas. That was only four years ago. He shot the doctor at point blank range in church. Murder in God's house. I bet everyone thought that man seemed pretty harmless, too, right up until they arrested him for murder."

"I'm not sure he's a good example, Tanisha. Scott Roeder had psychiatric issues. He had been associated with a number of militant fringe groups in the years prior to that shooting out in Wichita. But, I get your point.

"In some ways, we've been lucky here. I just read an article about abortion clinic violence. Since Roe vs. Wade in 1973 there have been something like 200,000 incidents of violence and disruption at clinics in North America."

"Yes." Tanisha nodded. "Every single person who works here knows about the seven clinic workers who were murdered before Dr. Tiller. Dr. Kopp, shot in his own kitchen in New York. Those two receptionists in the Boston clinics. The two doctors and the clinic escort in Florida. The security guard killed by a bomb in Alabama. Not to mention all the other assaults, kidnappings, stalkings, bombings, and arsons. Believe me, this job is not one that any of us do lightly. But we've never had any real problems here."

"I know. And, I guess it's too easy to lay the blame on our friends across the street. We all know that abortion is a divisive issue. But, the majority of people in the pro-life movement would never resort to criminal behavior."

"Honey, can you go back and find out something for me from the doctor and the police?" Tanisha asked. "Just ask them how much longer they expect to be. If the police are gonna be here for a while, we might need to send all these ladies back home and reschedule them for another day. Some of them are pretty jumpy just seeing a police car sitting out front."

After checking with the group closeted in Dr. Kearns' office, Alexa and Tanisha decided to close the clinic and send the patients home. It took about a half an hour to reschedule the six women sitting in the waiting room. Tanisha had a nice, reassuring way of handling the women, several of whom were pretty upset. Some had been sitting out there for nearly two hours and were not happy that they had to leave without seeing the doctor.

Alexa helped get birth control supplies from a physician's assistant for a couple of young women who needed immediate refills. Then, she began calling to cancel the rest of the patients on the schedule.

When the frenzy died down, Tanisha said to Alexa, "I know that Dr. Crowe really deserves a vacation. That man works so hard that he absolutely needs two weeks on a tropical island. But the timing sure is bad. If he was working, he would have been able to see all of these women today. At least he's back this weekend."

Alexa silently agreed that having Dr. Crowe back in the clinic would be for the best. He was the head doctor and physician administrator for the clinic. When Frank Crowe was around, everything seemed to run more smoothly. He had an air of calm that seemed to soothe everyone who came into contact with him, especially Dr. Kearns.

Elise Kearns was a wonderful, dedicated doctor, but in Alexa's opinion, she could also be a bit of a flake. Not that a death threat wasn't a legitimate cause for a freak-out, but when Alexa had poked her head into Dr. Kearns' session with the police she could tell that Elise was out of control.

"How about I put the CLOSED sign on the door? We'll still be here in case someone missed their phone message, but maybe it will send that crew across the street away," Alexa said. When she flipped the sign hanging on the door, Alexa stood there a minute looking at the protesters. There were ten today, and they looked like the same group as always. She recognized some of the faces, but their dress was what she really recognized. Most of the protestors looked like Mennonites or maybe settlers from an old movie about how the West was won. The men wore black trousers and plain, long-sleeved shirts. The women wore cotton dresses that dipped below their knees. Today, most of them wore sweaters or jackets against the crisp autumn air.

As she was about to turn away, Alexa noticed two younger men wearing jeans and lightweight fleece jackets join the group. She thought the one guy might have been the man she had seen last week, but she wasn't really sure. The other was a tall, thin African-American who looked totally out of his element.

When Alexa walked back to the desk, Barb emerged from the back to tell Tanisha that the police wanted to talk to her. Barb seemed visibly upset. In her early thirties, she was much younger than Tanisha. Barb strived to look like a tough cookie with her black outfits, heavy make-up, and the Celtic cross tattoo that crawled out of her shirt collar and up the right side of her neck. Alexa thought of Barb's look as Carlisle Goth, slightly shocking for this small town but one that would barely be noticed on a New York City street. Today, Alexa could see Barb fighting back tears, so she busied herself at the desk to give the young woman some space.

A few minutes later, Dr. Kearns appeared. She had taken off her white lab coat and wore a fashionable loose blazer, probably Eileen Fisher or another designer from her beloved Bloomingdales. Elise was a tall, thin woman with pale skin and ash-blonde hair who was always well dressed and usually quite striking. Right now, her skin was chalk white and even the normal bright luster of her hair seemed to have dimmed. She looked totally distraught.

"I'm going home for the rest of the day. You can call me if there is a real emergency, and I'll be here tomorrow. But this whole thing has just been too much for my nerves."

"Do you want me to call your husband for you?" Barb asked, pulling herself together as the doctor entered the room.

"No. He's got a full day of surgeries scheduled. He'll be home soon. I just need to rest for a while." She continued speaking as she walked toward the front entrance. "My car is parked down the street because there was a UPS truck blocking the staff lot this morning." The doctor's voice lost energy as she spoke.

Alexa jumped up from her chair and offered to walk the doctor to her car. She thought that the least she could do was run interference with the crowd across the street if they hassled Dr. Kearns. She felt a little guilty for thinking of Elise as a flake and over the top in her reaction to the death threat.

After all, she thought, I didn't react too well to finding a dead body. We all cope with trauma in different ways.

"What do the police think?" Alexa asked the doctor as they walked down the street. She asked the question mainly to distract Elise from the chanting across the street. It was unlikely that the police would have offered any conclusions yet.

"They really didn't have much to say. Just that this note could be a real threat or it might just be someone yanking my chain. I told them that it's felt like someone has been watching me for the past several days. I don't think the police took that part very seriously. I asked them if I needed police protection. Hah, police protection in Carlisle. They probably never had anybody ask for that before. Since I don't live in the borough, they said that they would tell the state police to patrol by our house at night." Apparently, the doctor had regained her energy. She sounded pretty pissed.

"I know this must be scary," said Alexa. "You need to be cautious."

"Yes, I will be cautious," Dr. Kearns replied. "But I can't let this take on a life of its own. This could just be one of those crazy anti-abortion fuckers playing with my head. And if I believe in a woman's right to choose, I can't let some half-wit intimidate me with a few letters pasted on paper like some kid's kindergarten project. Crazy fuckers. This threw me for a loop, but I'll be OK by tomorrow."

Alexa was glad to see that Elise was beginning to pull herself together and get angry, but she was still concerned. As the doctor climbed into the car, Alexa told her, "Stay mad at this creep and get some rest. But be careful, too." She thought of her recent experience in the forest as she said, "Crazy fuckers can be both crazy and dangerous. So, be on alert until the cops figure this out."

Walking back to the clinic, she thought about the irony.

One of the reasons I came back home was to get away from all the madness of the city, including the danger and violence. And, look at this. A dead body and a death threat. Maybe I should go back to New York City for some peace and quiet.

When the police officers finally left, the nurses and physician's assistants checked out, too. Alexa, Tanisha, and Barb were soon alone in the quiet clinic. They wrapped up some filing, rehashing the day as they worked. The threatening letter had obviously made an impression on the two clinic staff members, despite their attempts to shrug it off.

Barb usually affected a bored attitude at all times. Today, she was jumpy, shifting from one foot to the other as she described for at least the fourth time what happened when they opened the letter. The young woman had just gotten to the part where she and Tanisha had taken the threatening message to Dr. Kearns.

Alexa had a sudden thought and interrupted Barb's tale. "It's sort of strange that the threat came to Dr. Kearns. Dr. Crowe is the one who performs most of the abortions here. So, why would they send a threat to Elise but not Frank? It's weird."

"It is strange, now that you mention it," Barb agreed.

"How did you know that the message was for Dr. Kearns?" Alexa asked, seeing the look on Tanisha's face. "It was addressed to her, right?"

"Oh, my Lord, child. I think we made a mistake." Tanisha said. She turned to her co-worker. "Barb, didn't the envelope just say DOCTOR? It was in those cut out letters, too, just like the note. We just assumed it was for Dr. Kearns because she was on duty in the clinic."

Barb nodded her head in agreement and added hastily, "We gave the envelope to the police, but I'm not sure Dr. Kearns saw it. Oh, my. This threat could be for Dr. Kearns, but what if they were threatening Dr. Frank? And he's over there in Hawaii and doesn't even know that this is happening." By the time Barb had finished she was almost wailing in consternation. Clearly, Barb was much more concerned about the beloved Dr. Crowe than prickly Elise, who had a more uneven relationship with the office staff.

"Ladies, ladies," Alexa tried to calm them. "You were upset when you opened that envelope. Dr. Kearns was on duty today. The letter itself didn't specify who was being threatened. Everyone was on edge. It was an honest oversight. Tomorrow, one of you should call those officers and make sure they know that another doctor works in the clinic. You should tell Dr. Kearns that the envelope was not addressed specifically to her. Tanisha, maybe you want to call her at home now?

"Don't disturb Frank while he's on vacation. I doubt that the person behind this threat followed him to Hawaii. But you ladies or Dr. Kearns should let him know about this as soon as he steps back into the country. He should be on his guard. You all need to be on guard, actually."

Around four o'clock Alexa suggested that they leave. Emotionally exhausted, Barb and Tanisha agreed with little hesitation.

Driving home, Alexa reflected on the bizarre communication.

Although a letter like the one today could just be a crackpot blowing off steam, Alexa's recent brush with homicide made her realize that this threat should not be treated lightly. She hoped that the police would be able to quickly find the person who had sent the note. She admired the clinic's two doctors for their dedication to a difficult job and worried about their safety. Alexa made a mental note to check in with Elise Kearns the following day to see how she was doing.

Friday evening, Alexa and Scout went to Graham's house for pizza night. About once a month, Graham and Kate hosted a family evening. Scout was always welcome. When Alexa's parents weren't somewhere roaming the globe, they often hosted the get-together. The routine never varied. The Williams family ate take-out pizza from Rocco's, with Scout begging some crusts from the kids. Then they played board games until the children's bedtime.

"What game shall we play?" Graham asked when the pizza boxes were empty.

"Chutes and Ladders. Chutes and Ladders," six-year-old Courtney yelled.

Her seven-year-old brother, Jamie, protested, "That's a baby game."

"How about I make you a deal, kiddo," Alexa intervened. "If you agree to Chutes and Ladders, I'll read you a story while Courtney gets her bath."

After two rounds of the game, Kate gathered Courtney up in her arms and lifted her off her chair. Alexa wondered how much longer her petite sister-in-law would be able to lift her daughter. Courtney, with her tumble of honey curls, took after Graham, who was tall but sturdy.

"Come on, princess, it's time for a bath and then bed." Kate deposited her daughter on the floor and steered the reluctant girl toward the stairs. As they reached the top of the steps, Courtney wailed, "But Jamie is staying up. It's not fair."

The young man in question was already standing at the corner bookcase. Jamie seemed tinier than most seven-year olds. Alexa knew that Graham fervently hoped that his son would grow by leaps and bounds as he got older, reaching the six-foot threshold achieved by most of the Williams men. He adored Kate and her petite frame but shuddered to think that his son would favor his mother in stature. Jamie had already inherited her strawberry-blonde hair.

When they finished reading from *Hank the Cowdog*, Graham told his son that it was time for bed.

"Goodnight, Aunt Lexie." Jamie gave her a kiss and ran upstairs.

Graham turned to Alexa. "How are you doing? I see that they still don't know who that dead girl was."

"No, as far as I know, they still haven't identified her." Alexa told Graham about remembering the van on the road that morning and her conversation with the state police. "I know you were concerned about me getting involved without a lawyer, Graham, but there is no way they suspect me of anything. I just happened to be the one who found her dead body." She didn't mention the question regarding her whereabouts on the day of the girl's death.

Graham ran a hand through his sandy hair. Alexa knew this gesture.

"If you speak to the police again, whether you call them or they call you, I want you to make sure I am there. For Christ's sake, Alexa. You're an attorney. You know the rules."

"Speaking of police," she interjected, knowing that the brotherly advice was just getting started, "I had an encounter with the borough police this week as well."

"Speeding ticket? Or maybe they just pulled that rust-bucket Land Rover over on general principles," Graham jibed. He loved to tease Alexa about her Defender, a family hand-me-down with well over two hundred thousand miles on it.

"No, this was serious business, but I was just a bystander." Alexa filled him in on the threat received by the clinic, answering his questions about the incident. By the time she finished, she had gotten angry.

"I have a really hard time with people who become so caught up in their opposition to abortion that they turn to violence. What hypocrites.

"Mom always talks about the old days when a woman's choice was between a back alley abortion with a coat hanger or an unwanted child.

"But, I've got my own opinions on a woman's right to choose. Of course, birth control is always the best option. But, let's be real. Birth control can fail. Young girls have unprotected sex. Women are raped. And some single women and even couples just aren't in a position— financially, medically, or emotionally—to bring a child into this world.

"When I did that internship with the New York City DA's Child Abuse Unit, I saw some horrifying consequences of people who weren't ready to be parents. That's when I came up with my guiding principle: it's far better for a pregnancy to be terminated safely and legally than for an unwanted child to be born into a life of neglect or abuse.

"Of course, I respect an individual's right not to choose abortion. That's the whole point of choice. A lot of women and their families decide to raise the kid. And, there are loving families out there willing to adopt.

"But, it really ticks me off when someone tries to impose their beliefs on someone else's choice. Abortion is a legal medical procedure, not the murder of an unborn child."

"Down, girl. Down. I haven't seen you this wound up for a long time. You know you're preaching to the choir." Graham's amused expression turned serious. "What worries me is that I'm pretty sure whoever sent that note to the clinic has a very different, and probably dangerous, point of view."

Kate walked back in the room. "Two sleepyheads are tucked away for the night. Those kids can be a handful, especially when Aunt Alexa is here," she smiled.

Alexa laughed as she rose. "Come, Scout," she called to the dog dozing in the corner. "We have to go. I've got some sort of all-day event with Caleb tomorrow. It's at a lodge over in Perry County where his parents are members."

Kate's ears perked up. "Parents? He's taking you to meet the parents? This must be getting serious," she said, clearly excited.

Despite her own misgivings about Caleb's intentions, Alexa played things down. "I don't think so. It's an annual event for his family and friends and he needed a date. There is nothing serious about my relationship with Caleb. We're just having a good time."

"Isn't that what the guy is supposed to say?" her brother cracked.

Kate, always the matchmaker, frowned at her husband. "I don't really know Caleb Browne well, but we've met a few times. He's an established businessman in the community. He's incredibly good looking. Alexa, that sounds like the right combo for serious to me."

Trying to get out the door before Graham and Kate could dissect her love life any further, Alexa grabbed Scout's collar and walked to the foyer. As she left, she said, "I'm just not ready for anything serious, Kate. And, if I was, I'm pretty sure it wouldn't be with Caleb. He's a nice guy, and you're right, he's really hot. But, for me, he's just not going to be a permanent relationship."

Chapter Ten

When Alexa returned from Graham's house, she caught up on some chores. As she hastily ran the sweeper through the house, she made a mental note to take the screens out and put them away in the next few weeks.

Alexa's final chore was to mix a batch of brownies for tomorrow's party. Baking was not her strong suit, but box brownies were pretty hard to ruin. Open up the package, stir in eggs, water, oil, and voilà. For really special occasions, she made her Nanny Emma's devil's food cupcakes with coffee icing. Since Alexa didn't expect to know anyone at this party tomorrow except Caleb, she stuck to brownies.

With the brownies cooling on the counter, Alexa made herself a pot of tea and found some gingersnaps in the cupboard. Settled into one of her most comfortable chairs, she broke one of the cookies in half and offered it the mastiff at her feet.

"Between you and me, buddy," she said, "I'm a little nervous about tomorrow. I've basically never heard anything about Caleb's family, let alone met them. I don't really know any of his friends. And then, boom. Tomorrow, I get to party with the whole gang."

The dog moved closer as she spoke and rested his giant jowls on her lap.

"Nice try, Scout. Acting all sympathetic to get another gingersnap?" She offered him a few more bites. "I'm sorry to leave you alone on a Saturday. We'll have fun on Sunday, though. We're going on another hike with your favorite park ranger."

As she climbed into bed, Alexa wondered what the next day would bring. Her anxiety ratcheted up another notch when she remembered Caleb's call yesterday to mention that most of the women at the lodge would be wearing casual dresses. A dress to a picnic in Perry County? Was this the New Bloomfield Country Club or what?

Finally, in exasperation, she concluded: Alexa, you are making too big a deal out of this. Like Dad always says, just go with the flow.

At eleven the next morning, Caleb's big pick-up truck pulled up to the cabin. When she heard the big truck out front, Alexa threw an alpaca shawl around her shoulders and walked out to meet Caleb. After some indecision about what exactly a casual dress might mean to Caleb's crowd, Alexa had picked out one of her favorites: a Johnny Was black boho chic dress with colorful embroidery around the smocked neck and a pair of short Frye cowboy boots.

"Am I overdressed?" she asked as she hoisted herself onto the running board and saw that Caleb was wearing camouflage pants and what looked like an old hunting coat.

Damn, I thought he would bring his Explorer, she thought. It was quite the challenge to remain ladylike climbing into the huge Ford F-150 in this outfit. Alexa didn't even want to contemplate what the reverse process would look like when she had to reach the ground at the picnic. She hoped that there would be no audience— probably not the best way to make a good first impression by exposing her underwear to Caleb's friends and family.

"No. You look great."

On the drive over North Mountain to Perry County, Alexa tried to elicit more information about the lodge and Caleb's family. "Does your family live in Perry County? I thought you were from Carlisle."

"My parents live in a small village over here in Perry County, which is where I grew up. This lodge is a nice place for them to get away. The property has over 200 acres, so my friends and I come over here on Saturdays to hunt or fish. In deer season, we stay in the lodge for a few nights. And then, family and friends get together her for this annual party."

"Will your sister, Rebecca, be there?"

"Rebecca?" Caleb repeated in a shocked tone. A pained look fleeted across his face. "No. She's not here anymore."

Alexa was surprised to hear that his sister had left the area. As she reflected upon the times that Caleb had mentioned her, however, she realized that all his stories had been about Rebecca as a child ...

Several miles passed in silence. After they crested the mountain and began the descent into Perry County, she tried again. "What type of work does your father do? And your mother, does she work?"

"My father is a minister. As for my mother, being a minister's wife is a full-time job."

"A minister," Alexa exclaimed in surprise. In attempt to hide her astonishment at this revelation, she joked, "Are you one of those preacher's kids who were wild and got in a lot of trouble in high school?"

She never got an answer to her mischievous question. "Here's the lane," said Caleb as they turned. A small sign with the words "Kingdom Lodge" burned into an unfinished slab of wood marked the entrance.

"Kingdom Lodge?" Alexa queried. "That's an unusual name."

"Back in the day, this whole section of the county was called Kingdom Valley. That's where the name comes from. Now, only the old timers still call the area Kingdom Valley."

The gravel road opened into a large parking area filled with pick-up trucks and oversized SUVs. A row of pines partially concealed a large structure beyond the parking area. Alexa breathed a sigh of relief when she saw that no one was in the parking lot to see her clamber over the running board of the big pick-up truck. When Alexa reached the ground, Caleb led the way to a slate path in a gap in the pines.

Alexa gasped when she saw the lodge. A lovely mix of stone and timbers, the old building sprawled out along the hillside. The ground sloped downward, and Alexa could see the glimmer of water in front of the massive structure.

Caleb smiled at Alexa's reaction and said, "This is just the back. The front deck that overlooks the lake is spectacular. Just go up these steps."

The view was truly outstanding. The lodge's deep wraparound porch faced out over a long, narrow lake that nestled below a steep mountain ridge, blazing orange and red with the last of autumn's color. Alexa only got a few brief seconds to take in the scene before Caleb took her elbow and began steering her into the lodge itself.

Caleb seemed nervous. He nodded at several people but kept marching her through the main great room. The room was two stories high with a large, double-sided stone fireplace in the center. The impressive room reminded Alexa of the Old Faithful Inn in Yellowstone, though on a smaller scale. Mounted deer heads and other taxidermy served as the primary decoration.

Alexa was surprised to see so many people at this party. There were fifty or more adults in the great room, and they had passed others on the spacious porch. At least another twenty kids were running through the place and around the lake. From Caleb's description of family and friends, she had expected a fairly small group.

Caleb stopped in front of a couple sitting near the fireplace. The older couple rose, and Alexa turned her attention to the man and woman in front of her.

"Father and Mother, I would like to introduce you to Alexa Williams. Alexa, these are my parents, Reverend and Mrs. Browne," Caleb said rather formally.

"How nice to meet you. This is a beautiful place."

"It is nice to meet you as well, my child." The reverend spoke while his wife stood smiling at his side. Caleb's father was a giant of a man, tall and broad shouldered with a flowing gray beard that came to a point just above his belt. His mother was a thin woman with moss green eyes. Her brown hair was gathered in a tight bun behind her head. Wearing a simple but dated charcoal dress, Mrs. Browne had an air of faded elegance.

Alexa imagined that the mother had been quite the beauty when young. The father, however, was imposing and a bit overwhelming. The black suit and clerical collar went with the job, she supposed. But, the beard made Reverend Browne look like one of the guys from ZZ Top, although not nearly as laid back.

The reverend spoke to Alexa. "Caleb has told us quite a bit about you. A lawyer, yet you look so young to carry such a burden."

"I love the law," Alexa responded. "I don't think of it as a burden at all. Every day is a challenge, and I enjoy that."

Mrs. Browne laid a hand on her husband's arm. "Now, Jebediah, let's give Caleb and Alexa a chance to get some food and enjoy fellowship with the other young people. I'm sure we'll have time to talk later. I am so glad to meet you, my dear. As the scripture says at Hebrews 13:2, 'Do not forget to welcome strangers, for by so doing some people have entertained angels without knowing it.' Although I must say you don't seem a stranger to us since Caleb has mentioned you so frequently."

Caleb, who had stood by silently during the conversation, jumped in. "Yes, we will certainly spend time with you later, but we haven't had anything to eat yet. I hope you brought your pumpkin pie, Mother."

"Son, you know that your mother would not come to this annual fall picnic without at least four of her famous pumpkin pies. Go and enjoy."

In the dining area there were several tables piled high with food. Alexa saw fried chicken, several hams, deviled eggs, and too many versions of macaroni and potato salad to count. Alexa slipped the brownies she'd made onto the dessert table; they looked forlorn among the elaborate pies and cakes already on display. Caleb and Alexa filled their plates and made their way to one of the tables set up on the porch.

"Your parents seem very nice," Alexa said, mentally crossing her fingers. "Your mother is lovely. Your dad is a little intimidating, though."

"Yeah, growing up with Reverend Browne as my father wasn't always the easiest. He lives and breathes the whole man of God thing, and that comes with very high expectations." Caleb grew pensive. "You were joking about me being a preacher's kid earlier. I don't think I ever went the typical road that you hear about. I wasn't a wild teenager. I didn't get in trouble or do drugs. But, I think that I have taken a somewhat different path than my father would have liked. Maybe that's been my way of acting out."

Caleb became more somber as he continued. "I have to admit, though, that my father's lessons run deep. I find that the man I've become in recent years is much more like the boy Reverend Browne raised. I always try to do the right thing in my life, just as my father taught." He looked at Alexa ruefully. "Perhaps my path isn't as different as I would like to believe."

After a pause, Caleb declared, "Enough deep talk. We're here for a party. If you've finished that plate of food, let's go wander."

Surprisingly, Alexa enjoyed the afternoon. After lunch, she and Caleb stopped to chat with several groups of people. Caleb seemed to know everyone, and she sensed an undertone of deference in the way people treated her date. The preacher's son thing, perhaps?

Caleb introduced one couple as the Lehmans. "Paul and Charity own a farm near my parents' house. I spent a lot of time there when I was a child."

"I still remember you and Paul Junior raising Cain in the barn on rainy afternoons," Charity laughed.

"How is Paul Junior?" Caleb asked.

"Well, he and Mary couldn't make it today. They have been dealing with their young boy, Thomas, who has been very sick," Paul explained.

"Reverend Browne has been so wonderful to our family and that child. He visited every day during the crisis and encouraged the congregation to help out with the medical bills. Your father is a wonderful man, Caleb."

By mid-afternoon, Alexa had forgotten more names than she remembered. However, she would remember three young men, who seemed quite close to Caleb. He had introduced them as his hunting buddies. Clad in camouflage pants and jackets like Caleb, Daniel, Joel, and Gabriel all looked like they lived for the outdoors.

Caleb may have mentioned hunting with Gabriel and Daniel. She had a hazy recollection of those names, but she didn't remember hearing about Joel. However, she had a tendency to zone out when Caleb waxed eloquent about his outdoor sports. She hadn't met any of them before.

The three friends seemed quite different. Brown-haired Daniel came across an affable guy, who always had a joke at the tip of his tongue.

Small and wiry, Joel moved like coiled spring. Alexa wondered what had him wound so tight.

Gabriel was tall with copper hair, a dusting of freckles across his nose, and the face of an Irish angel. He was one of the most physically beautiful men Alexa had ever seen in her life.

Of the three, only Joel and Daniel had women with them. Joel's plain wife, Leah, was nice but rather subdued. Leah was pregnant and shared that she was in her sixth month, so Alexa attributed her somber demeanor to exhaustion. Leah's voluminous dress was as dull as her expression. Alexa didn't think she had ever seen maternity clothes quite that awful.

Daniel's date was a perky brunette named Georgia, who looked like a tomboy with her spiky short hair. She apparently hadn't gotten the dress code memo and was wearing blue jeans and a leather jacket.

The gorgeous Gabriel appeared to be at the party on his own.

Caleb and his three friends had an endless supply of hunting stories. When the guys decided that they wanted to go to a range on the outskirts of the grounds for target practice, Alexa decided to stay on the front porch with Leah and Georgia. She didn't think she could take one more story about a giant buck that got away.

"These guys really love hunting, don't they," she remarked to Leah and Georgia after the men left. The three women claimed rockers on the front deck and watched a group of kids boating on the lake. Most of the other adults had migrated into the great room, so they had the broad porch to themselves.

"Boys will be boys," drawled Georgia. "I hunt a bit myself, but it's not a major obsession. Actually, that's how I met Dan. We were both looking at some archery equipment at the Outdoor Show in Harrisburg last winter. His bow made me quiver and that was that."

Alexa dissolved into laughter at Georgia's infectious giggle. Leah pursed her lips as if she had eaten something sour. "Men hunt," she pronounced in a whispery voice. "That's what God intended, and I'm thankful that Joel can bring home food to the table. I don't know how you can hunt, Georgia. It's just not natural."

Although it didn't seem like Leah was joking, Alexa decided not to pursue this issue of God's intention. "How long have you and Joel been married, Leah?"

"Two years. We waited until he came home from the army."

Georgia asked Alexa, "What's the story on you and Caleb?"

"We've been dating for a few months. He's out of town a lot, so I don't see him that often."

"You are such a lucky girl to be dating Reverend Browne's only son. There are so many girls in the congregation who would love to settle down with Caleb," Leah enthused.

"We have a lot of fun together." Alexa was tempted to shake Leah up a bit by telling her how hot Caleb was in bed, but she feared precipitating a premature delivery.

Georgia had fewer inhibitions. She turned to Leah and asked, "Where is that little blonde that Gabe was getting it on with? I thought I would see Beth here today."

"Yes, Gabriel had been seeing her for a while. But, Joel says they ended their relationship. Beth was not the Christian girl Gabriel thought she was."

"Wow. That's a surprise. I thought they were pretty into each other. I really liked Beth. We always found a lot to talk about. Maybe I'll give her a call."

Alexa was spared hearing more about the love lives of the hunting buddies by Caleb's mother. When she walked out and glanced in their direction, Alexa rose to join Mrs. Browne at the timbered railing.

"Are you enjoying yourself, my dear?"

"Yes, Mrs. Browne. It's a lovely day, and the lodge is quite spectacular. I had no idea that there was a place like this in Perry County."

"Please dear, call me by my given name, Joanna. I am so glad to finally meet you. Caleb rarely tells us much about his social life, and he seldom brings a young woman to meet us. You must be very special to him. He has often spoken of you to the reverend and me; and now, here you are."

In the afternoon sunlight, Caleb's mother showed her age. Fine lines etched the corners of her soft green eyes and the bright sun highlighted the silver strands that streaked her hair. However, the woman held herself ramrod straight, which gave her an almost regal air.

Mrs. Browne was clearly making an effort to be kind. But, Alexa couldn't imagine calling this distant and rather otherworldly woman, Joanna. "I'm not sure how special I am to Caleb, but we enjoy each other's company.

Although, now he's abandoned me and is off somewhere shooting with his buddies."

"Oh, yes. Those four have been such good friends for as long as I can remember. I think they met in Bible School and have stayed close ever since. Of course, Caleb can't see his friends quite as often since he moved over the mountain to Carlisle."

Alexa smiled inwardly at the way she said this, as if Caleb had moved to another country and not just an hour away.

"He doesn't come to visit his father and me as often either. The Good Book speaks pure truth when it says at Psalms 127:3 that 'Children are a gift from the Lord.' Caleb has certainly been our gift. I would like to see him more often, but I understand that young men must have their own lives. I am blessed that we remain close. Caleb is very much his father's son."

Mrs. Browne's Bible verses discomfited Alexa. Maybe it came with the territory when you're married to a preacher. Still, she was ill-prepared for the next question.

"What congregation does your family worship with, Alexa?"

"Umm, my family has always been Presbyterian." She failed to mention that, except for weddings and funerals, Alexa hadn't gone to church since she was sixteen.

Searching for more neutral ground, Alexa said, "Tell me more about yourself, Mrs. Browne. Have you ever worked outside the home or is being a minister's wife a full-time job?"

"Sometimes I think I would have enjoyed a job of my own, but I married Reverend Browne right after school. He had just completed his studies for the ministry and had been assigned a congregation. I stepped into the role of minister's wife and helpmate quite young. When the children came along, there was even more to do. Although the house seems empty now with just Jebediah and me, the work of the church keeps us both busier than ever."

Hearing raucous laughter, Alexa looked across the lawn to see Caleb and his friends goofing around. "Looks like they had fun shooting."

In a few seconds, Caleb danced up the front stairs and onto the porch. "What a lovely pair the two of you make." He wrapped an arm around his mother's shoulders.

Alexa was relieved that Caleb had interrupted the awkward conversation with his mother. "Target practice was good, it appears."

"It certainly was. I won three out of five. I just don't know how I lost the last two to Joel. The gun started to pull high toward the end."

"You always were a good shot, son. I'm glad we had a chance to chat, Alexa. Caleb, come and speak to your father before you leave." Mrs. Browne headed back inside.

Dark shadows fell over the lake. For a brief moment, a narrow band of trees at the top of the ridge dripped crimson in the last rays of the setting sun. Alexa hugged her shawl a little tighter.

"It is absolutely beautiful here, Caleb. You and your family are lucky to have this place."

"Yes," he replied almost wistfully. "The lodge is one of my favorite places on earth. Not that I've seen much of the rest of the world, but I can't imagine many spots that could compare. I've put a lot of Perry County behind me, but I'll always come back to the lodge."

Caleb had never shared anything that was truly important to him. In one short afternoon, she was learning more about this man than she had during their entire relationship. Today certainly was providing a new perspective on Caleb Browne.

"Let's go eat. I'm starving again. Caleb pulled her toward the great room door.

"Eat again? It's only been a couple of hours since I devoured a huge plate of food."

"That's what picnics are all about, isn't it?"

The dining room still overflowed with food. Alexa could swear that she saw ten new things on the entrée table and an entire new table of desserts. These people had gone all out for this picnic. Caleb filled a plate, and Alexa couldn't resist some chicken wings and another piece of pumpkin pie. They filled their cups with cider.

Caleb led Alexa into the great room where they grabbed two seats on an aging leather couch against the wall. "So, tell me about these friends of yours," Alexa asked.

"I've known Gabriel, Daniel, and Joel my whole life. We were best friends at church and in school. We sowed our wild oats together and stayed friends even after we left Perry County. I moved to Carlisle after college and opened my business. Daniel worked at a sales job in Harrisburg for a few years until I hired him as a sales manager. Gabriel is an artist. He sells his handcrafted wooden furniture in artisan shops up and down the East Coast. Joel did a stint in the army. Then he married and came back to work on the family farm. These days the four of us get together to hunt here at Kingdom Lodge."

"I could tell that you're pretty tight with these guys."

The conversation ebbed when Caleb tackled the mound of food on his plate. Alexa nibbled at a chicken wing and took in the large gathering before her. The room hummed with activity. Kids tore through the room, dodging furniture and weaving through clusters of adults. Many of the men stood around the roaring fireplace, which threw off enough heat to warm even the edges of the room. A number of women sat together, many holding babies and small children in their arms.

Alexa felt like she was watching a movie. Then it hit her. Something was missing: color. Everything here had been filmed in sepia tones. The men wore faded flannel shirts and brown hunting clothes. The robust-looking guy right in front of Alexa sported brown camouflage pants and a well-worn plaid flannel buttoned up at the neck. Most of the men had adopted a similar uniform.

Even more subdued, the women looked like a flock of pigeons, cooing together in their plain garb of gray and brown. Perhaps they sewed their own clothes and had all used the same pattern for their modestly cut dresses? Alexa searched in vain for bright colors, even among the children. Bizarre. Was brown the new black here in Perry County?

During the afternoon, Alexa had caught a few women whispering when she passed by. She assumed they were gossiping because she was Caleb's date. Now she realized that her bohemian designer dress, especially paired with the cowboy boots, was way out of the norm for this crowd. She had walked onto the wrong movie set. Georgia was probably the only other woman here today who looked like she belonged in the twenty-first century.

A hush fell over the room. When Alexa glanced at Caleb to ask what was going on, she followed his gaze to the center of the room. Reverend Browne stood by the big fireplace with his hand raised. Everyone in the room had turned toward the minister, who let the silence linger a few seconds. Holding a large red Bible, he began to pray.

"God, our heavenly Father. In Jesus' name, we pray. Today, we thank You for all Your many blessings to those assembled here. As 1 Thessalonians 5:18 says, 'It is a key to faith and it is natural and right that we give thanks always to the One from whom all good things come.'

"Thank You, Father, for the blessings of this day, for this wonderful food, for the fellowship of our church and of Kingdom Lodge. Thank You for each day we live and faithfully do our humble best to carry out Your Word and Your will.

"We are all brothers and sisters in Christ who take into our hearts Psalm 100, 'Know the Lord is God. It is He that made us and we are His: we are His people, and the sheep of His pasture. Enter His gates with thanksgiving.' We come to You today in thanksgiving and seek to live our lives in Your service."

As the Reverend continued, Alexa tuned out and studied the others in the room. Everyone she saw, even the toddlers, sat completely still, hanging on to every one of Reverend Browne's words. The tall, bearded preacher did cut a fascinating figure. In this mode, he looked less like the ZZ Top guys and more like some old time prophet ready to lead the faithful to the Promised Land. She was jolted out of her reverie when the minister's voice rose to a thunderous level.

"As we rejoice in Your blessings, Father, we also pray to vanquish the powers of darkness. We vow to continue our vigilance against those who do not honor Your work here on earth or seek to subvert Thy will. We pledge to continue our work to bring the sinners to the light and drive the demons back into the darkness and the hellfire from whence they came."

Reverend Browne's eyes, the same eerie silver-gray as his son's, smoldered. "We are Your Christian soldiers in the war against evil and the holy fight to help Your Son save the world. John 3:17, 'For God did not send His Son into the world to condemn the world, but in order that the world might be saved through Him.'

"We ask for Your help in this sacred task and ask You continue Your blessings to this flock. In Jesus' name. Amen."

Amens echoed across the room as he finished. The chorus of Amens rang with a peculiar similarity, just like the crowd's clothes. Caleb whispered an Amen, and then sat in silence.

Alexa felt like she had stumbled into another country. Hers was not a family who prayed in public at weekend picnics. Ambivalent about the idea of God and turned off by organized religion, Alexa never prayed at all. The closest she came to prayer was when she practiced meditation. Add on this group's slavish devotion to drab as a fashion choice. This whole experience was weirding her out. She was ready to leave.

"Caleb," she said, much more lightly than she felt. "Can we head out of here soon? I'd like to get back to the house. I didn't make arrangements for anyone to take care of Scout. He's been alone for hours."

"Sure. Things will start to wind down here soon, anyway. Why don't we leave now?"

Caleb headed toward his parents, who were holding court by the fireplace. "Goodnight, Father. Goodnight, Mother. I'm taking Alexa home, so we're saying goodbye."

"Yes," said Alexa. "It was a lovely day. It was nice to meet you both."

"Drive safely," Mrs. Browne told her son, then turned to Alexa. "I'm so glad to finally meet you, my dear."

Reverend Browne put his hand on Caleb's shoulder. "It is always good to see you, son. Come to dinner soon. And bring Alexa so we can get to know her better."

He raised his hand above Alexa's head and chanted, "May the grace of the Lord Jesus Christ, and the love of God, and the fellowship of the Holy Spirit be with you."

It seemed like the ride home would never end. Caleb rattled on and on about his friends and target practice. Alexa just let his words wash over her and tried to reconcile the Caleb she had been dating for months with the Caleb she had met today. This Caleb was unexpectedly formal, almost diffident with his parents. This Caleb had a tight bond with three guys he had barely mentioned. But, Alexa had been most freaked by the ultra religious atmosphere at the lodge, one that this Caleb blended into so seamlessly. The old Caleb had kept this entire part of his life secret.

When they reached Alexa's cabin, Caleb walked her to the door. "Thanks for coming with me today. I hope you had a good time."

"The lodge is beautiful. I can see why you love the place." Alexa stepped into the house. Scout slipped past her, headed for the trees.

Caleb stopped at the threshold and grabbed her hand. "I can't come in tonight. I have to fly to Atlanta tomorrow. I might not be home again until next week. But, I'll call you as soon as I get back." He leaned over to kiss Alexa, drawing her into a tighter embrace, then sighed, "No. I've got to go."

"It was a long day. If you're traveling tomorrow, you need your rest. Call me when you get back."

Alexa followed Caleb onto the deck. Long after the afterglow of his taillights faded, she continued to gaze down the lane ruminating about the revelations of the day. When Scout ambled up the steps and pushed his cold nose into her palm, she finally let the thoughts go and walked into the house.

Chapter Eleven

Wednesday, November 21, 1934.

Folded so close ...

As the car drove down the endless road, Dewilla stared in wonder at the big white and red barns that punctuated the miles of fields. Some of the structures had fanciful paintings on them. When the family first passed paintings like these a few days earlier, Winifred told the girls that they were Pennsylvania Dutch Hex signs.

Dewilla hadn't learned anything about these Dutch people in school, but the family moved around so much that her lessons had been interrupted many times. Dewilla thought that she would like to learn more about these Hex signs when she enrolled in her new school in the East.

Dewilla didn't understand why they left California to make this long journey east. It didn't make sense. Daddy said that something called the Depression made it hard for people to find work. But, Daddy had a good job in California, working at the fruit company. He had even made enough money to buy this big blue Pontiac Essex sedan for their trip.

Now Daddy needed a new job. She had heard him ask about work at several stops along the way, but he'd had no luck. So, they just kept driving. Now, Daddy had turned west again, and Dewilla didn't know where they were headed.

Sometimes, Dewilla thought that she had been traveling her whole life. In those ten years, the Noakes had lived in Utah, California, and then moved back to Utah. When Mama died two years ago, Daddy packed the girls up and took them to California again.

That's when Winifred came to take care of them. Dewilla had so admired her beautiful cousin. "Norma," she sighed, "I wish I had stylish dark hair like Cousin Winnie. Instead, I look just like you and Cordelia with our light brown hair and dumb freckles."

"She's pretty, I guess. But, Winnie is stuck on herself."

"Since Aunt Pearl is Daddy's sister, you would think that we would look more like Winifred."

"Maybe you and Cordelia, but not me since Daddy's not really my father. My real father still lives in Idaho, you know. So, Winnie's not my blood cousin.

"I'm glad that you came with us after Mama passed. I don't know what I would do if your real father took you away from us. I miss Mama so much."

"I miss Mama, too. And I don't mind us having light brown hair because we look like our Mama, not that prissy Winifred. I don't know why Daddy wants that girl here anyway. I've been taking good care of you and Dewilla since Mama died, and Winnie is just a few years older than me."

"Norma, Winifred is six years older than you; she's almost a grown woman. But, I hope she will be a lot of fun, like another big sister in the house."

After a few months, Dewilla concluded that Norma had been right. Winifred was a disappointment, more interested in Daddy than the girls. Norma said that Winifred was the reason they were heading east. She told Dewilla, "People in town started calling Winifred a harlot, so Daddy wanted to get her away from California."

Dewilla didn't exactly know what a harlot was. Harlot sounded a lot like Jean Harlow, who Dewilla had seen on movie posters at the picture palace. With her platinum hair, Miss Harlow's beauty put even Winifred to shame.

It seemed strange that Daddy wanted to get Winfred away from people who were calling her beautiful. Of course, Daddy always told the girls not to be vain. Maybe he didn't want Winifred to hear everyone comparing her to Miss Harlow and get a swelled head.

This harlot thing was a puzzle though. Winifred didn't look a whit like Jean Harlow.

As Dewilla watched the countryside pass by, she hoped that Daddy would find a place to live soon. The excitement of a trip across the country had waned. After a week and a half on the road, Dewilla was bone tired—tired of traveling, tired of sleeping in shabby tourist camps, tired of the relentless hunger that stalked her every waking moment.

Monday, the girls nibbled at stale Parker rolls that Norma had pocketed from their feast at the diner. After a stop at a filling station, Daddy climbed into the Pontiac with his shoulders slouched. Dewilla cried when he whispered, "I am so sorry. The rolls will have to do for today's meal. I used all of today's food money to fill up the car."

On Tuesday, her father fed the family. Afternoon was slipping into evening before he pulled over at a rundown cafe. By that time a fog had claimed Dewilla. She couldn't surface from the dense mist that filled her head.

"Dewilla. Get out of the car now, girl." Dewilla latched onto Winifred's whispery voice and climbed out of the thick miasma that enveloped her. When Dewilla's feet touched the pavement, her legs nearly buckled. Driven by the prospect of a hot supper, she forced herself to walk into the restaurant. When Daddy ordered only one meal to divide among the three sisters, Dewilla's tiny portion left her desperate for more.

Dewilla had never experienced hunger before. In California, the family had a garden, and Daddy put meat on the table at least once a week. On this trip, the farther they traveled, the less they had to eat. Daddy said that he had to budget their money and that meant cutting back on meals.

Dewilla worried most about Cordelia, who acted fretful and sickly. The eight year old just couldn't understand why they had so little to eat. The baby of the family, Cordelia had always been cosseted, and she often seemed much younger than her years. Although all three of the sisters had been devastated by Mama's death, Cordelia had turned into an even bigger baby.

Norma and Cordelia had been sneaking extra food onto Cordelia's plate whenever they could. But, now, none of the sisters had been getting enough to eat, and it was getting harder to share.

Daddy drove on, leaving the barns with Hex signs far behind. Dewilla stared at an endless procession of barren fields until the dun-colored blur made her drowsy. She drifted on the edge of sleep until a pang of hunger jolted her awake. Fighting tears, Dewilla had an alarming thought: what would they do if the money ran out and Daddy still hadn't found a job?

Chapter Twelve

When the sunlight streaming through her bedroom windows awoke Alexa, she pulled the covers to her chin and thought about Kingdom Lodge. Yesterday seemed like a bad dream. Reverend Browne's unsettling prayer. Mrs. Browne's Bible verses. Leah's take on appropriate gender roles. All those dreary clothes.

Let's be honest, she admitted. Seeing Caleb right at home in that ZZ Top gospel show is what really has you freaked out.

A faded orange leaf fluttering against the windowpane captured Alexa's attention. It called to mind the image of a dying brown leaf tangled in white-blonde hair. It had been two weeks since Alexa and Scout found the body in the woods. Every time Alexa thought about the way the girl had been dumped beneath the mountain laurel, she got angry.

A thump of the mattress interrupted Alexa's reverie. Scout was bouncing his chin on the edge of the bed, so she rolled out of bed to let the dog out for his morning romp.

The phone rang as Alexa poured water for her tea. "Hey, this is Reese. Are you still up for a hike? This weather is supposed to hold all day."

"Absolutely. What time?"

"One of the guys called in sick this morning, so I'm covering his shift. I can't get there before one o'clock. Is that too late?"

"No, that gives me time to finish some work around the house. There are some trails nearby the cabin that we could explore. Do you want to stay for dinner? I made spaghetti sauce earlier this week."

"Sounds like a plan. See you later."

Alexa loved Sunday mornings at the cabin. After breakfast, she spent some time meditating on the deck, soaking in the crisp autumn air. Plunging into fall clean up, she put flowerpots into storage and swept leaves. She took screens out of the back windows. In hopes of more warm weather, she left the front screens in place. Before she knew it, Alexa heard Reese's Jeep crunching the leaves on the lane.

They started their hike near the cabin. Alexa told Reese, "If you follow this trail south, it climbs Hunter's Ridge and eventually intersects with the Appalachian Trail. This is one of several small trails that circle through the forest. I thought we could do a loop that takes us by Weaver's Pond and then come back through the pines."

Scout led the way. For the first twenty minutes they climbed slowly upward. At the top of the incline, they came to a big outcropping of rocks. Alexa hopped from rock to rock until she stood on the largest boulder. Reese scrambled to keep up.

"No panoramic view like Flat Rock, but the trees are pretty spectacular this time of year. See the roof of the cabin down there? Sitting on the border of the state forest is a real plus; nothing for miles except the cabin and a sea of trees."

"This is pretty sweet. Not too many people can walk out their front door and get a view like this."

Alexa and Reese continued to hike in companionable silence for another hour. Soon, the path wound downhill to a small pond. When Scout ran up to the edge, several frogs splashed into the quiet pool. The dog cautiously bent to take a drink.

"Is he a swimmer?" asked Reese.

"No. He won't go any farther into the water than this. I don't know if he can swim. Can you imagine rescuing this big lummox if he started to sink?"

After a quick pause for a drink, Alexa and Reese pressed on. Alexa guided Reese onto a path that paralleled the state road. They were close enough to see an occasional car. A few of the motorists waved as they passed.

After a few minutes, Alexa stopped in front of a simple blue sign that said: 'Here Were Found Three Babes in the Woods, November 24, 1934.'

Reese touched the sign. "I've seen this from the road and always wondered what it meant."

They rested on a log while Alexa told Reese the story. "The sign commemorates three young girls who were killed by their father and his lover, who was also his niece. As you can see from the date, this happened during the Great Depression. Two men who were cutting wood found the three girls' bodies on the ground covered with a blanket. The children were lying in a row; the middle sister had her arms around the youngest.

"When they searched nearby, the police found suitcases that contained information on the girls' identities. A few days later they connected the girls to a murder-suicide in the train yards near Altoona, Pennsylvania. The father had shot the niece and then turned the gun on himself.

"The press dubbed the girls 'the Babes in the Woods.' The scandal made the news all over the country. Thousands of people came out to see the girls' bodies and attend services at a local funeral home. The sisters were buried in Westminster Cemetery near Carlisle.

"When Graham and I were kids, we would come out here and play. We went on a school field trip to the local history museum for an exhibit about the Babes. We saw a picture of the dead girls; three young girls in winter coats, lined up on a blanket on the ground. The exhibit also had death masks of the sisters' faces, made by the police. They were really creepy but fascinating.

"The exhibit made such an impression on my brother and me that we began playing a game about the Babes. Graham and I would take turns lying on the ground and pretending that we were dead.

"Now, I shudder to think about how we could make a game out of something so tragic, but I think Graham and I were too young to totally understand the concept of death at the time. Besides, I think it's in children's natures to be macabre. I liked to pretend that I was the middle sister, perhaps because of her unusual name, Dewilla."

Alexa paused for a moment before confessing, "I know this sounds crazy, but when I found that young girl dead in Michaux, for a moment I thought that she was one of the Babes."

After leaving the blue memorial, Alexa broke away from the trail. In less than fifteen minutes of steady walking, Alexa led Reese to a rustic little building nestled beneath acres of tall pines.

"This is a church?" Reese nodded at the cross on the top of the small limestone structure.

"Yes. Our Lady of the Forest—a Catholic Church. It's been here forever. When the iron forge was in operation at Pine Grove Furnace, people would come here for regular services. Today, it's not used much. They open it up for services a few times in the summer. A priest comes up from Shippensburg, I think. Every once in a while a couple gets married here. I think it would be a very romantic setting for a wedding.

"I brought you here to show you a secret piece of Our Lady's history." Alexa headed to a small stream a few yards beyond the church. They followed the gurgling stream into a grove of towering pines. The pine needles dampened the sound of their steps.

Catching sight of the small stone springhouse ahead, Reese exclaimed, "What a great spot."

Alexa smiled and cupped her hands to catch water flowing from a pipe. "This is pure spring water and great for drinking." She took a sip from her hands. "Try it. Luckily, this is off the beaten path, so people don't come here to collect the water. But, the state does test it periodically to make sure it's safe to drink."

Reese tasted the water and gave it his approval. Scout lapped thirstily at the small pool of water that had collected below the pipe.

"Was this spring the reason they built the church here?"

"I'm not sure, but it makes sense that they would build near a spring. It's so beautiful here. These trees are old growth pines; they must have been tall even when the church was built almost two hundred years ago."

As she spoke, Alexa moved toward a huge rhododendron bush at the rear of the springhouse. When Reese joined her, she leaned over to grasp a rusted ring at the foot of the bush. It was partially concealed by the vegetation.

"What's this? I didn't even see that ring until you grabbed it."

"This is the real surprise," Alexa said as she lifted the door attached to the ring. When Alexa lifted the trapdoor, the dog poked his nose into the open cavern, immediately started whining, and dashed back to the front of the springhouse. "This is an old way station on the Underground Railroad. Very few people know that it's here, but it has fascinated me since I was a kid. Dad used to bring Graham and me here."

She took a flashlight from her pocket and illuminated the hole in the ground. A rickety-looking ladder descended into a fairly large cavern. It looked like the stones of the springhouse extended underground to form one wall of the cave. The other walls were timbers and dirt. Despite its proximity to the spring, the cave looked fairly dry. Several old wooden boxes were scattered on the floor.

"So, Our Lady of the Forest was more than a simple parish at one time," Reese observed.

"I'll tell you the story at dinner," Alexa told him as Scout whined again. "Scout, you are such a baby. Come on, we're leaving. I'm closing the door, so you're safe. Graham is so right about you—you are a wuss."

Reese seemed surprised that the walk from the church back to Alexa's cabin took them less than thirty minutes. They headed through the grove of pines. The angle of the light that filtered through the tall trees indicated that they were headed south. When they emerged from the pines, Scout broke into a lope toward Alexa's cabin dead ahead.

Reese insisted on helping Alexa with dinner despite her protests. "It's only spaghetti, and the sauce is already made. I just need to heat that and the pasta. How hard can that be?"

Alexa was happy to have the tall park ranger bustling around her small kitchen. Reese prepared garlic bread and set the table while Alexa heated the pasta and sauce and made a simple salad. As usual, Scout managed to be under their feet at every turn.

Alexa opened a bottle of red wine as they sat down to eat. She turned from the counter and gestured to the shelf above her, "Can you reach the wine glasses for me, Reese? I usually use a stool." She stopped abruptly as Reese walked behind her and reached above her head to take a wineglass in each of his hands. Although he hadn't touched her, Alexa felt slightly short of breath.

"Thanks," she said as they sat at the table. "Being vertically challenged has its drawbacks sometimes."

Reese gave her a slow smile. "Anytime you need a hand, just let me know."

Over dinner, Reese discussed the search for the young girl's identity and killer. "Once again, there's not much to tell. The police have had no success in tracking down the van. No one has contacted them with information about either the girl or the homicide. Corporal Branche told me that they plan to step things up a notch to identify the girl, but he didn't clue me in on the plan."

"I hope they make some progress. She deserves justice."

"I have two sisters who are about the same age as the victim. I shudder to think about something like that happening to either of them. My parents and I would be heartbroken."

"It's hard to imagine how devastated her family will be when they find out that she's been killed. I can't get the sight of her body out of my mind. She haunts my dreams."

As they cleaned up after the meal, Reese made Alexa laugh with his stories about his new rugby team. "I played rugby in college, but it's been a while. The team needed more players, but they are still not sure whether I'm worthy enough to play for the All Punks."

"Did you say, All Punks?"

"Yeah. I think it's their homage to the legendary New Zealand team, the All Blacks."

"Aren't you good enough?"

"Ouch. You know how to hurt a guy. Actually, they know that I'm a pretty good forward. I can run. I can pass. But, a rugby team doesn't want any sissies. They haven't seen enough of me in the scrum. That will prove my manliness."

"Men." Alexa snorted.

When she found herself admiring the way Reese's brown curls tumbled over his forehead, Alexa realized that this evening was feeling a lot like a date. She decided that Reese needed to know that she was seeing Caleb.

"Meeting a crowd of people all at one time, like your new rugby teammates, can be a little crazy," she said. "Yesterday, the guy I've been dating took me over to Perry County to a place called Kingdom Lodge. I hadn't met his family or many of his friends before. But it turns out that Caleb's father is a minister of a fundamentalist Christian church and his friends are all avid hunters. I felt like a fish out of water most of the day."

"I hear Perry County has some beautiful areas. I have a friend who's stationed over there at Little Buffalo State Park. Someday soon I want to get over to see him."

"Yes. Perry County has some nice spots. This place I went to yesterday is a beautiful old timbered lodge set on a little lake. It reminded me of a Swiss chalet. I had no idea it even existed until yesterday."

"This boyfriend, Caleb," Reese said carefully. "I hope he has been helping you through the trauma of finding the dead girl."

"I wouldn't exactly call Caleb my boyfriend ... although we've been dating for a few months." Alexa felt compelled to clarify. "We haven't discussed the dead girl."

"You didn't tell him about finding her in the woods?" Reese asked with raised eyebrow.

"No, my brother advised me not to discuss it. I haven't told anyone except Graham and his wife. I haven't talked about her with anyone else but you."

As Reese absorbed Alexa's answer, an uncomfortable silence fell between them. To break the silence, Alexa asked if he wanted more wine.

"No, thanks. It's late, and I really should be going." Reese broke into an impish smile, "But not until you tell me about the Underground Railroad."

Alexa's mood lightened. "OK. You know we are only thirty miles or so from the Mason-Dixon Line. During the Civil War era, there was a lot of Underground Railroad activity in this area. Some of the houses in Chambersburg had secret rooms with tunnels to the river. There were places in Lancaster with hidey-holes in the barn. Here in Cumberland County, people dug several caverns to hide runaway slaves, like the one we saw today. All of these places were way stations on the Underground Railroad.

"Slaves were smuggled in from Maryland or West Virginia. A standard route wound from Boonsboro, Maryland through what is now Caledonia State Park to the chapel. The runaways received food and shelter for a day or two, and then were moved on to the next station farther north.

"During those days, the priest at Our Lady of the Forest was a man named Father Roberts. A passionate abolitionist, he volunteered to become a conductor on the Underground Railroad. Apparently, he convinced some of his congregation to join him in providing for runaway slaves. They say that Father Roberts had seen a slave beaten when he was a young boy staying with friends down South, and that's why he became both a priest and an abolitionist. But, no one really knows for sure. What we do know is that he and his parish dug that cavern and housed hundreds of escaped slaves who were running north toward freedom.

"According to the historians, Confederate cavalry got into a confrontation with Father Roberts at Our Lady of the Forest. This took place in late June of 1863, just a few days before the Battle of Gettysburg. When the small cavalry unit trotted up to the church, Father Roberts had twenty men, women, and children hidden in that cavern behind the chapel.

"Father Roberts didn't panic when the Confederates arrived. Instead, he offered the soldiers food and gave them water from the spring. The lieutenant of the Rebel riders was a Catholic from Virginia, who asked the priest to hear his confession.

"Several of the parishioners, mostly old men and women, were at the church when the Rebels arrived. Father Roberts asked them to sing hymns to cover any sounds from the slaves in the cavern. Just think how brave those men and women were to stay in the chapel and sing. They were probably terrified that the cavalry would kill them all.

"Father Roberts heard the lieutenant's confession, and in return, the Confederates spared the priest and his parishioners. After a short while at the church, the soldiers rode on to join General J.E.B. Stuart's forces in an attempt to take Carlisle. Union soldiers turned Stuart's attack away.

"But the cavalry didn't set a torch to Our Lady as they did with many buildings in the area. A nearby town, Chambersburg, was burned to the ground while the chapel and its hidden Underground Railroad way station remained unscathed. That night, the slaves hiding in the cavern moved on to the next station. When word got out, Father Roberts became a bit of a local hero."

"Wow. Thanks for telling me the story. I learned about the Underground Railroad in school, of course, but seeing that cavern today really brings it home." Reese rose from the table and walked to the door. "Thanks for showing me your local hiking trails. It was a great day and a great dinner."

"I had a good time," Alexa said as she moved with him to the front door. "There are a lot of other trails out there to explore. Just let me know if you want to try one next weekend or later in the month." She glanced at her mastiff sleeping on a nearby chair. "It looks like Scout is too tired to say goodbye."

Reese stopped at the threshold and turned toward Alexa. For a brief moment, Alexa thought he might kiss her. Instead, he touched her shoulder lightly, said goodnight, and walked out the door.

Chapter Thirteen

Home from their latest vacation, Alexa's parents invited her to dinner on Tuesday evening. She had missed them and enjoyed hearing about their trip.

Her mother bubbled over with enthusiasm. "The Amazon was wonderful. Each day the boat traveled upriver we got farther and farther away from civilization. I spent hours just watching the miles drift by on the riverbank. It was mesmerizing."

"Susan," her father interrupted, "don't exaggerate. We stopped at a lot of villages and markets in the early days of the trip. There are many people, called *ribereños*, who make their homes near the river. Also, there was a huge amount of traffic on the Amazon itself. The river acts the main route for transportation of goods and people. However, the traffic and the villages thinned out when we traveled into some of the narrower tributaries."

"Alexa, the wildlife was outstanding. Birds, blue morpho butterflies, pink river dolphins."

"Pink dolphins, Mom? What were you drinking while you lounged in that riverboat? Too many pisco sours, perhaps?"

"They exist. We even swam with them one day upriver."

"And don't forget those lovely capybaras, dear," her father jibed. "They look like giant rats."

"Like the ROUSes from *Princess Bride*?"

"The what?" her mother asked.

"Rodents of Unusual Size." Alexa and her father responded in unison, laughing hysterically.

Alexa's mother bustled into the kitchen to cut three pieces of homemade pumpkin bread while her dad recounted their climb to the Sun Gate at Machu Picchu.

As they ate dessert, with Scout closely monitoring, the travel tales finally came to an end.

"So, Alexa," asked her mom, "what's been going on with you while we were away?"

"Yes, dear," her dad interjected. "Is everything OK up at the cabin? I need to get out there soon and help you winterize."

"Everything has been good." Alexa mentally crossed her fingers. She would eventually tell them about the crazy things that had been happening, but not on this first night together. In the six weeks that her parents had been gone, she had found a dead body, been questioned by the police about death threats at the clinic, and met Caleb's really conservative and borderline cult-like parents. Alexa just wasn't ready to deal with the parental angst that disclosing this would bring.

"I'll fill you in later; Scout and I need to get home. I've got an early day tomorrow. Great dinner, Mom. I missed you guys, and I'm glad you're back." Alexa grabbed her jacket and herded Scout out the door.

At the clinic the next afternoon, things seemed fairly calm. Back from his Hawaiian vacation, Dr. Crowe was seeing patients. With two doctors, the appointments flowed more smoothly.

In the late afternoon, Alexa had chance to ask Tanisha and Barb, "Has anything happened with the death threats? Do the police have any leads?"

Barb replied in disgust, "Nothing. At least we haven't gotten any new notes. But, the cops don't have a clue who sent that letter or whether it was directed at Dr. Kearns or Dr. Crowe."

Tanisha chimed in, "And, honey, I don't think they give a rat's behind about any threats to this place." She nodded her head toward the group across the street. "The cops are tired of dealing with those people and see this clinic as one giant hassle. I don't think they're looking real hard."

"I spoke to Elise on the phone late last week," Alexa replied. "She seems to be dealing with the threat and has put it behind her as much as she can. I think she's operating on the assumption that the threat could have been against either her or Dr. Frank. I'm hoping that this was just a one-time thing from a pissed off patient or some anti-abortion wacko."

"We can only hope," Barb said as she stood to call the next patient into the examining room.

Privately, Alexa still worried about Elise, Frank, and the clinic. She studied the small band parading up and down across the street. They didn't look dangerous in their sober dresses and suits. The same two young men who had looked so out of place last week were there again. Dressed in jeans, they walked with the group but did not carry any signs. "I wonder what their story is ..." Alexa murmured.

Shortly before Alexa left for home, Dr. Crowe sought her out to discuss the threat. "We don't know how serious this threat really is. But we must be cautious. In a way, we've been lucky up to now. Here at Cumberland, we've gotten a little complacent. We've been focused on all the restrictive new rules coming out of the state capital. Meanwhile, we've forgotten about the violence that has plagued other clinics across the country.

"You know how it is. We spend nearly all of our time here providing preventive care and contraceptives. But the pro-life movement only focuses the abortions.

"Alexa, you are a volunteer here. We would all understand if you took a few Wednesdays off until the police find out who is behind this."

Dr. Crowe's kindly face wrinkled in concern as he studied Alexa. He lowered his six-foot frame into the chair next to her as he continued. "Elise and I have made a personal choice to provide family planning and abortion services to women in need. The other staff here views these services not just as a job, but as a cause. We know that you feel strongly about our services; you're one of our most dedicated volunteers. But, child, I could never forgive myself if you got hurt."

Alexa smiled at this man, whom she had known forever. Dr. Crowe was nearly seventy, although only his steel gray hair gave any indication of his age. He was one of her father's best friends, and this dedicated doctor had always been one of her role models. However, for Alexa, volunteering at the clinic went well beyond hero-worship for Dr. Crowe.

"Doc, it's fine. I'm fine. You know that I've been passionate about a woman's right to choose since high school. I became an even stronger pro-choice advocate in college. One of my good friends struggled with a decision about abortion after a date-rape incident. I'm in this for the long haul. I am not going to be scared off by a threatening letter.

"I admit that the threat note is scary. Those people who picket across the street are pretty creepy, too. But, I'll continue to be here every Wednesday to help out."

Dr. Crowe grasped her hand. "There was no doubt in my mind that you were going to hang in there with us. Is there any possibility that you could stay after hours next Wednesday? I have a procedure scheduled. The nursing staff will be here to assist me, but Tanisha has to attend her daughter's school concert. Could you help with the paperwork?"

"No problem. I'll stay." Alexa knew, of course, that the procedure Dr. Crowe was talking about was an abortion. The clinic often scheduled its abortions for the evening, after the protesters left for the day, so that the anxious patients could have privacy.

Alexa had come into the clinic one night about a month ago to help with abortion paperwork for the first time. She hadn't really seen the patient, other than a quick glimpse of the woman's blonde curls and small shoulders hunched over her knees when she came to collect the completed forms from the nurse. Alexa believed that even the small role that she played had helped this woman. The patient had told the clinic staff that she was fleeing an abusive relationship and could not handle the responsibility of a child. In some ways, this volunteer work at the clinic was more satisfying to Alexa than her day job as an attorney.

Alexa's chickens came home to roost on Friday pizza night at Graham's house. While she had dragged her feet in coming clean to her parents about the dead girl and the clinic threats, Graham and Kate had no such qualms. By the time Alexa reached Graham's house, her parents had been fully briefed. Both her mother and father jumped all over Alexa the minute she and Scout walked through the front door.

"Alexandra, why didn't you tell us about finding that young girl's body? Graham told us what you have been through. Are you all right?" Her mother was full of concern for Alexa's wellbeing.

True to form, her dad, the attorney, first addressed the legal aspects. "You should never have talked to the police without Graham in the room. Didn't law school teach you anything?" Then, he jumped to his feet and hugged his daughter.

When he released her, Alexa said, "Mom, I'm fine. I wasn't hurt in any way. It was terrible, though, finding her like that.

"Dad, it's OK. I was never a suspect. I was just in the wrong place at the wrong time. It was a pretty horrible experience. I still feel like I should do something to help find out who she is."

Kate rose to swoop up the two kids in her arms, "Jamie and Courtney, come and help Mommy get drinks in the kitchen. The pizzas will be here pretty soon."

Her mother led Alexa to the couch. "Honey, we want to hear everything that happened."

Alexa described the day when she and Scout found the young girl lying under the bushes in the state forest. "It was so surreal to find her there, dead. Her eyes were still open. I can't stop thinking about her." Surrounded by her sympathetic family, Alexa broke into tears.

She had finished describing the police interview when the doorbell rang. When Graham rose to get the pizza, her father said, "After the kids go to bed, we want to hear about this trouble at the clinic, too."

On the drive home, Alexa confided in Scout, "Big guy, you're still my best buddy. I have to tell you, though; it's nice to have Mom and Dad home. I guess I've downplayed the effect of everything that has been going on in my life. Finding that girl and then the problems at the clinic—no wonder I'm a little shaky about these things. It's not like the parents can make everything better, but it's nice to know that they're on my side."

The big dog settled down in the back, and they drove the rest of the way in silence. However, Alexa couldn't quiet her mind. She vowed that she would call the investigators next week for a status on their search for the unknown dead girl's name and her killer.

Maybe she would try to track down Reese the next day to find out what news he might have. Thinking of Reese made her realize that she hadn't heard from him since Sunday and that she sort of missed him ...

At least Graham didn't know anything about her day at Kingdom Lodge with Caleb, so no need to tell the parents that story. She was still trying to figure out how she felt about Caleb after seeing him in this new context. She hadn't been with him since the party although he had called her from the road on his business trip. He was down South again and said that he would be there for another week.

She welcomed the breathing room. She sensed that Caleb wanted their relationship to become more serious. That wasn't something she was looking for right now. Or maybe, she concluded as she pulled up to the cabin, she just didn't want a relationship with Caleb.

Alexa stood on her deck and watched the moon rise over the trees. As Scout ran through the forest, the fawn mastiff was bathed by golden light. He abruptly plunged into darkness when he reached the pines. A shiver ran down Alexa's spine when she lost sight of the dog in the shadows. She was about to call for Scout when he emerged from the grove of pines and trotted up the stairs. Turning to open the door, she shrugged off the sudden chill and followed the dog into the house.

Chapter Fourteen

Alexa's mind whirled while she drove into work on Monday. The weekend had been a busy one. On Saturday, her father had come out to the cabin and, together, they had gotten the place ready for winter. They stored most of the deck furniture and cut logs for the woodstove. She devoted Sunday to a brief that was fast coming due.

Earlier this morning, Alexa's meditation practice had been totally unsuccessful. She could not empty her mind. Thoughts of the dead girl, Caleb, and Reese tumbled through her head, one after the other.

Those thoughts still distracted her.

I've got to calm down or I'll never be able to concentrate on work, Alexa thought.

Stopped at a traffic light just a few blocks from the office, Alexa glanced at the iPhone on the console. She sighed to see two emails that she needed to handle right away.

Looking back up at the light, Alexa saw a filthy white van shoot across the intersection in front of her, sailing through on the orange, just before the light changed to red. She sat bolt upright and, without any conscious thought, turned right to follow the van down High Street. "That's the van I saw in the woods," she said aloud. "I know it is. There's a roof rack, it's the same color, and it's all beat up." She accelerated to catch the van, shifting the old Land Rover quickly through each gear in an attempt to get close enough to read the license plate.

Within two blocks, she had nearly closed the distance and was only a few car lengths away from the white van, close enough to see the license plate. "Damn," she fumed. It was covered in mud. The only number she could see was a three, and she wasn't sure where it was in the number sequence. The back window looked like a stone had hit the glass, with several cracks radiating out from a single point.

Alexa's next thought was to try to pull up next to the van and get a look at the driver, maybe at the next stoplight. At the next light, however, the van, which was still a few car lengths ahead, took the orange again. The light changed to red, and Alexa slammed on her brakes. In the middle of the next block, two college kids stepped into the pedestrian walkway halting Alexa again and dashing any hope of catching up with the white van.

She traveled a few blocks to park in the office lot. The minute she turned off the ignition, Alexa scrambled through her purse for the state police trooper's card. Her finger fumbled when she tapped in the numbers on her cell phone, so she had to dial a second time. Finally, Trooper Taylor came on the line.

"I'm sure that this was the van from that morning. I last saw it about five minutes ago. It was heading west on High Street, near the college. I had to stop for the light, and I lost sight of it."

"Thanks for reporting this. You shouldn't have tried to follow the van on your own. But, we'll take it from here. Thanks, Miss Williams."

Alexa's heart was still pounding when she walked into the office. The first person she saw was Brian Stewart, who looked at her and said, "Seen a ghost, Williams? Or did you just skip the makeup and beauty routine this morning?"

"Fuck off, Stewart," she replied just as Graham emerged from his office.

"Alexa, in here please," Graham commanded, stepping back through his door. With a smirk on his face, Brian stepped aside to let her pass.

"What is with you?" Graham demanded. "You know it's not appropriate for the attorneys, or anyone for that matter, to curse in the office. And you look a mess."

"Graham, I'm sorry. That piss ant Brian always knows how to push my buttons. But, I'm all keyed up because I just saw the van." She proceeded to tell him about chasing the van to try to get information.

"Alexa, why didn't you call the police immediately? What would you have done if you did catch up to the van? You could have been in danger if these people had something to do with that girl's murder. I'm worried about you. You haven't been thinking rationally since you found that dead girl."

Taken aback by Graham's verbal assault, Alexa took a deep breath. "You're right, Graham. This whole thing has shaken me to the core. For some reason, seeing that lifeless body made me feel responsible for finding out who killed her. I know that's not logical. And, I didn't really think about danger when I saw the van this morning. I just reacted."

When Graham saw tears come to Alexa's eyes, he reached out to wrap her into a hug. "Hey, midget. I know that it's easy for me to tell you what to do and how to feel, but I wasn't there and I didn't see her. But remember, you aren't CSI Carlisle. Let the cops track down the killer."

When Trooper Taylor showed up just before noon, Alexa could hear the whispers running through the law firm. When they were settled in her office, she described the entire incident. "I just know that was the van. The minute I saw it, I knew."

"We put out an alert the minute you called. Then, we had troopers drive around the area where you saw the vehicle. But, so far, no success in locating it. The van could be parked in a garage or on its way to Florida at this point," Trooper Taylor said in frustration. "Did you get a license number?"

"Not really. The plate was covered in mud. The only number I could make out was a three. And, truthfully, that could have been an eight."

"Could you tell if the plate was from Pennsylvania?"

"Yes. Even though it was dirty, I'm sure it was a PA plate—a regular one, not a 'Conserve Wild Resources' one or one of those with tigers or trains."

"Well, just one number will be hard to work with, but it's more than we had before. Did you see the make of the van?"

"No, I was concentrating on the license plate. I didn't even think to look for the name of the vehicle," Alexa admitted.

With another stern lecture on being careful and instructions to call immediately if she saw the van again, the trooper thanked Alexa and left the office. As she walked him to the door, Alexa could see the administrative staff and paralegals watching while pretending to work. She wasn't surprised to see Brian at his office door, making zero effort to conceal his interest. Somehow the office radar had pegged Trooper Taylor as a cop, despite the plainclothes. Ignoring them all, Alexa walked back to her office, shut the door, and returned to her work.

Caleb called Alexa at home that evening. He had stayed in Atlanta through the weekend but would be back later in the week. Usually, Caleb's calls were short and to the point. But this evening, he was surprisingly chatty and spent a lot of time talking about his trip. Still trying to sort out her feelings for Caleb, Alexa didn't contribute much to the conversation. He didn't seem to notice and ended the call by mentioning how much his parents had enjoyed meeting her. They made plans to get together when Caleb returned.

"I miss you. See you Saturday," he closed.

Alexa placed the phone on its stand and sank to the couch, Scout at her feet. During the conversation she had paced back and forth with the wireless unit, her feet expressing her nervousness at Caleb's tone.

"Little buddy, I wish you could give me some advice here." She spoke to the dog. "I'm clearly uncomfortable with where Caleb seems to be headed. Practically overnight, we've gone from casual dating and a little great sex to meeting the parents. And, oh, by the way, we're all religious conservatives."

Then Alexa veered in another direction, "But I'm off my game ever since I found the girl in the woods, so I might be overreacting. Hell, maybe Caleb's just lonely down there in Atlanta and wanted someone to talk to."

Scout lifted his head onto Alexa's knee as he listened attentively. She scratched his ears as she debated the Caleb situation. "If he's looking for some sort of commitment, I'm going to have to break things off. I like Caleb, but I don't want to lead him on.

"Look at the way I've been thinking non-stop about Reese. If I was into Caleb, Reese would have no place in my thoughts. But, there's no need to make a hasty decision here, is there, Scout? We'll just have to see how Caleb plays things on Saturday."

Chapter Fifteen

Wednesday morning's newspaper created quite a stir in the law offices and throughout the town. The front-page carried an article about the dead girl and the continuing efforts to identify her. The police had taken the extraordinary step of publishing the only photo they had of the unidentified victim, a picture of the young woman's face taken in the morgue.

Alexa didn't have a chance to read the article closely, so she took her copy of the newspaper along when she left for the clinic. Running late because a client meeting had gone long, she rushed past the protestors with hardly a glance.

Things were so busy at the clinic that it took nearly an hour before there was a break in the patient flow. Finally, Alexa asked Tanisha about things at the clinic.

"Bad news. We received another death threat yesterday, and this one was addressed specifically to Dr. Crowe. It was almost identical to the initial note, even down to the message: 'RETRIBUTION IS MINE SAYETH THE LORD. YOU WILL BE THE THIRD TO DIE.'"

"Do the police have any leads?"

"If they do, they haven't told us. Heck, the one detective told Dr. Kearns that they're still trying to figure out what the threat really means—the part about 'the third to die.'"

Barb, who was passing by, added, "Duh. It doesn't take a rocket scientist to figure out that anything that says 'die' can't be good."

Tanisha continued, "Everyone is concerned. But, we've got to provide healthcare to these women. We had a staff meeting this morning about the situation, but we all agreed—the doctors and the staff—that it's business as usual. We can exercise caution, but we can't stop services because of a few pieces of paper. Dr. Crowe is talking about hiring some sort of security, especially for after hours. That's going to put a hole in the budget for sure."

A client interrupted Tanisha's update. The woman, a longtime patient, sashayed through the door and came directly to the front desk. All of her 250 pounds swathed in fake leopard fur, quivered in indignation, "Who is them crazy people out there with signs? Calling me a baby killer. I ain't no baby killer. I'm just here for my annual. They people need to mind their own bidness. Why, they even got a pregnant woman marching around out there. When I leave, I might just give them crazies a piece of my mind."

"Well, Miss June, I'm not real happy with those folks either." Tanisha tried to calm the woman. "But, the law says they can be there. I don't think it will do much good for you to mix it up with any of those people. Let's get you signed in, and you can think about it while you wait."

When the solid stream of patients finally ended shortly after five o'clock, Alexa flipped the sign on the main entrance to CLOSED. She looked across the street and saw that the protestors had gone. She giggled to Tanisha, "It was probably best that we took Miss June out the back door after her appointment, but I really would have liked to see her go ten rounds with one of the protestors. I'd put my money on Miss June in a cage match with that tall thin woman who's always here, the one that carries the sign about the blood of lambs."

Tanisha cracked up as she put on her coat and gathered her purse. "That protestor woman might surprise you, honey. Sometimes the skinny ones are stronger than they look. I need to get to my daughter's school. The concert starts at six o'clock. Here are all the papers you need to have the patient fill out. Dr. Crowe will come out and talk to you in a few minutes about tonight. The appointment isn't until six-thirty, so you might want to slip out for some food first."

After Tanisha left, Alexa reread the article in the morning paper. The written story didn't have any new information, so Alexa studied the picture of the girl. Seeing this photo disturbed her. A chill crept through her, just like on the morning she had found the body. They had closed her eyes for the newspaper photo, but the waxy tinge of the young woman's skin made it clear that her rest was permanent.

Looking at this photograph of the dead body made Alexa realize what had been off about the earlier sketch in the newspaper. The pen and ink sketch had not been able to depict the distinctive silvery-blonde color of the victim's hair. Although newsprint wasn't the perfect medium for a crisp picture, the tones in this photo conveyed the light hair that, even in death, gave her the girl an ethereal look.

As Alexa examined the picture, Dr. Crowe walked into the room and sat down beside her. "I thought I'd take a few minutes and walk through what I need from you tonight," he said, but stopped as his eye caught the front page picture. "What's this?"

"This is a photo of a young woman who was found dead in Michaux State Forest last month. They are trying to identify her. Did you see the sketch a few weeks ago in the paper?" Alexa asked, and then answered her own question. "You know, you might have been on your Hawaii trip when the first picture came out. I guess the police thought that showing an actual photograph of her face might help someone identify her."

"I know this young woman," Dr. Crowe sighed. "She was a patient. She had a procedure here shortly before I went on vacation. In fact, that's the night you were here to help. Let me try to remember; yes, her name was Elizabeth." The doctor moved toward the file cabinet.

The news that this girl could be identified electrified Alexa. "That's why she looked familiar. I saw her that night, just from the back, but those white-blonde curls were striking."

"Oh, you recognized her from the picture, too?" Doc extracted a file from the cabinet and waved it in the air. "Yes, I was right. Elizabeth Nelson was her name. Does the article say how she died? She was fine when she left here, and she never called about complications, or for that matter, came back for a follow-up."

"Don't worry about any issues with her procedure, Doc. The article doesn't talk about cause of death, but I know that it was strangulation."

"How have you come by that information, dear? Gossip among the lawyers in town?"

"Not exactly. I didn't recognize Elizabeth from this picture. I was the person who found her body."

After she explained the circumstances of her involvement, Alexa located the card with Lieutenant Trooper Taylor's number. She seemed to be using that card a lot lately. While Dr. Crowe called the investigator, Alexa copied the officer's phone number into the contacts list in her phone.

Dr. Crowe put down the phone. "He wants to meet me in the morning."

"This is a real breakthrough. They've been trying to identify her for weeks. What do you know about Elizabeth?"

"Well, you are a staff member, so I feel comfortable sharing information with you. But, I really know only what she told us. She had a Carlisle address. She said that her pregnancy was unplanned due to a birth control failure. And, she didn't believe she could handle a baby on her own.

"Apparently, Ms. Nelson found out that she was pregnant just as she was breaking up with the father. I remember she made a cryptic statement about the father being too dangerous to love and especially too dangerous to raise a child. I wasn't completely sure what she meant, but I assumed it had something to do with domestic violence.

"She was early in her second trimester. Ms. Nelson was young and quite healthy. There were no complications whatsoever. We kept her here a little bit longer than usual because she didn't have anyone to take her home. I wanted to be completely sure that there would be no problems stemming from the termination. Even then, she was ready to leave the clinic within two hours following the procedure."

"I remember now that she was alone. One of the nurses asked me to schedule a taxi for the patient before I left for the night."

"Yes. Ms. Nelson had mentioned that she was still fairly new in town and didn't have many close friends here. She even talked about going back to her hometown in the near future."

After a short discussion of the paperwork that needed to be completed by tonight's patient, Alexa ran to a nearby deli for sandwiches. An hour later, with the paperwork complete and the patient settled into the exam room, Dr. Crowe told Alexa that he and the clinical staff could handle everything else. He urged her to go home.

"OK. Scout has been alone since this morning, so he'll be happy to see me. Doc," Alexa turned back as she reached the door. "No one but my family knows that I found Elizabeth's body. Graham advised me not to discuss it with anyone."

"Don't worry, child. I won't say a thing."

As the Land Rover's headlights illuminated the dark roads to her cabin, thoughts of the dead girl churned through Alexa's brain.

Check that; thoughts of Elizabeth. Alexa was so glad that Dr. Crowe had recognized her from the photo in the newspaper. Now, she could put to rest that nagging sense of familiarity she had experienced ever since the day in the woods. Her distinctive blonde curls, almost a Scandinavian blonde, had triggered that impression of familiarity. But, since Alexa never saw Elizabeth's face that night in the clinic, she hadn't been able to pinpoint the connection.

Elizabeth had lived in the area. Why hadn't anybody reported her missing? Why hadn't anyone recognized the earlier drawing in the paper? Alexa fervently hoped that the police would be able to locate Elizabeth's family after they spoke to Dr. Crowe tomorrow.

Before she left the cabin the next morning, Alexa received a phone call from Reese. Trooper Taylor had told him that the dead girl had been identified. He was surprised to find out that Alexa already knew. They agreed to compare notes on Friday evening.

"Are steaks OK?" Alexa asked. "Pick me up around seven o'clock at the cabin, and we can go to Florentine's."

When Reese skipped up the steps to her cabin on Friday, Alexa did a double take. He was dressed in khakis, a light sweater, and a scuffed brown leather jacket. "You're looking quite nice," she remarked. "I realize now that I've never seen you dressed in anything but your uniform or hiking clothes. You clean up pretty good."

"I could say the same of you." Reese gestured at Alexa's gray wool turtleneck, charcoal suede miniskirt, and black boots. "You've turned into a fashion plate."

"I have all these designer clothes from my days in New York City. I've got to wear them somewhere."

Over porterhouse for Alexa and filet mignon for Reese, they discussed the latest developments in the Elizabeth Nelson case. Alexa explained that she had been with Dr. Crowe when he recognized the picture.

"Here we have been looking for the girl's identity for all these weeks while it was right under my nose. I even glimpsed Elizabeth from the back when she was in the clinic one evening."

"But, I understand that this doctor, what's his name, Crowe?"

"Yes. Doctor Frank Crowe. He's head of the clinic."

"He was away when she was killed, so he never saw the press coverage, right?"

"Correct. With all the chaos at the clinic over those threatening notes and the backlog of appointments, it seems he hasn't had the time to catch up on the local news."

"I've had several conversations with the state police investigators in the past few days. They're making some progress now that they know who the victim is. They found Elizabeth's apartment and interviewed the neighbors. No one seemed to know Elizabeth very well. They all described her as a nice young woman and a good neighbor. Apparently, she kept to herself and spent long stretches of time holed up in her apartment."

"So, she lived alone and didn't mix with the neighbors?"

"That seems to be the story. But, she lived in one of those rental condos on the east end of town. I hear they cater to a transient clientele. Someone recommended that I look at a place there, but it was too far away from the park for me. I doubt that they spend much time talking over the fence in that neighborhood."

"What about friends or family?"

"Most of the neighbors, at least the nosy ones, had seen Elizabeth going in and out of the apartment with a man. But, Trooper Taylor said that the descriptions of the boyfriend were all over the waterfront.

"The landlord told the police that Elizabeth had moved in from out of state this past winter. Elizabeth gave him notice that she planned to vacate the apartment within the month. Since she didn't have an exact date for the move, Elizabeth and the landlord had agreed that he would keep her security deposit and the place would be hers through the end of November. Taylor said that a look at the boxes in the apartment confirmed that story. She had already started packing."

"What about an employer?" Alexa continued to drill for information.

"Not yet. The state police didn't find any pay stubs. Everything is online these days; who needs paper? But, they are researching her financial records so they should figure out if she had a job and where."

"I wonder if the boyfriend killed her ... on the cop shows, they always look at the boyfriend first."

"I'm sure he's on their radar. It's odd that the guy hasn't stepped forward to identify her or report her missing. But, maybe he moved out of town or is a soldier who just shipped out to Afghanistan. Anything is possible, so you can never leap to conclusions."

After exhausting the topic of Elizabeth Nelson, their conversation drifted. Alexa spoke of her volunteer work at the clinic, and the threats that they had been getting. Reese told her about a new project for the park rangers.

"It's crazy, but we have some indication that a militia group is using the state forests as a training ground. We've gotten all these reports from people who have heard automatic gunfire and reported a lot of off-road vehicle activity in Michaux as well as state lands in Franklin County."

"Militia? Around here?"

"Hard to believe, isn't it? Plus, it is so difficult to confirm with the thousands of acres of state land around here, some of it fairly remote. This investigation could take weeks, if not months, and who knows if there is anything to these reports. Could just be hunters and people on ATVs."

"Or hunters riding ATVs?"

Alexa didn't get to hear any more of the story about the search for militia. Reese broke off the discussion when Alexa's friend, Haley, stopped by their table. Alexa introduced her childhood friend, "Haley, this is Reese Michaels. Haley and I have been friends forever. Reese is a ranger at Pine Grove."

"I just wanted to say hello. Blair and I are here for our fifth anniversary dinner."

"Wow. I can't believe you've been married that long."

115

"Well, you should remember. You stood next to me during the entire ceremony." Haley directed the next comment to Reese.

"Watch out for this one, Reese. She's a handful."

"I'll keep that in mind."

"Great outfit, by the way, Lexie. What is that, Armani?"

After a few more minutes on fashion, Haley returned to her husband.

The rest of their evening was lighthearted. Reese was easy company and had a knack for making Alexa laugh. As Reese drove her back home, Alexa studied his profile in the flashes of light from passing cars. The kinetic illumination created a dreamy effect that was almost hypnotizing.

This evening felt like a date to Alexa, but she wasn't sure that Reese was on the same wavelength. Was there an attraction? Or were they just pals? When he dropped her off at the cabin, Reese made no move get out of the Jeep. When Alexa was safely inside, he drove off with a beep of his horn.

The weather on Saturday reflected Alexa's mood. Strong gusts of wind blew the last leaves from the trees, and sporadic showers doused their brilliance when they hit the ground. Usually, Alexa loved hearing the wind in the trees, but today it set her on edge and heightened her anxiety about this evening's date with Caleb. She hadn't seen him since their afternoon at Kingdom Lodge. Alexa now felt a lot of ambivalence about their relationship and how this date would play out.

As it turned out, Alexa had a good time with Caleb at a very nice restaurant in nearby Harrisburg. He seemed just like the guy she had been dating all summer.

When they returned to the cabin, Alexa had no hesitation about inviting Caleb in, and the sex was as good as always.

Lying next to him in a pleasant daze, she thought, maybe we can continue this relationship and keep it casual.

Perhaps she had overreacted to the unsettling afternoon at Kingdom Lodge. She was still in this frame of mind when Caleb got up to leave.

With his hand on the doorknob, Caleb asked, "Are we on for next Saturday night? I would really like to start spending time together during the week, but I'm still pretty tied up most evenings with the business. And, of course, my parents want us to start coming to Sunday dinners after church. But, we can talk about that later. For now, can we confirm next Saturday?"

"Sure," Alexa responded with a sinking heart. When Caleb left, she huddled on the couch with her arms wrapped around her knees. What a fool. She had deluded herself tonight, lulled by the familiarity of a relaxed dinner and great sex. Now, she realized with certainty, things had changed.

Caleb wanted more than a casual relationship. Even before Kingdom Lodge, she had known that Caleb Browne was never going to be a permanent relationship. She had thought he was just looking for fun, too.

How did I miss the signs that Caleb was becoming more serious, she fretted.

"Next Saturday, I'll have to break things off," Alexa announced to Scout. "I can't lead him on any longer."

Haley couldn't wait to flag down Alexa after yoga class on Tuesday night. Melissa missed class, so it was just the two of them. Over huge cups of chai tea at the Om Café, Haley pumped Alexa for information on Reese Michaels.

"OK, give. I thought you were dating Caleb Browne, who in my opinion is really hot. But, then I walk into Florentine's on Friday night, and there you are with this other really fantastic looking guy. Are you two-timing Caleb? Have you moved on? You know, now that I am happily married, I need to get my thrills by living vicariously through you and Melissa."

"Reese and I are just friends. I met him a few weeks ago, and we've been doing some hiking together. I really like him, though." Then, Alexa proceeded to tell her friend about the turn that her relationship with Caleb had taken.

Haley sympathized with Alexa over the situation with Caleb. "But, honey, you've got to tell him. It sounds like he's way more serious than you are. I think you need to break it off clean."

"I know you're right. That doesn't make it any easier."

Haley leaned her head over the table toward Alexa and lowered her voice, "Just in case you're thinking about a rebound relationship with this Reese Michaels, I want to tell you what I heard about him. When Blair saw me talking to the two of you at Florentine's, he told me that he had heard about this new ranger from some of his Elks buddies that work up at the park. They say that Michaels transferred here from a park out in the western part of the state after a big public incident. Apparently, a young girl who was staying in the campground accused him of sexual assault. I guess there wasn't enough evidence to convict him, but the park officials moved him out of the area because of the scandal."

"I can't believe that. Reese is one of the good guys. He seems to be up front and open with nothing to hide. That's one of the things I like about him. The story can't be true."

"Maybe there is more to it. You know how rumors get out of hand. Ask him about it and hear what he has to say. In the meantime, honey, be careful with that guy. Ted Bundy seemed like a good guy, too, until they found out how many women he killed."

"My God, Haley. We started this conversation with you telling me that Reese looks fantastic. Now, you've gone from rumors of an alleged sexual assault to accusing the guy of serial murder. That's a pretty big leap." They both broke into laughter, although Alexa quickly sobered as she thought of Elizabeth Nelson dead in Reese's state forest.

Chapter Sixteen

Wednesday, November 21, 1934.

In slumber which broken shall be ...

A lurch of the car jarred Dewilla awake. Groggily, she realized that Daddy had pulled the Pontiac to the side of the road and turned off the motor. Rubbing sleep from her eyes, Dewilla saw Norma awkwardly propped against the other corner of the wide back seat. Her sister's arms were wrapped around Cordelia, who was still fast asleep. These days it seemed like Norma had stepped into Mama's shoes and taken on a responsibility well beyond her twelve years. Cousin Winifred, who had come to take care of the family after Mama died, never really knew how to manage the girls. Lately, she barely even tried and spent most of her time with Daddy.

Winifred opened the car door next to Dewilla and said in her breathy little girl's voice, "Your daddy wants you to come out for a drink at this spring." Winifred held the door for Dewilla while she clambered out. Norma eased from under Cordelia without disturbing the sleeping child and slipped out the far door.

When Dewilla stepped out of the Pontiac into the cold November day, Daddy was bent over a stream of water that gushed from a pipe in a wall. The steep hill above the spring blocked the sun, and icicles clung to the rough stones surrounding the rusty old pipe.

Daddy filled a tin cup with spring water and passed it around. When her turn came, Dewilla recoiled at the touch of cold metal on her lips, but she took a big sip to quench her thirst. Norma drank the rest and passed the empty cup back to Daddy while Winifred went to rouse Cordelia.

When his youngest child emerged from the car, Daddy handed her a fresh cup of spring water. Cordelia gulped greedily then wailed when the cold water hit her empty stomach. "It hurts. It hurts," she cried.

"Silence, girl." Daddy shouted. "I cannot abide your constant caterwauling." His handsome face turned ugly with anger.

Dewilla shrank away and pulled Cordelia into her arms. They both ran to Norma's side. "She's hungry." Norma protested.

"We are all hungry. Don't keep harping on me. I know I haven't been providing for you right. Your mother would be ashamed of me." As he spoke, Daddy's anger vanished to be replaced by the saddest look Dewilla had ever seen. He looked even sadder than the day Mama went home to heaven. His voice sank, "I am going to fix things so you young'uns won't be hungry anymore."

Winifred put her arms around Daddy and whispered in his ear. Dewilla strained to hear but could only catch part of what Winifred was saying. "Elmo, you know it is for the best. We can manage better without." Winifred's remaining words were swallowed up by the bitter wind.

Dewilla shivered uncontrollably. In the swift twilight of winter, afternoon had dissolved into evening. As Dewilla watched, deep shadows reached out and folded Daddy and Winifred into their darkness.

Late November in Pennsylvania was cold, and the biting wind that whipped down this mountain road only added to Dewilla's misery. However, the chill that filled Dewilla now was a different kind of feeling. Something she couldn't name gripped Dewilla with an unspeakable dread that gnawed at her even stronger than the hollow space in her empty stomach ...

Chapter Seventeen

Thoughts of Caleb and Reese preoccupied Alexa when she jumped out of her car near the clinic on Wednesday around noon. After jamming the parking meter full of quarters, she rushed down the sidewalk. Running late, she didn't notice the young man from the picket line walking toward her until he was a few yards away.

"Miss, could I speak to you?" She recognized him as the odd man out with the protestors; the one who wore jeans and a fleece jacket instead of the sober attire of the rest of the group.

Alexa stepped off the curb and hurried across the street without replying. The last thing she wanted right now was a philosophical discussion with an anti-abortion activist. When Alexa reached the clinic door, she halted on the threshold and glanced back. The young man had returned to the group. She noticed that an immensely pregnant woman was brandishing a sign, perhaps the same one who had Miss June in an uproar last week. The pregnant woman looked familiar. Perhaps, Alexa thought, she was a regular who had been here before her pregnancy began to show.

Alexa's mind was not really on family planning business today. Even the news that the clinic was now receiving new threat letters almost daily, while alarming, could barely wrest Alexa's focus away from her personal life.

Dr. Kearns spoke briefly to Alexa about the threats. "Dr. Crowe and I don't like that we've been backed into a corner, but we're hiring security during business hours. Because the threats haven't stopped, the board approved the expense. Everyone agrees that our first obligation is to protect patients and staff. It's better to be safe than sorry."

"Security is a good idea. Maybe these threats are just words on paper and nothing more. If that's the case, they've already had an impact. Clearly, the notes have put everyone on edge. But, I think you and Frank are wise to take precautions. With the history of violence against abortion clinics, you've got to be careful."

By mid-afternoon, Alexa had developed a splitting headache and told Tanisha that she was going home to rest.

"Honey, it's no wonder you're stressed with all these threats and talk of security. You go home, take some aspirin, and lie down for a while." Tanisha admonished.

"I wish it was that simple, Tanisha. The stress that is causing this headache comes from not one, but two guys. And, I don't think either aspirin or a nap is the answer."

When she left the clinic, Alexa kept an eye out for the young man in the fleece jacket. However, he and the other protestors were gone.

Alexa's father walked into her office around ten o'clock the next morning. When Alexa looked up in surprise, she was shocked at the haggard look on his face.

"I didn't think today was one of your days in the office, Dad. Is something wrong? Is Mom OK?"

"Your mother is fine, Alexa. But, I do have bad news, and I wanted you to hear it from me. Alice called to tell me that Frank Crowe has been shot. It happened last night around nine when he was leaving the clinic. He wasn't even on duty. He had just stopped by to pick up some notes for a newsletter article."

"Oh, no." Alexa jumped to her feet in consternation. "So, these threats we've been getting were real." Tears filled her eyes. "Who would do something like this to Doc?" She hesitated, dreading the reply, then asked, "Is he dead?"

"I'm sorry, honey. I should have told you right away that Frank's alive. He's holding his own at the hospital, but it is very serious. Apparently, the shot missed his heart, but they had to remove part of his lung. The doctors are concerned about more than the initial trauma. With Frank's age, recovery from almost any surgery becomes tricky."

"Dad, I can't believe this. I came home partly because the city was too dangerous. But, now I seem to be surrounded by violence. A dead girl in the woods. Frank Crowe, one of your oldest friends, shot. All the staff at the clinic threatened. What is going on?"

Her father moved to fold Alexa in his arms. "I know you're upset, baby. I'm sick about this, and your mother is frantic. We are both worried about Frank surviving this gunshot wound. However, what frightens us the most, Alexa, is that all of this has come too close to you."

"I think I should go over to the clinic and see how everyone is doing. Elise and the staff must be so worried about Dr. Crowe. He is the heart and soul of that place. They all must be freaked out about their own safety as well."

"The clinic is closed today. The police have the place cordoned off and are processing the crime scene. All the staff members are either being interviewed by the police or were told to stay home. I expect that the place will be closed for the next few days."

Alexa struggled to concentrate on work. When she called the hospital, they could only say that Frank was in critical condition. Just shy of seventy, Dr. Crowe was in great health, but she worried about his capacity to recover from a serious gunshot wound. He was no spring chicken.

She called Elise Kearns to find out how she was coping. Knowing that Elise rattled easily, Alexa was pleasantly surprised to find the doctor in a fighting mood.

Elise declared, "The clinic will be open for business as soon as the police give the word. The new security company will be patrolling the building night and day. We're not going to let this stop us from providing services."

Alexa worked late to finish a project that Graham needed the next day. When she left the law office by the back door and walked to her car, Alexa felt a little jumpy. The familiar parking lot seemed darker than usual, even though Alexa knew she only saw danger in the shadows because of what had happened to Dr. Crowe.

On the way home, Alexa stopped at the supermarket for milk and dog food. She had been away from home a lot lately and had been neglecting Scout a bit. She didn't want to add insult to injury by making him go hungry. Although she didn't have much of an appetite, Alexa picked up a take-out order of ham and green beans, too.

In the parking lot, Alexa hefted the twenty-five pound bag of dry food into her Land Rover and closed the back door. When she turned to lift the smaller bag from the shopping cart, she saw the young man from the clinic who wore the fleece jacket walking toward her. At his side strode another young man wearing a baseball cap. When the second man lifted his head, she recognized him as the tall black protestor who she had also seen on the clinic picket lines.

"Can I speak to you for a minute?" the young white man called out as he approached. "You work at the clinic, don't you?"

Alexa panicked. She grabbed the grocery bag in one hand and with a hard push, shoved the empty shopping cart toward the two men. She leapt into the car and turned the ignition key. The parking space ahead was vacant, so she floored the Land Rover and lurched forward, squealing the tires. Alexa looked in her rearview mirror. The young men stood in the parking lot watching her leave.

Alexa drove several blocks then pulled over to fasten her seatbelt. Her hands were shaking so badly she had trouble inserting the belt into the buckle. Keeping watch in the rearview mirror, she called 911 and reported the incident. She told the 911 operator that these men picketed the clinic and could have something to do with Dr. Crowe's shooting. The operator asked her name and location. Alexa gave her name and address but said, "If the police want to speak to me, they can find me at home or at my law practice tomorrow."

Watching to make sure that no one followed, Alexa drove home. After she carried the groceries into the house and greeted Scout, Alexa collapsed onto the couch. She was so weary that she could barely lift her head.

Maybe this is a reaction from the adrenalin rush, she thought. Or, maybe everything is just catching up to me. I always thought the protestors were harmless. But, those two guys scared me. What if they're the ones who shot Dr. Crowe? What did they want with me? Is everyone associated with the clinic in danger?

Alexa lay on the couch absently stroking Scout, who was nestled on the floor beside her. One thought after another ricocheted around her mind—Dr. Crowe crumpling to the ground with a bullet in his chest; the guys in the parking lot; Elizabeth Nelson sitting with her back to the door in an exam room; the same delicate blonde dead beneath a mountain laurel.

As she ruminated, Alexa wondered for the first time: could Dr. Crowe's attack and Elizabeth Nelson's death be related?

The ringing telephone roused Alexa from her thoughts. A borough policeman reported that they had not located any men at the supermarket matching the description. An officer would interview Alexa in the morning.

While she was nuking the take-out ham and green beans in the microwave, the phone rang again. Reese had heard about Dr. Crowe. Alexa was pleased that he called, but that pleasure was overshadowed by mistrust. Haley's story about Reese's involvement in a sexual assault scandal was still fresh. Given her recent experiences, Alexa wasn't in a particularly trusting frame of mind. Still, Reese had sounded so concerned that she wanted to believe in him.

Police filled Alexa's Friday. First, an officer named Starke with the borough force came to the office to interview her about the parking lot incident the night before. Alexa told him that she had seen the two young men several times on the anti-abortion picket lines. "The white guy approached me once before outside the clinic. I admit that I'm on edge about Dr. Crowe's shooting and the threats to the clinic. When these guys started walking toward me in the dark parking lot, I just freaked."

"Understandable, Miss Williams," Officer Starke said. "Did they threaten you in any way?"

"No. They just said that they wanted to talk, but the whole thing was sketchy. No one else was around. I wasn't going to give those guys the opportunity to attack me."

"Also understandable. At this point, we don't have enough information to track down these two men. We've reviewed the videotapes from the supermarket but didn't see anyone matching your description. We will continue to try to locate these two so that we can question them. Because of their presence at the clinic as protestors, we regard these two as persons of interest in the felony committed upon Dr. Crowe.

"As a lawyer, you must realize that at this point we have nothing to hold them on. Although, understandably, you felt intimidated by these two young men, technically, they did not threaten or harm you in any way. Even if you file a formal complaint, it would be difficult to charge them with any crime. We will, however, continue to track them down."

When Officer Starke left her office, Alexa sat back to reflect. The discussion left her torn between feeling somewhat foolish and somewhat pissed at Officer Starke. As the interview progressed, his questions took an increasingly condescending tone. By the end, the cop's skepticism was so apparent that Alexa imagined he was mocking her.

The policeman's behavior had been very unprofessional, but his questions had forced Alexa to reconsider last night's encounter.

Did I jump too quickly to the conclusion that those two men were trying to harm me? Perhaps. But how could I know what they intended? I did what I needed to protect myself. Either way, that policeman was a jerk, and his attitude was uncalled for. Doc Crowe was just shot; yet, Officer Starke acted like I'm some hysterical woman jumping at shadows.

Alexa decided she would stay on high alert until they found whoever shot Doc and was terrorizing the clinic. And she wouldn't apologize to anyone, including that jackass, Starke. "Understandable," Alexa lisped aloud and laughed hysterically.

Melinda knocked on her door, puzzled when she saw Alexa sitting alone in her office laughing. "Corporal Branche and Trooper Taylor are here to see you, Alexa." Shutting the door behind her, Melinda whispered, "Is everything OK? You've been getting all of these visits from the police. Everyone out front is worried. You aren't in trouble, are you? Should I call Graham?"

Alexa smiled ruefully. "Thanks for your concern, Melinda, but I'm not in trouble. You know I volunteer at the Cumberland Clinic. Dr. Crowe, one of the staff doctors, has been shot. The police are just talking to me as part of the investigation. No need to call Graham. He and my dad are both aware of this." Alexa deliberately avoided the fact that the state police were here primarily because of Elizabeth Nelson's death. At this point, Alexa's connection to the case was still not public knowledge.

When the investigators asked Alexa about her contact with the living Elizabeth Nelson at the clinic, it became clear that they had already considered a possible connection between the murder and the shooting of Dr. Crowe.

"I only saw her that night very briefly from the back. I never even saw Elizabeth's face. I organized her signed paperwork, scheduled a cab to pick her up, and then left the clinic.

"Last night, it occurred to me that there could be a connection between Elizabeth's murder and Doc getting shot. You've probably thought of this, but the notes coming to the clinic say 'You will be the third to die.' What if they considered the baby to be the first, Elizabeth the second, and Dr. Crowe the third? Maybe the father or someone is opposed to abortion and wanted to punish Elizabeth and Doc for what he considered killing the baby?"

Corporal Branche nodded his head. "We have been exploring that possibility."

Alexa filled them in on her encounter in the supermarket parking lot. "They may not have meant me any harm, but I erred on the side of caution."

"We'll talk to the borough police about the incident. Maybe it was nothing more than two guys wanting to talk to a pretty young woman, but you are right to be on guard. You were at the clinic the night that Elizabeth Nelson got an abortion. You found her body, and you may have seen witnesses or the perpetrators of the crime. Like it or not, Ms. Williams, you are involved in this case. I advise you to use caution at all times and call us at the slightest hint of danger."

"You're on my speed dial now. And, I will certainly be careful. However, no one knows that I found Elizabeth's body so I shouldn't be a target from that angle."

Trooper Taylor told her, "Yes. We have protected your identify for that very reason. But, in our experience, news like this often leaks out, even inadvertently. Family tells a friend. The friend tells someone else, and soon the whole world knows. So, be careful."

"Have you found Elizabeth's family or her boyfriend?"

The corporal answered that question. "Her family is coming to town next week from Oregon. Her mother and father have only had sporadic contact with Elizabeth since she moved east, so they had no idea that she was missing. Apparently, it was not unusual for two or three weeks to go by between phone calls. Since they had spoken to her only a few days before her death, they weren't alarmed that they hadn't heard from her.

"Elizabeth told her parents that she was thinking about quitting her job and coming back home to Oregon. She said she missed the Portland scene. Her mother sounds like a pretty sharp woman. She read between the lines and figured that things with Elizabeth's latest boyfriend had ended badly. The mother thinks that the move back to Oregon had as much to do with putting distance between Elizabeth and the boyfriend as it did with coming home.

"Apparently, the Nelsons weren't all that close to their daughter anymore. They characterized Elizabeth as 'having an independent streak.' Still, this news hit them hard. They clearly loved their daughter and were distraught to learn that she was dead. They were broken up to hear that she had been murdered and died alone in a place so far from home."

"I still don't understand why no one identified Elizabeth earlier or reported her missing."

"It is puzzling. She's lived in this area for a while and must have interacted with a lot of people during that time. We did find out where Elizabeth worked and why they didn't miss her. Turns out that she was some kind of child prodigy computer whiz. Her parents danced around the subject but eventually told us that she had been a hacker in high school and didn't need college to land a job.

"She worked for Technostorm in Harrisburg, developing computer software programs. That's why she moved here from Portland to begin with. They offered her a deal big enough to justify a move across the country. Like most of their employees, Elizabeth spent most of her time working at home. She only checked into the office a few times a month.

"The supervisor says that many of their computer geeks don't even know each other because they work at home and set their own schedules for visiting the office. He said that Elizabeth got more attention than most because she was so pretty. But, as a group, the boss said that his people are not big on current events so, it's possible none of them saw the coverage of her murder. The supervisor said that he doesn't watch the news. He spends most nights reading tech blogs, whatever they are.

"He told us that Elizabeth had given notice at work, but the date was sort of open-ended because she agreed to complete her current project before she left the job. He expected to hear from her sometime later this month when the new software program was finished.

"The boyfriend is still a wildcard. We don't know who he is or why he didn't recognize her picture in the news."

After the state police investigators left, Alexa ate a sandwich at her desk and processed this new information. Finally, it made some sense why it had taken so long to identify Elizabeth. The original sketch published in the paper had not been the best likeness, and a lot of people didn't even read the local newspaper or watch local news on TV anymore. Many of the people she knew got their news online or tuned into Fox, CNN, or MSNBC because the local news was so lousy. Like her friend, Melissa, said, you could only read so many stories about bears, car accidents, and school board meetings before you cancelled your subscription to the local newspaper and fled to cable. The unfortunate result was declining revenues to the local news media and coverage that became even less meaningful.

Despite the news gap factor, Alexa couldn't understand why Elizabeth's boyfriend, other friends, or neighbors hadn't stepped forward. She had been a striking young woman, unusually pretty with her Scandinavian coloring. It seemed impossible that Dr. Crowe was the only person who had seen that picture and recognized Elizabeth. The big question was: Why hadn't those people stepped forward?

Chapter Eighteen

While she dressed for her date, Alexa ran through the breakup speech another time. She shouldered all the blame. She just wasn't ready for a serious relationship. She had been burned too badly by her failed romance with Trent. She had enjoyed their time together. She knew that Caleb wanted more of a commitment, but she didn't want to lead him on.

She would leave out Caleb's parents, hunting, religion, conservative politics, and all the things that were the real issues.

"So long, farewell, auf wiedersehen, adieu." Alexa burst into the familiar refrain from the *Sound of Music*. "OK, OK. You have totally lost it, girl," she said to herself in the mirror. "Let's just get this over and done with. We'll go to dinner. When the time is right, I'll say my piece and that will be it. Good-bye, Caleb." The intense feeling relief surprised her.

When Caleb parked in front of the cabin, Alexa grabbed her coat and headed to the door. She couldn't conceal her shock when she opened the door to find Caleb standing there with an Antonio's Italian Ristorante bag in his hand.

"What's this?"

"I thought we could eat in for a change. I brought you penne carbonara. Isn't that your favorite?" he said with a tight smile. "I have something important to discuss with you, and I thought it would be best to do it in private."

"Yes," Alexa stammered. "What a surprise. What would you like to drink?"

"Water is fine for now."

"I think I'll have a glass of wine."

As Alexa got drinks, she dithered about how to deal with this unexpected development. All her careful planning was blown.

Go with the flow, she decided. You can't just dump him the minute he walks through the door—especially since he went to the trouble to buy dinner.

Perhaps it was the forced intimacy of the quiet cabin. Perhaps it was Alexa's anxiety about the bombshell she was about to drop. But, the conversation seemed strained. She chattered desperately about neutral topics like her latest yoga class and local news.

"I took an extra yoga class this week. The studio had a yogi from India who taught several classes. He really emphasized the spiritual side of the practice. It was a great experience," Alexa said.

"I don't get this whole yoga thing. How can you call an exercise class spiritual?"

"Yoga is so much more than exercise. I'm always so busy at work. Taking a class at the end of a hectic day is so calming."

"A lot of things keep you busy."

"I guess you're right." Alexa decided that this was going nowhere fast, so she searched for another topic. "I read that the college is expanding again. They bought that old warehouse near the campus."

Caleb seemed to pay little attention to Alexa's mindless chatter. He barely spoke and seemed withdrawn. A few times during dinner, Alexa saw him rock back and forth in his seat. Baffled by his unprecedented decision to eat in and his increasingly strange behavior, Alexa couldn't fathom his mood.

"How was your week, Caleb? Did your business trip go well?"

"Fine."

"We had good weather here. Chilly in the morning, but warm by the afternoon."

"Perfect for hunting."

As the tense meal drew to a close, Caleb still hadn't broached the important item that he wanted to discuss. Could he have sensed that she was going to break things off? Was he going to break up with her?

Alexa rose to clear the dishes. She fed a few scraps of Italian bread to Scout, who had spent the entire meal glued to her side. Then, she let the dog out into the night for a run. She almost had to push the big mastiff out the door.

"Do you want a piece of this tiramisu?"

"Dessert can wait." Caleb pinned Alexa against the kitchen counter. He brushed her hair aside and kissed the back of her neck. "I had a different type of sweet in mind right now."

Alexa giggled. "Has that line worked for you at any time, ever?" She debated how to handle this second unexpected turn of events. Nothing this evening was going as planned.

Against her better judgment, Alexa allowed Caleb to lead her to the living room. Finding the right time to deliver her breakup speech was getting harder and harder. Doing it now, while Caleb had romance on his mind, just seemed too cold. Maybe afterwards when Caleb was on his way out the door?

Caleb stopped in the middle of the room. Without speaking, he brought his lips to hers and kissed Alexa with a fiery intensity. Alexa responded to Caleb's passionate embrace and arched her body closer. When he broke off the kiss, Caleb shocked Alexa by ripping off her blouse. Turned on by Caleb's urgency, Alexa melted into his arms.

From there things heated up quickly, and Alexa pushed that breakup conversation to the back of her mind. Sex with Caleb had always been electric.

Why not have one more for the road, Alexa rationalized as she surrendered herself to the moment.

Caleb's kisses were greedy as he ran his hands up and down Alexa's body. He paused long enough to unfasten her bra and fling it to the floor. He tangled his fingers through Alexa's hair, arching her head back until her neck was exposed. She moaned as his tongue drifted from the hollow of her neck to the cleft between her rising breasts.

Caleb was still completely dressed. When Alexa reached to unfasten his belt buckle, he grabbed her wrists and pushed her hands away. He slid Alexa's panties down her hips until they cascaded into a silken pool at her feet. When Alexa was fully naked, Caleb placed his hands on her shoulders and pushed her down onto the sofa. The chill of the leather couch on her bare skin telegraphed Alexa's vulnerability, a sensation that was both unnerving and exciting.

Alexa watched with impatience as Caleb unfastened his belt buckle. Instead of disrobing, Caleb unzipped his fly to expose his rigid member. He took a condom from his pocket and ripped open the foil. He dropped the wrapper to the floor and slowly and deliberately rolled the condom over his erect penis.

Light from the kitchen cast Caleb's shadow onto the wall. Drawn by the dark motion, Alexa studied the elongated silhouette. A massive, hulking shadow-beast pranced on the wall, brandishing an angry penis. Alexa felt a frisson of unease.

Caleb hovered above Alexa, lying nude on the wide couch. Disoriented, Alexa thought the shadow-beast had stepped down from the wall. Then the creature snarled in Caleb's voice, "I think you're going to like this new game."

When Caleb leaned in, Alexa knew that something was wrong. Towering over her, Caleb's eyes were stormy. For an instant, Alexa could see her apprehension reflected in the gray opacity of his gaze.

When he lowered himself to the couch and straddled Alexa's body, things turned rough. Caleb grabbed Alexa's arms and swept them above her head. With one hand, he held her wrists so forcefully that Alexa could barely move.

With his other, Caleb clawed at Alexa's breasts and brutally pinched her nipples.

"That hurts," Alexa cried trying to twist her body away from the mauling. But, pinned beneath Caleb's muscular legs without control of her arms, Alexa could find no leverage. Ignoring her protests, Caleb closed his teeth over her nipples in a series of sharp painful bites. With a grunt, Caleb forced Alexa's legs apart with a knee and swiftly entered her.

Alexa's initial passion had turned to dust. His pounding shaft felt like sandpaper in the dry tissues of her delicate sex.

Sweat dripping from his body, Caleb continued to ride Alexa, seemingly oblivious to her distress. With Alexa now lying motionless beneath him, Caleb's punishing thrusts intensified until he groaned loudly in climax.

Within seconds, Caleb pulled away and rearranged his clothes, his back turned.

It took some effort for Alexa to peel herself from the couch. Haltingly, she stood and picked up her clothes from where they lay crumpled on the floor. After one look at her torn blouse, she used the strips of fabric to wipe Caleb's stale sweat from her chest and tossed it down. Then she slipped on a bulky sweater from a chair near the steps.

As she dressed, Alexa surged from shock to anger. "What was that all about? It might have been good for you, but it sure as hell wasn't good for me."

Caleb looked at Alexa without remorse. "I thought your type likes it rough. I just didn't know your type until now."

"What are you talking about? My type? And that was about as far from consensual sex as you can get. You were the only one having sex here a few minutes ago. No one has ever treated me like that. And I certainly didn't like anything about it."

Caleb sprawled into a chair and gestured insolently for Alexa to sit opposite. She lowered herself gingerly to the couch. She was still reeling from this entire experience, which felt more like an assault than an experiment with a little soft-core bondage or S&M.

In the lengthening silence, Alexa waited for Caleb to reply. When he said nothing, she realized that this encounter had crystallized her resolve. This jerk was history.

Just as Alexa opened her mouth to end the relationship, Caleb began speaking in a hollow tone. "You know what type of woman you are. But why didn't you tell me? All this time you have been working at that clinic, and you never bothered to mention that you were involved in killing unborn babies. I thought you were a good person. I know that you engage in promiscuous sex and have some crazy liberal ideas. But, I thought that, beneath it all, you were a good, clean Christian woman. Now I find out that you are part of that filth and desecration. You work at that charnel house that rips innocent babies out of their mothers' wombs. And you kept it a secret from me.

"If I had known, I would have never introduced you to my parents. I thought we could have a life together, but you have ripped that future to shreds with your godless actions. I can't believe I took you to meet my mother and Reverend Browne. They may never forgive me." His voice rose until, by the end, he was shouting.

Alexa sat in shock at this unexpected onslaught of words. She had no idea who this man was—standing here, ranting about abortion and God. She shrank back into the couch as Caleb leapt up and grabbed her arm. The gray of his eyes shimmered like shards of glass.

"You whore. You need to be punished for your sins against children and against God."

Alexa collected herself enough to say, "Caleb. I want you to leave. We can discuss this some other time, but I didn't deliberately keep my volunteer work at the clinic secret. I just never thought to mention it." She unsuccessfully tried to twist her arm from his grasp and rise to her feet.

"I'll gladly leave. But, you needed to be taught a woman's place." Caleb shoved Alexa back onto the couch.

"Caleb, you are out of control and I want you out of my house. Now. Get your coat and leave right now." Alexa's unease morphed into fear. Outside, Scout was barking and crashing his body into the door.

Caleb grabbed Alexa's hair. "You are a whore just like Rebecca was. God will punish you, too, you bitch. You're a whore and a liar, and you should be ashamed for shedding the blood of innocents." With that final insult, Caleb released her and moved away.

Anger overcame fear. Alexa leapt to her feet. "I want you out of here immediately, Caleb, and I don't ever want to see you again. Get out. Get out now."

Caleb grabbed his jacket and walked deliberately to the door, his parting words dripping with contempt. "Why would I want to stay now that I know who you really are, you Jezebel?"

When Caleb opened the door, he stepped to the side as Scout rushed into the room. The frantic dog raced to Alexa. Caleb bolted, closing the door before Scout could turn on him.

Seconds later, Alexa collapsed onto a soft wing chair and heard Caleb slam the door of his pick-up truck. Stones peppered the front deck like bullets as Caleb gunned the motor and spun his tires in the loose gravel. Finally, the truck raced away down the driveway, and a heavy stillness descended on the cabin.

Alexa couldn't bring herself to move. Scout snuffled over her in concern. Oblivious, Alexa remained glued to the cushions, her mind a blank. After several minutes, Alexa became conscious that she was sobbing and snapped back to reality. Using the mastiff's big back for leverage, she pushed herself into a sitting position. Then, she walked to the front door and slammed the bolt shut.

"I need a shower," she said, shuddering. "I need to wash that bastard off me."

She had been a willing participant when Caleb initiated sex this evening. Even though it had quickly turned into something more disturbing, Alexa couldn't call it rape. Still, Alexa felt compelled to scrub away this feeling of violation.

Glancing at the clock, she was amazed that it was just nine o'clock. Caleb had walked in here less than two hours ago. This nightmare of an evening had seemed so much longer.

When she left the shower, the water had turned cool. Alexa stood in front of the full-length mirror on the back of the bathroom door. Although her skin was unbroken, red marks covered both breasts. Her stomach and inner thighs were bruised from Caleb's knee. Her right wrist was black and blue where Caleb held it as he pinned Alexa to the couch. Seeing these injuries only pissed Alexa off more. She straightened up and declared, "If you let this get to you, that bastard is going to win. He wanted to destroy you—don't let him. You are better than that. You are better than Caleb Browne."

Alexa hobbled slowly back downstairs to make herself a cup of tea. Scout crowded next to her on the loveseat, his head resting in her lap. Huddled beside the healing warmth of the woodstove, she wondered how she had gotten to this point.

I have been dating this man for months without a clue to his real character. How could my judgment have been so flawed? Was I so intent on a casual fling that I overlooked any warning signs?

Though, to be honest, she'd never really invested in a relationship with Caleb. Then, after that day at Kingdom Lodge, she'd realized that their differences were too fundamental to ignore.

Even then I had no idea what I was dealing with. With his conservative background and minister father, abortion is a hot button issue for Caleb. When he thought

I was deliberately deceiving him, he just lost it. I think he really was getting serious about me. That must have sent him further around the bend when he found out about the clinic. I wonder who told him ...

The thoughts swirled endlessly until Alexa just couldn't deal with them anymore. Rising, she checked the locks and trudged upstairs to bed with Scout at her heels.

Chapter Nineteen

Scout settled into bed beside Alexa, as if knowing instinctively that she needed comfort. Exhausted, she fell into a restless sleep almost immediately. When she woke, Alexa was surprised to find that it was nearly ten in the morning. Swinging her feet to the floor, Alexa discovered that her bruises throbbed and she ached in places that had felt fine last night. Caleb's angry and punishing sexual assault had drained her both physically and emotionally. Even though she had slept for hours she was still tired.

Alexa pulled on sweatpants and one of her favorite old sweaters before she followed Scout downstairs. She opened the door to let the anxious dog out, saying, "Thanks, buddy, for letting me sleep in. I really needed it." Alexa busied herself with making breakfast, but when she tasted the oatmeal in her bowl, she pushed it away. There was a hard sick knot in her stomach, and she couldn't eat. Once Scout was back in the house, Alexa stoked up the woodstove to ward off the chill.

Scenes from last evening crowded Alexa's mind. Caleb screaming at her, calling her a whore. That minute when she realized that the sex had turned into something twisted and unpleasant. Standing in the shower trying to wash the whole experience away.

Last night, she had just wanted to bury the encounter with Caleb by going to sleep. In the clear light of Sunday morning, Alexa realized that the experience was not going to just disappear—she was going to have to deal with it.

"Scout, take a nap or something. I'm going to see if meditation can focus my mind."

Five minutes later, Alexa gave up any pretense of meditation. She just couldn't quiet her turmoil.

The ringing phone provided a welcome interruption. Elise Kearns told Alexa that Doctor Crowe's condition had been downgraded from critical to serious. "They are talking about moving him out of ICU in a few days if his condition remains stable. I believe Frank will be hospitalized for quite some time yet. But, he has turned the corner and will almost certainly recover."

Alexa was so pleased to hear about Doc. "Maybe I can get in to the hospital to see him as soon as he's moved from ICU. Do you know if the police have any leads on who shot him?"

"Not that I know. There is one good piece of news though. The police are finished with the clinic, and we'll be opening again on Monday. I told the police that women depend upon us for their medical care and that we need to be back in business as soon as possible."

"Thanks for the update, Elise. I'll see you at the clinic on Wednesday." Alexa thought about mentioning the protestors who had accosted her in the supermarket parking lot a few days ago, but she didn't want to alarm Elise over an ambiguous incident. After all, Officer Starke didn't think there was much to be concerned about.

The phone rang again. Without so much as a greeting, Alexa's mother chirped, "Since Thanksgiving is fast approaching, I wanted to make sure you are bringing pumpkin pies and cranberry salad. Kate is making sweet potatoes, and I'm doing everything else."

"Of course, I'll bring the pies and cranberry. Don't I always?" The thought of Thanksgiving dinner made Alexa smile. Even when she was in the city, she always made it home for the annual celebration of overeating and family togetherness. And, thanks to the miracle of frozen pie crusts and canned pumpkin mix, even Alexa had mastered the pumpkin pie.

As they finished the conversation, her mother asked with concern, "Is everything all right, Alexa? You don't quite sound yourself today."

"I'm fine, Mom," she lied. "I just don't feel up to par. I'm just going to hang around the house for the rest of the day and take it easy. Luckily, it's a week and a half until Thanksgiving, so I'm sure I make a full recovery in time to make pies."

A few minutes later, the phone rang one more time. Reese asked if Alexa wanted to ride with him to Long Lake Dam. "I got tapped to drive some supplies up to a ranger working on a project near there. The ranger mentioned that a flock of snow geese had landed on the lake. I thought you might like to see them."

"Thanks, Reese, but no. I actually would like to see the snow geese. But, I'm not feeling well today. I'm burrowed in for the afternoon."

"Get well. I'll talk to you soon."

Reese Michaels, thought Alexa as she put the phone down. Just speaking to him lifts my mood. However, after last night's disastrous end to my most recent relationship, it's way too soon to be thinking about a new one. It's even more bizarre to consider getting involved with Reese, given the circumstances. Caleb used sex as a way to lash out at me last night. Now, less than twenty-four hours later, I'm mooning over a man who, according to Haley, may have a history of sexual assault.

Alexa wondered again about the coincidence of Elizabeth Nelson being found in Michaux, a place that Reese worked every day. Was he the mystery boyfriend who dumped her in a place he thought no one would find? Even as Alexa formed the thought, she rejected it. From what she knew of Reese, she didn't think he was capable of murder. But, how well did she really know this guy?

Even taking a more rational perspective made Reese an unlikely suspect. The man was too intelligent to kill his girlfriend and dispose of her body in the same state forest where he worked. What was it her dad always said, "You don't crap in your own backyard?" Plus, Reese had only been on the job since late spring, while neighbors had seen Elizabeth with the same boyfriend for many months.

Alexa didn't want to believe that Reese could be either a rapist or a murderer. But, her judgment about men had just been proven to be lacking. She could be wrong about Reese, too.

To make sure she didn't have to speak to anyone else, Alexa tuned the phone ringer to silent. She needed time alone to process what had happened with Caleb. She added more logs to the woodstove, wrapped an afghan around her legs, and sat on the couch to brood. Scout parked himself on the floor at her side, studying her mournfully as if he sensed her distress and confusion.

Alexa was bewildered. How could she have let herself get into a situation where she knew so little about this man? Alexa realized that she had always stayed detached from Caleb and never allowed herself to get too involved. Did keeping an emotional distance from Caleb mean that she'd always had reservations? Or, did it mean that she feared commitment, period?

Alexa concluded that the sexual mistreatment was not her biggest concern from last evening's nightmare with Caleb. Surprisingly, she was most upset that the incident had exposed her physical vulnerability. Despite her attempts to break away from Caleb, she simply had no leverage against a man of his size. Alexa had always thought of herself as physically fit and strong. Last night had taught her an uncomfortable lesson about the limits of that self-image.

Thinking about Caleb, she shifted from introspection to anger. Regardless of what she may have done wrong, Caleb's actions were inexcusable. Instead of agonizing over whether to break up with Caleb, she should never have had anything to do with him in the first place. She tried to recall the things he had said last night as he lashed out at her.

Clearly, abortion was the major issue. Perhaps she had always known that her volunteer work at the clinic would be much too liberal for Caleb's taste. Maybe that's why she had never once mentioned it.

Although her connection to the clinic was hardly a secret, Alexa wondered how Caleb discovered that she worked there. Could he know the young guys in the fleece jackets? Possibly. But, did they even know her name? It came to her in a flash. It was the pregnant woman with the protestors. Although Alexa had only chatted briefly with Joel's wife at Kingdom Lodge, she now realized that Leah was the woman on the picket line who had seemed so familiar. She probably couldn't wait to tell Caleb about seeing Alexa.

Wait a minute.

Alexa considered a new possibility. Did all of the protestors come from Reverend Browne's church? The women on the picket line all wore long dresses similar to the women Alexa had seen at Kingdom Lodge.

If she was correct, Alexa could almost understand why Caleb had lost it. For Reverend Browne's son to be caught dating an abortion advocate would surely embarrass Caleb among the congregation. Caleb's father didn't seem like a man who would easily dismiss such an error of judgment by his own son. Frankly, Caleb seemed almost afraid of his father that day they were at the lodge.

Then, there was Caleb's accusation of promiscuity. Alexa said to Scout, "Funny isn't it? Mr. Religious didn't seem to mind the promiscuity so much until last night. What a double standard. It was fine for the two of us to have sex, but I'm the one who's promiscuous. I guess that goes right along with his comments on 'a woman's place.' After all these months, I find out that this guy is a complete asshole."

What else had Caleb said last night? Something about Rebecca? Yes, he said that I was a whore "just like Rebecca." Rebecca, the sister who Caleb said wasn't here anymore. Had she left the area because she had gotten pregnant? Maybe she even had an abortion. With that family, either an out-of-wedlock pregnancy or an abortion would cause Reverend Daddy to throw her out. Rebecca was obviously a sore subject for Caleb. Surprising, in a way, since he always spoke so fondly of her as a child. Alexa wondered where she was now ...

Alexa resolved to learn from the experience with Caleb, although it might take her time to figure out all the lessons to be derived. As the afternoon waned, Alexa needed some respite from her thoughts. She spent an hour stretching out her sore muscles with yoga. By the time she finished a brief period of successful meditation, Alexa was ready to put Caleb and last night behind her. She was ready to move on.

Alexa rushed out to Melinda's desk with another document to format. This week was crazy with three court-imposed deadlines on the horizon.

"It never rains but it pours," Melinda sighed, as always having a pithy saying to fit the situation at hand.

"True," acknowledged Alexa, "but the office is closed for three days over Thanksgiving, so we'll have time to rest after this is done."

"Rest? I have to cook Thanksgiving dinner for fifteen people on Thursday. Friday is Black Friday, so my daughter and I will be shopping all day. Then, on Saturday, I have to help George pack for deer camp, which is always a major production. I won't have any time to relax until at least Sunday. There's just no rest for the weary."

"Enough with the clichés, Melinda. Next thing I know, you'll be telling me to 'Throw the cow over the fence some hay.'"

Just then, Brian sidled by and remarked snidely, "I think it so charming that you two speak Pennsylvania Dutch to each other." He then focused on Alexa. "Williams, how many visits do you expect from the police this week? If you need an attorney who's not a family member, I'd be happy to represent you, for a reasonable fee."

"Brian, thank you, but I don't need an attorney. I'd love to chat some more, but I'm really slammed with work this week. What is it that you're working on? Or maybe you don't have enough to do, and that's why you're trying to drum up business from me?"

When Brian moved on, Alexa said, "I don't know why that guy always rubs me the wrong way. But, he seems to go out of his way to antagonize me. Who knows what he's saying to other people about these police visits?"

"Personally, Alexa, I think Brian is more worried about himself than you. Maybe that little squirrel has some nuts in his cage that he doesn't want the police to find out about. Did you ever think of that?"

"What do you mean? Do you have some dirt on Stewart?"

"Well, apparently that new clerk, Tiffany, saw Brian at a concert down at Hershey last month. I think it was one of those rock 'n' roll revival acts, maybe the Beach Boys. No, I think it was Black Sabbath."

"Big difference. Melinda, I don't think the police are going to arrest Brian for his musical tastes, no matter how criminal. Seriously, Black Sabbath? And this Tiffany was there, too?

"No. No. It's not the music. It's who Brian was with. Tiffany said that Brian had his hands all over this little blonde who looked like she was about sixteen. Jailbait. Maybe that's what has Brian worried ..."

"Although Brian and I have our differences, I can't imagine he would date a teenager. The girl could be a lot older than she looks. I see these kids come into the clinic sometimes, thinking that they can't be more than thirteen, and it turns out that they're college students. I don't think you should spread Tiffany's gossip any further."

"You're probably right. Loose lips sink ships."

Alexa groaned as she retreated back into her office. She quickly forgot about Brian Stewart as she turned her attention to the pile of legal work.

Alexa thought that she might have to forgo her volunteer afternoon at the clinic on Wednesday. But, after yoga class she skipped the usual trip to the Om Café and went home to spend a few hours editing documents. Work was a good way to avoid thinking about the fiasco with Caleb. Plus, Alexa just wasn't ready to talk to Melissa and Haley about any part of the experience.

By noon on Wednesday, Alexa had nearly completed her projects and decided to go to the clinic. She hadn't heard any updates on Doc's condition since her short phone conversation with Elise on Sunday, so she hoped for a progress report.

To be honest, Alexa also wanted to walk through the clinic door to confirm that Caleb's diatribe on Saturday had not affected her commitment to freedom of choice. Although work had claimed her attention over the past few days, it had not eclipsed her brooding about the ugly scene with Caleb. It didn't help that Caleb had left messages on her home phone on both Monday and Tuesday, apologizing for his actions and wanting to work things out between them.

Alexa was furious. How could Caleb possibly imagine that she could forgive him or that there was anything left to work out? He had treated her badly, caused her physical harm, and said unforgivable things. She had been wearing long sleeves all week to cover the bruise on her wrist. And the bruise on her abdomen throbbed during spinal twists in yoga class. Walking into the clinic today was partly a way for Alexa to say, "Fuck you" to Caleb.

A few minutes early, Alexa strolled slowly toward the clinic, taking time to study the group of six protesting across the street. Neither Leah nor the young men in jeans were there today. Looking at the others, however, made Alexa wonder how she could have missed the link between these austere and vaguely old fashioned people and the ones she had seen at Kingdom Lodge. Now that she had made the connection, it seemed glaringly apparent that this group was part of Reverend Browne's congregation.

Alexa walked through the clinic door but stopped in alarm when she saw the young man in the fleece jacket standing over Tanisha. Her hand went into her pocket for her cell phone to call the police. To her surprise, Tanisha looked up with a smile as the young man approached Alexa.

"Have you met Eric Goldman yet, Alexa?"

Still cautious, Alexa moved toward the man, who had extended his hand to her. Tanisha continued to say, "Eric and another young student at Dickinson are doing a study about societal attitudes toward family planning and abortion. Is that the best way to describe your project, Eric?"

"Ms. Williams, I must apologize to you." The young man's words tumbled over each other. "Although entirely unintended, I believe that my friend, Tony Kennedy, and I scared you last week in the Garden Fresh parking lot. We've been trying to catch you, hoping we could arrange an interview as part of our project. I tried to talk to you a week or so ago when you were walking into the clinic. I couldn't get your attention that day and didn't want to leave my discussions with the Blood of the Lamb group. So, when Tony and I saw you at Garden Fresh, we just rushed up to you, not even thinking about how you might react to two men accosting you in a parking lot at night.

"I'm sorry if we frightened you. But, we would really like to interview you for a volunteer's perspective on family planning and abortion rights issues. Tanisha says that you're a lawyer, which is really awesome. An interview with you would totally enhance our study."

By this time, the five women who were sitting in the waiting area were watching Alexa and this Eric Goldman like the latest episode of *General Hospital*. Alexa moved past them and behind the reception counter with Eric trailing behind.

"Let's sit back here and discuss this," she said moving into the chart area in the far corner. "Mr. Goldman, you and your friend did frighten me. It is not a good idea for two strange men to approach a woman alone after dark unless they're her friends. We're programmed to go on high alert in a situation like that.

"Also, you must be aware of what has been going on here at the clinic recently. Doctor Crowe's shooting and the threats that we've been receiving were reported in the news. We're all on edge. Put yourself in my shoes. I know you only as one of the people who stand across the street protesting the clinic's work. I thought you and your friend wanted to threaten or harm me."

"We never thought. I'm such an idiot." Goldman slapped his forehead in consternation and seemed very affected by her words. Obviously, none of this had occurred to him, although at least it had registered that Alexa was frightened at the Garden Fresh. "When you pushed the cart at us and jumped into the car, we knew we had scared you. But we didn't think about all this stuff. That's some heavy shit—I mean, heavy stuff."

Face to face, Alexa could see that Goldman was very young. He reacted to her words as if he had just received a lecture from the high school principal.

"I understand if you don't want us to interview you. We've spent a lot of time interviewing the protestors. We've spent some time with the doctors and the staff here, too. But, we've never been inside the clinic on one of your volunteer days. I'm sorry," he said a final time and rose from his chair.

"Wait. I didn't say you couldn't interview me. But we have a few more things to discuss. First of all, I need to tell you that I reported you to the police."

"Oh, man. If I'm arrested, my father will be so pissed. And, I'll get thrown out of school. What a dumb ass I've been. Tony, too."

"Calm down. I would almost like to see you spend a night in jail, just to scare you as much as you guys scared me last week. But, that's not going to happen. Now that I know what was really going on, I'll call the police and explain. They won't come after you." Alexa thought it unlikely that Officer Starke had looked very hard for them anyway.

She continued, "When is your project due?"

With a look of abject relief, Goldman replied, "At the end of the semester, on December fifteenth. Thanksgiving break starts Friday, but we'll be back at school on December first. Can we talk to you then?"

"Yes. How about, this time, we schedule an appointment and you can come to my office for the interview?" Alexa fished one of her cards from her pocket. "Call my assistant, Melinda, at this number. I'll tell her to find a time after you return to school, one that suits you and Tony. OK?"

"Thank you. We'll call her tomorrow. I appreciate this so much, especially since we were such jerks. Thank you, Ms. Williams." Goldman backed away from Alexa, grabbed his coat, and nearly ran out the door.

Tanisha, who had overheard most of the conversation, offered her opinion. "You left that young man off awful easy. I didn't know anything about him and that other kid, Tony, accosting you in the parking lot. You must have been petrified."

"Yeah, Doc had just been shot the night before then here were these two guys hurrying toward me in the parking lot. I just reacted. I pushed my shopping cart at them, jumped in the car, and sped away. I was scared to death. They probably thought they were dealing with a crazy woman."

"These young people just don't have any sense these days. They should have just come here to the clinic if they wanted to talk to you."

Alexa gritted her teeth and dialed Officer Starke's number. She was glad to get his voicemail, where she left a detailed message that the incident with the two young men had been a false alarm. As she clicked end on her cell phone, she imagined a visit the next day from Officer Starke, who certainly wouldn't miss an opportunity to say, "Told you so," in his condescending way.

She then called Trooper Taylor to alert him that these two students would likely not be a lead in their search for Elizabeth Nelson's killer. The policeman still asked for their names. He thought Eric and Tony might have seen something that could help in their investigation.

As the afternoon wound down, Tanisha took a call from Dr. Crowe's wife. She told Alexa, "Alice says Doc will move to the critical care unit tomorrow. So, that must mean he's improving."

"Good news. Critical care isn't limited to family members. I'll try to drop by for a visit."

The security guard at a desk in the waiting room had been a constant reminder that the clinic still might not be safe. Alexa was skeptical about how much security this guy could actually provide. He was dressed for the role in a khaki uniform with a pistol in the holster on his hip. However, the guard looked to be well past sixty and had quite a paunch. With his dyed black hair, Alexa thought that this Ryan Murphy looked a lot like Wayne Newton in his Vegas years.

The guard's presence in the waiting room clearly bothered the women who had come for medical care. When Murphy left for his periodic patrols around the outside perimeter of the clinic, the patients whispered among themselves about the guard. Alexa could tell some of the women were anxious.

And who wouldn't be anxious? she thought. They know one of the doctors was shot, and then they come in here and see a security guard. That doesn't do much to raise the comfort level, does it?

Alexa asked Tanisha how she felt about the security situation.

"It makes me feel safer. My husband has been really worried since Dr. Crowe got shot, so he's happy that there's a guard here. But the threat letters come almost every day. They look the same as the others with letters cut out of magazines. The police take every single one to analyze. But I don't think they're getting any closer to solving the case."

"I hope they are making some progress. Maybe we'll be surprised and they'll make an arrest." Alexa tried to be more reassuring than she actually felt. This case didn't seem any closer to being solved than Elizabeth Nelson's murder.

"Oh, I forgot. The messages have changed. Now they say 'YOU WILL BE THE NEXT TO DIE.'"

This change in the message disturbed Alexa. The fact that the notes were evolving was frightening. If Alexa understood the new message, the attack on Frank could just be the beginning.

"We are all being extra careful," Tanisha told Alexa. "And you should be, too. But, really, what can we do except keep coming to work every day and hope that the cops catch this nut? Whoever did this should be arrested for shooting Dr. Crowe."

And stopped from doing any more harm, Alexa silently added.

Chapter Twenty

By the time Alexa pulled the Land Rover in front of her cabin, daylight had faded. Sunset arrived earlier every evening especially since the switch from Daylight Savings Time. She was surprised to see Reese's SUV sitting in front of the house. He opened the door and stepped out.

"Hi. What brings you here?" she asked.

"I have a few things I wanted to talk to you about." Reese helped her with the bags she pulled from the Land Rover."

"Sure. Come on in." Alexa pushed away her instant of hesitation about inviting Reese in. She was certain that the things Haley had heard about Reese weren't true. She believed this even though a quick Internet search the day after the conversation with her best friend confirmed that Reese had been accused of sexual assault. The news stories also said that the charges had been dropped. She wasn't clear why she was so certain of Reese's innocence, especially when she had been so wrong about Caleb. Perhaps she needed to believe that her judgment about men wasn't totally screwed up.

Scout was ecstatic to have both Alexa and Reese open the door. He smiled and wagged his entire body before he dashed outside.

"You're in luck. These bags contain way too much Chinese food for one person to eat. I hope you like emperor's chicken and spring rolls."

"I didn't mean to invite myself to dinner," Reese demurred. "Mainly, I wanted to check on you. You didn't sound yourself on Sunday." As Alexa took several large cartons out of paper bags, he said, "But I do love Chinese food, and it looks like you've got enough here for four people."

"I couldn't make up my mind, so I bought all three of my favorites. If you hadn't shown up, I would be eating Chinese food for the rest of the week. Do you want something to drink?"

Alexa brought Reese a beer and kicked off her shoes. She picked up the heels and said, "I need to change out of these work clothes. Can you let Scout into the house when he comes back?"

Reese sat at the kitchen counter and began leafing through a Sierra Club magazine. When Alexa walked through the living room toward the stairs, she noticed the light blinking on the answering machine. Turning the volume to low, she pressed play. The first message came from a friend in New York City, asking Alexa to call so they could touch base. The second was the one she dreaded—another apology message from Caleb, asking her to give him a chance to explain. She erased Caleb's message when it finished and walked upstairs to change into jeans, trying to shake off the negative energy that Caleb's voice had unleashed in the house.

By the time she came back downstairs, Alexa had shrugged off the message from Caleb. Her mood lightened even further when she saw Reese sitting in her kitchen. The tall ranger was engaged in a serious discussion with Scout that entailed major ear rubs. Together, she and Reese microwaved plates of food and brought them to the table. Between bites of spring rolls, spare ribs, chow mein, and emperor's chicken, they tried to carry on a conversation.

Reese had heard from the state police about the two guys approaching Alexa at the Garden Fresh. Somehow, in telling Reese about today's news that her would-be attackers were actually Dickinson students working on a project, Alexa's original terror in the parking lot morphed into a funny story. They were both cracking up by the time Alexa described the way she had launched the shopping cart toward the two guys and peeled rubber in the Land Rover.

"I can see it in the morning paper now." Reese drew his hand across an imaginary headline. "Local lawyer discovers new use for shopping carts. Pentagon investigates possible application as new weaponry system."

Alexa laughed. "How were the snow geese? I'm sorry I couldn't go with you, but I felt lousy." She self-consciously tugged at her right sweater sleeve to hide the bruise on her wrist.

"The geese were beautiful. The lake looked like it was covered in snow. I understand that it's fairly rare to see an entire flock touch down in this area. But that's only partly why I'm here tonight. You said you were sick on Sunday, but I thought there was something else in your voice when I called. Then, I started thinking that I haven't seen you for more than a week, not since we went to Florentine's that night." Reese's clear blue eyes clouded with concern. In an unconscious gesture, he ran a hand through his thick brown hair. "It seemed like we were becoming good friends and I wanted to make sure that nothing was wrong. That I haven't done something to upset you ..."

"Reese, you haven't done anything wrong. It's just that my life has been really crazy. I've had a lot of things to deal with. Finding Elizabeth dead in the woods, threats at the clinic, Doc being shot, my pseudo assault in the parking lot. Plus, my workload in the office has been pretty full." Alexa stopped short. One of the lessons learned from the Caleb mess was not to avoid the truth.

"But ... I'm not being completely honest," she admitted. "I do have some questions for you. I heard that you are here in Michaux because you were transferred. That you were involved in a scandal out in the western part of the state ... something involving sexual assault."

Reese hung his head. "I'm never going to get away from that. I should have told you instead of letting you find out from someone else. But, I liked you the minute I met you, and I was afraid that this albatross from my past would scare you off."

He put down his fork and sighed before continuing. "This is the straight story. When I was at Roaring Falls State Park, part of my job was to patrol the campgrounds. Every once in a while we would get a bunch of kids partying and bothering the other campers. Even though alcohol is not allowed in the campgrounds, we pretty much turn a blind eye if people are discreet. But when we get a crowd of teenagers or college kids who are openly drinking and creating a ruckus, we have to shut them down.

"One night, I was on a routine patrol of the campgrounds. Several adults flagged me down about a group of high school kids camped at the end of the cul-de-sac. The adults complained that these kids were drunk and shouting obscenities. Of course, I had to deal with it. When I got to the teens' campsite, ten kids sat around the campfire in front of three tents. They were singing loudly, clearly drunk. A few of them were dancing. When I pulled up, they didn't seem to notice the car. I walked over to the campfire and identified myself in a loud voice. I actually had to shout before I finally got their attention.

"Then, all hell broke loose. One of the guys yelled at the others to run, and they scattered into the woods. It was one of those incredibly stupid things people do when they're drunk or high. They left their cars and their tents. They had no way out of the park, yet they all went charging into the dark woods.

"I radioed for backup. What should have been a simple warning to these kids had turned into a major clusterfuck. Now we were going to have to track them down, charge them with disturbing the peace and underage drinking, and call their parents. We might even have to bring in the state police because of the drinking and drugs. Believe me; I was not happy about this.

"While I was waiting for the other rangers to show, I surveyed the campsite. When I looked into the tents, there was a young girl lying in the third one. The screen door was partially unzipped, and when I shined my light through the opening, I could see that she was breathing. At first I thought she was sleeping, but then I realized that she was either faking it or under the influence. I spoke through the screen, 'Miss. I'm Ranger Michaels with the park service. I need you to get up and come out. I'm going to back away and give you a chance to exit the tent.' She was on top of one of the sleeping bags, fully dressed. I could tell she had heard me, even though she still pretended to sleep. I said, 'I'll give you one minute.' I backed away and went on the check the last tent.

"Maybe two or three minutes passed. I heard some shuffling in the tent but she still didn't come out. I could hear some of the other park SUVs crossing the bridge at the entrance of the campground.

"All of a sudden, the girl bursts out of the tent, screaming at the top of her lungs. She starts shouting, 'Help. Don't touch me. Help.' Her clothes were a mess. Her blouse was ripped down the front, and she didn't have any jeans on. People from the other campsites rushed in our direction when they heard her screaming. Just then, two of the other ranger vehicles pulled up.

"When the other two rangers joined me, this girl started sobbing and pointed at me, 'That man. He raped me.'

"That was the beginning of a nightmare that lasted several months. The park service had to take the girl's accusation seriously. They called an ambulance to take her to the hospital. They took me back to headquarters and called the state police. It took them most of the night to track down the rest of the kids from the campsite. Then, the police had to interview me, the first two rangers on the scene, and all of the campers nearby.

"I kept telling them I was innocent. Truthfully, I think that everyone in the park service and even the state police believed me from the very start. I called in my position when I arrived at the campsite before I exited of the car. I called for help about five minutes later when the kids scattered. How plausible was it that I would come across this young girl and rape her in the short time it took the other rangers to reach the site—especially when I knew they were on the way?

"But, she stuck by her story and the hospital rape exam showed that she had sexual intercourse and some vaginal bruising. They also found both alcohol and ecstasy in her system. This girl was the daughter of a big shot in Pittsburgh politics. So, the police were under a lot of pressure.

"Finally, the DNA testing came back and confirmed that, while the girl might have had sex that night, it wasn't with me. When they confronted her with the evidence, she finally broke down and admitted that she lied. She didn't want her parents to know that she had been drinking, doing drugs, and having sex. She came up with the rape story on the spur of the moment. I guess she thought Mom and Dad would focus on the rape and ignore the fact that she had been at a wild camping party. It almost worked.

"You know how it goes. The news carried the story that I had been cleared, that the accusation was a hoax. The girl was underage, so she was never charged with anything. But, good news never gets the amount of coverage that the original story does. Although I was never arrested or even formally charged, people looked at me with lingering suspicion.

"The park was relieved when I asked for a transfer. I wanted to get a fresh start somewhere else. They arranged a transfer down here because it was the first opening that came up. I thought I could escape by moving halfway across the state, but I guess I was kidding myself."

Reese finally stopped speaking. He looked dejected as if telling the entire story to Alexa had drained him.

"I knew that there was more to the story than the little I heard. It must have been terrible experience for you.

You were doing your job. Then, in an instant, everything went to pieces."

"That's it exactly. What was so difficult to deal with was that it felt so out of control. I had done nothing wrong, but the minute she said that I had assaulted her, things just spiraled away."

"I can see how it felt that way. I spent a summer doing an internship with a criminal law firm. Some of our clients were guilty and often in jail for their third or fourth offense. They knew the drill. What I remember the most, though, were the first time offenders. I learned to pinpoint the ones who might actually be innocent. They were in total shock. One day their lives were normal, then a cop knocks on the door and their universe turned on its head. It's good that you were never formally charged, but the experience sounds similar."

"It's discouraging. I feel like this is always going to be hanging over my head. I moved 300 miles away to Michaux, but the rumors came right along with me. Am I always going to be 'that ranger from the sex scandal'?"

"Reese, you are a decent guy. Even if people hear about it, once they get to know you, they will dismiss the rumors. Or, maybe they'll just come right out and ask about it like I did. As far as I'm concerned, we never need to discuss this again."

"Fine with me." He reached for another helping of emperor's chicken.

For the rest of the meal, they kept to lighter topics. As they cleaned up after dinner, Alexa asked, "You said that there were things you wanted to talk to me about. What things?"

"We covered one already, maybe in more detail than I expected. Should I take our conversation to mean that you still want to spend time with me? I don't have many friends around here yet, so I don't want to lose you."

"Yes. I like hanging out with you, so we can still be friends," Alexa mocked him gently.

"I also wanted to tell you about a new development in the Elizabeth Nelson case. The parents are due in town tomorrow."

"I am still astounded that no one has come forward with more details about Elizabeth's life. She must have had some friends here. Why hasn't the ex-boyfriend come forward?" Alexa's voice, which had risen in concern, dropped to a whisper. "I think it is very sad. It's almost as if Elizabeth Nelson didn't exist here in Carlisle."

"It is sad. But there is at least one person out there who interacted with Elizabeth Nelson—her killer. Just be careful because that person is still out there. And the police have not ruled out the possibility that this is the same person who shot Dr. Crowe. We were laughing earlier about the two kids who scared you at Garden Fresh, but you were right to be cautious. Those two turned out to be harmless, but they could just as easily have been the people who shot the doctor. Even though you are a volunteer, you are at the clinic every week. I'm not sure that a loose cannon looking to gun down an abortion clinic worker is going to make a fine distinction about your employment status."

Alexa nodded. "Can you throw a log in the fire?" she asked Reese. "It's getting chilly in here. One of the downsides of living here is heating with the woodstove. It's a whole lot of work."

After stoking the fire, Reese sank into one of the big leather chairs in the living room. Scout ambled over to stretch out at his feet.

Alexa was about to join them when the phone rang. The phone sat on a small table next to the couch. Alexa could see from caller ID that the call was from Caleb. She didn't want to speak to him. But, if she didn't pick up the phone, Caleb's message would be audible to Reese, sitting only a few feet across the room. Quickly, weighing the options, she decided to pick up the phone.

"Excuse me," she said to Reese. "I need to take this call." As Alexa picked up the receiver, her sweater slipped down her arm, exposing her bruised wrist.

Walking into the kitchen, Alexa answered, "Hello."

"Alexa. I am so glad that you picked up," Caleb said. "I hope you got the messages that I have been leaving all week."

"I got them."

"I want to apologize for my outburst on Saturday. I am so sorry, but when I found out that you worked at the clinic, it came as such a shock. I realized that I didn't know you as well as I thought. But, the way I spoke to you was way out of line. I hope you can forgive me."

Alexa turned her back to Reese and spoke softly into the receiver. "Caleb, I'm not sure that I can ever forgive you. Please stop calling."

"Alexa, just give me a chance to explain. Can we meet face to face to discuss this? I know you're angry. I have to talk to you about this in person. Please, can we get together?" Caleb grew increasingly agitated.

"It seems to me that enough has been said already. I need to go now," Alexa said and ended the call. She was angry and didn't want to give Caleb another chance; she just wanted to get him off the phone.

Even though Alexa had walked into the kitchen area, the downstairs was really one big room. It was clear that Reese had heard Alexa's side of the conversation. He asked, "Is everything OK? It's really none of my business, but you sounded upset."

Alexa decided to share an edited version of what had happened with Caleb. "That was the guy I've dated most of the summer. I wasn't looking for anything serious, and I didn't think he was either, until recently. Then I got to know a little bit more about him. He took me over to Perry County to meet his family at this place called Kingdom Lodge. It turns out that he's way more conservative than me. Learning more about Caleb finally jolted me into a decision to break it off. I had been heading in that direction anyway.

"While I was coming to the conclusion that we should break up, apparently he was going the opposite way. He wanted to move the relationship in a more serious direction. Then, he found out that I volunteer at the clinic. He was over here on Saturday and just freaked out on me about the clinic because of the abortions performed there. It was ugly, and I told him that I didn't want to see him again.

"All week long, he's been calling to apologize and ask for a chance to explain. I'm not sure how to make him stop calling. I don't want to get back together."

Reese tried to look sympathetic, but the look of delight that passed briefly across his face undermined the effect. "I wondered about this boyfriend. Breaking up is never easy, but it sounds like he's not the man for you."

"I always thought that we were just having a good time together, with no real commitment on either side. Then, I realized that he was much more invested than me."

"Are you going to give him that chance to explain?"

"I don't know. My instinct says no, that we said everything that needed to be said last Saturday. On the other hand, I spent a lot of time with Caleb over the last few months and we had some very good times together. I sort of hate to end it on such a bad note. I know that I don't want to be alone with him if I do agree to talk. It's got to be in a public place."

"Why don't you want to be alone with this guy? Did he hurt you? I mean physically? Was that why you were 'sick' on Sunday?" He glanced at Alexa's right wrist, and it became clear that Reese had seen the bruise she'd tried to hide.

Alexa waffled. She had already told Reese too much about Caleb. "He was angry and lashed out a bit. I suffered no permanent damage. Don't be thinking that I'm in some domestic violence situation. This has never happened before, and it will certainly never happen again." She spoke the last words very forcefully.

"You are clearly not telling me the whole story, but that's your call. If you do decide to meet this guy, you shouldn't be alone. Just call me and I'll go with you. I'll ride shotgun."

"Right," Alexa finally found some humor in the situation. "I agree to hear Caleb's apology and probably a pitch about getting back together. And I bring you along to keep an eye on the conversation. I'm sure Caleb would be thrilled to have another guy there while he makes his case."

"I wouldn't be part of the conversation. But, I'd be somewhere nearby to make sure things don't get out of hand when you tell him no again. Because you're going to say no, right?"

"Right. But, we're getting ahead of ourselves here. I'm not sure that I'll even agree to see Caleb. I do appreciate your kind offer, sir. You're sort of like a modern day Sir Galahad, ready to ride to a lady's rescue at the drop of a hat."

"I don't really see myself as Sir Galahad, and I don't really see you as a lady. I'll be more like Goose to your Maverick." He paused. "No. Nix the *Top Gun* analogy. I forgot that Goose dies. We'll stick with Sir Galahad."

When they both dissolved into peals of laughter, Scout jumped up and ran around the room barking. That only made Alexa laugh harder.

Alexa's spirits were still high when Reese left.

What an evening, she thought. It certainly was a night for truth telling. I'm so glad that Reese was open about his trouble at Roaring Falls. I'll have to set Haley straight and make sure that she passes the real story on to her husband and his friends.

She then reflected on the conversation about Caleb. Real smooth, Alexa.

Telling Reese all about my last boyfriend? Well, she amended, nearly all. She had skipped any mention about the sex with Caleb. It had felt good, though, to talk about what had happened.

Talking to Reese came easy for Alexa. Spending time with him had helped crystallize all the things that were missing in her feelings for Caleb. However, she was wary of quickly bouncing from a failed relationship with Caleb into something new with Reese. Still, Alexa knew she was hoping for more than friendship from the good-looking forest ranger.

Chapter Twenty-One

Wednesday, November 21, 1934.

By his gentle voice whispering low ...

When Dewilla opened her eyes, she panicked. "Where am I?" she moaned. The sight of her sisters, fast asleep beside her, reassured the youngster. The three girls shared a lumpy old mattress, and her sisters hogged all the blankets, leaving Dewilla with only a thin sheet. She was cold.

Still disoriented, Dewilla rolled onto her back and stared at the ceiling. An anemic ray of light from the kitchen exposed a web of deep cracks etching the aging ceiling. The sickly light lacked the strength to reach the bed, which crouched low in the shadows.

Dewilla came fully awake and realized that she was in yet another dingy tourist court. Since the family left California a few weeks ago, they had stayed in a succession of these cheap cabins. Early in the trip, she and Norma could barely contain themselves at the excitement and glamour of sleeping in tourist courts.

Norma burbled, "Staying in a motor court. We'll be just like Claudette Colbert in It Happened One Night."

Dewilla reminded her sister, "Daddy put the kibosh on me seeing that picture, remember? He said I was too young."

"I wish you could have gone. Miss Colbert made me laugh every time she opened her mouth. I'm going to wear my hair like hers when I grow up; she's such a looker. And, Mr. Gable ..."

"Clark Gable is a keen number."

"And, how. But, what would you know about handsome men, kiddo?" Norma teased.

"Daddy's handsome. Winifred said so."

A thousand weary miles and countless shattered illusions had long since ground the glamour of the road to dust. The Pontiac, a real hay burner, guzzled dime after dime of Daddy's traveling money. Each motor court became more ramshackle than the last.

Of course, having a lumpy bed sure beat the few nights they camped beside the road, Dewilla thought. Daddy had tried to make camping an adventure, but the ground was too hard. And those spooky night sounds: coyotes and owls and who knows what else. She was glad it had gotten too cold for sleeping outdoors now.

Twilight had still lingered when Daddy coasted the Pontiac into tonight's tourist court near Lancaster. The girls had been so happy when Winifred found two cans of stew tucked in the back of a kitchen cupboard. The sisters bolted down their portions at the tiny table and went straight to bed. Dewilla fell asleep quickly, her belly still warm from the stew.

Now fully awake, a murmur caught her attention. The sound of low voices came from the same direction as the flickering light. It must be past midnight. What could Daddy and Winifred be doing at this hour?

Quietly, Dewilla rose onto her knees and peeked over the half-wall that separated the sleeping area from the kitchen. Daddy and Winifred perched on chairs at the table with their heads close together. They spoke so softly that she couldn't hear what they were saying. While Dewilla spied on the grownups, Winifred rose from the rickety white chair and sashayed over to Dewilla's father. Slowly, Winifred leaned over and kissed Daddy on the mouth.

Dewilla gasped. She had seen Mama and Daddy kiss a thousand times. The two of them always joked around and then turned lovey-dovey, smooching and hugging. But, it didn't seem right for Winifred to kiss Dewilla's daddy. Seeing Winifred with Daddy made Dewilla miss Mama so much she could hardly breathe.

Winifred ended the kiss and stood. Then, Daddy just stared at Dewilla's cousin with a crazy look on his face. Grasping Winfred's wrists he pulled her down onto his lap. Daddy seized Winifred's face with his big hands and kissed her fiercely. When Winifred snuggled closer to Dewilla's father, a strap from her flimsy shift slipped off her slender shoulder.

Dewilla's cheeks burned with embarrassment. She couldn't stand to watch any longer and ducked back down on the bed. Dewilla pried a corner of the blanket from Cordelia and curled into a ball. Silent tears streamed down her cheeks. The child wanted to wake Norma up to tell her what was happening, but she let her older sister sleep. What could Norma do?

Everything in Dewilla's life had changed. Her mama had left them and had gone to Heaven forever. The family abandoned their home and their friends to go on the road for reasons that she didn't totally grasp. Hunger had become a constant companion. And, her beloved daddy had turned into a different man, one with dark moods and a worrying bond with Cousin Winifred. Dewilla wished that she could understand everything that was happening.

Just before Dewilla drifted off to sleep, she said a prayer for herself and Norma and Cordelia. "Mama," she whispered. "I'm scared. We need your help. Now that you are an angel in Heaven, please ask God to take care of us. I fear that Daddy has lost his way."

Chapter Twenty-Two

Alexa found time after lunch to slip away for a quick trip to the hospital to visit Doctor Crowe. Doc was sitting up in bed reading when Alexa knocked at the door.

"Come in, my dear. I can tell I'm feeling better because this hospital is starting to drive me crazy. You are a welcome respite from this book Alice brought. I love the adventure novels in this series. However, I have to admit that being attached to all these monitors in a hospital bed tends to undermine that feeling of being there with the characters."

Alexa crossed to the bed and kissed the very pale Doc on the cheek. He seemed diminished by the sterile hospital room with its white walls, white sheets, and bank of machines and monitors.

"I have been so worried about you. I'm happy to say that you're looking pretty good for a man who was just shot. I should have known that a mere bullet couldn't keep you down."

"The doctors tell me that it was touch and go for a few hours after they brought me in here. But, I'm doing fine now. I just need to rest and give my body time to heal. I'm counting the days until they move me out of this critical care unit. When I hit the general care area, I expect that they'll discharge me in a snap."

"Do you mind telling me what happened?"

"When I got shot? There's not much to tell. After dinner, I wanted to finish an article for the regional newsletter. I realized that I had neglected to bring the flash drive with the draft document home. I'd also forgotten my research notes, probably because I was rushing to get home to dinner. One of Alice's hard and fast rules is: don't be late for dinner.

"So, around eight o'clock, I took a quick trip to the clinic to collect what I needed. I parked the car in my space near the back door, walked to my office, and picked up the flash drive and my research notes from my desk. I was in the clinic less than five minutes.

"Then, I made my way to the back exit, locked the door, and started toward my car. Out of nowhere, I felt this blow to my chest. It actually knocked me back a few steps, and I crumpled onto the ground. Then the pain hit, and I realized that I'd been shot. Luckily, I had my cell phone in my jacket pocket. I pulled it out and punched nine. Maybe it's my medical background, but I have 911 on speed dial on all my telephones. So, I had just enough time to hit the single digit before I lost consciousness. I never actually spoke to the 911 operator.

"About the same time I was dialing 911, the police received a flurry of calls from people who live near the clinic, complaining about gunfire in the alley. There was a patrol car in the area, and they found me almost immediately. Their quick action probably saved my life."

"I'm so glad that they found you so fast, Doc. What sort of sick bastard just lies in wait to shoot you? Did you see anyone?"

"No, Alexa. As I told the police, I have a vague impression of a metallic noise, maybe a boot scraping metal, from somewhere down the alley. But, I didn't see anyone. The cops think that whoever shot me could have been hiding in the shadows on the fire escape behind the Brenneman building. The calls were from people who live in those apartments.

"They also think that I might have been followed from my home. There's no way that anyone would know that I'd be visiting the clinic after hours. Heck, I didn't even know I was going down there until a few minutes before I left the house. I rarely return to the clinic after I leave for the day. Even on those evenings when we do terminations, I usually just stay at the clinic and have dinner brought in.

"If I was followed, I certainly wasn't aware of it. The police theory is that when I went into the clinic, my assailant found his position on the fire escape and just waited for me to come back to the car. The bullet they recovered from the scene was from a high-powered rifle. It was dark, and our parking lot isn't very well lit. This guy must be a pretty good shot."

"You seem awfully calm about nearly getting killed. Aren't you furious? I am. I'm furious and scared for you, all at the same time."

Doc paused a minute to take a sip of water. "This has been a sobering experience, Alexa. As you get older, you begin to realize that your time on this earth is limited. But, it's easy to ignore that looming inevitability. Getting shot in the chest and waking up in the hospital with part of your lung gone is a real reality check. Of course, any one of us could be gone in an instant. But, at my age, the odds of that increase rapidly.

"To focus on your question, yes, I am angry at this coward who hid in the shadows and shot me without even showing me his face. It saddens me that there is such hate in the world that a stranger would shoot me because I help women end unwanted pregnancies. But my focus right now is on my recovery, my family, and making sure I've got my priorities straight for the brief time I have left."

Alexa didn't quite know how to respond to Doc. She wanted to respect his emotional reaction to the near-death experience, but she was concerned about what he might be implying. "Doc, are you saying that you're going to quit the clinic?"

"No. That's not what I'm saying at all. The clinic is and always will be one of those priorities that I just mentioned. But, when I get out of here, I want to better balance my work at the clinic with the rest of my life. More trips to Hawaii. More time with Alice, my kids, and grandkids. That's all I'm saying, Alexa."

"You had me worried there for a minute. I can't imagine the clinic without you. I hope the police catch this SOB who shot you." Alexa grasped Doc's hand. "Now, I'm going to let you rest or get back to your adventure novel. I just wanted to say hello."

As she left the room, she saw Doc put the book down and close his eyes in exhaustion. It hurt Alexa to see this good and decent man in such pain.

Chapter Twenty-Three

By noon on Friday, Alexa had received eight additional voice messages at home and work from Caleb. She ignored them all. When he called yet again that afternoon, she sighed heavily and instructed Melinda to put the call through. The continuing phone calls were becoming a nuisance.

Caleb started off with the litany of apologies and excuses that had become familiar from the barrage of voice messages over the past week. He asked, "Have you thought about meeting me?" His voice took on an unattractive pleading tone that Alexa would never have envisioned from this man. "Talking on the phone is not a good way to resolve this, Alexa. Please just spend a little time with me so we can talk it through."

As she listened, Alexa reached an unwelcome conclusion. The only way to convince Caleb that she wanted nothing more to do with him would be to meet face to face. With a grimace, she assented. "OK, Caleb. I'll meet, but don't expect much from any discussion. Like I said on Wednesday, I might be able to forgive you, but I am not interested in dating you anymore."

"Can we get together tomorrow?"

Anxious to get this over with, Alexa agreed. "Yes. I could meet you for a few minutes in the afternoon. I have some errands to run in Carlisle."

"I was hoping we could have some privacy. I know it's a drive, but could you come to Kingdom Lodge around two o'clock?"

Alexa was so surprised at this request that she didn't know how to respond. She had envisioned a fast cup of tea at some diner while Caleb said his piece. Then, she would make a quick exit. Driving over to Kingdom Lodge was an entirely different proposition. Alexa's frustration edged into anger as she paused, speechless at this outrageous request.

Caleb seemed to sense her hesitancy. "I don't want to impose on you, but I'll be there in the morning hunting with the guys. By the afternoon, it should be calm there and we would have a chance to talk."

Alexa surprised herself when she abruptly consented. Now that she had agreed to meet Caleb, she didn't want to put this off any longer. If this was the only way to get it done tomorrow, she would make the trip to the lodge. It was clear that Caleb would keep pushing until he spoke to her. Alexa would rather that conversation take place soon so they could both just move on.

Alexa acknowledged that she shared some of the blame in this disastrous flameout. Nothing excused Caleb's anger or his rough behavior in their final sexual encounter. But, Alexa had to admit that she might have led the guy on. Her willingness to meet Caleb on his terms, she decided, was a way of taking accountability for her part in the relationship debacle.

"OK. I'll drive over to meet you, but I'm going to bring a friend along." Alexa wasn't so remorseful that she'd lost all reason. She was reluctant to be alone with Caleb in a place like Kingdom Lodge. She couldn't risk a repeat of the violent anger of last weekend. Having someone along would also make it easier to leave.

Alexa remembered Reese's offer to ride shotgun if she met with Caleb. She hoped Reese wasn't working tomorrow afternoon.

Reese answered his cell on the first ring. Alexa said, "I have a favor to ask if you are free tomorrow. I just agreed to have that discussion with my old boyfriend. He wants to talk at Kingdom Lodge over in Perry County. It's a place that his family owns. I wondered if you would be willing to ride over with me. Of course, the conversation is between Caleb and me, but I don't want to go alone."

"What time? I have a shift that ends at noon, but I can go after that. Meeting with him is your call, but it's not a good idea to go on your own. Driving over there will give me a chance to see some of Perry County."

Alexa arranged to meet Reese at her cabin the next afternoon. Before she turned back to work, Alexa thought about her instinctive decision to turn to Reese. She could have asked either Haley or Melissa to go along, but she had already confided more about her blow-up with Caleb to Reese than to her two best friends. She knew that Caleb would be hurt that she would bring another guy to this attempt at reconciliation. Although she was past caring much about Caleb's feelings, she would ask Reese to hang outside while they spoke.

When Reese arrived the next afternoon, Alexa asked, "Is it OK with you if I take Scout along? I'll drive the Land Rover so you don't get dog fur in your Jeep. I just hate to leave him alone on a Saturday." Scout bounded around the Land Rover in anticipation.

"The more the merrier," Reese said, laughing as Scout leapt into the back compartment of the Rover. "I'm just along for the ride, anyway."

Alexa tried to thank Reese for coming to Kingdom Lodge, but he brushed aside her words. He spent the ride commenting on the scenery, talking to the dog, and generally trying to distract Alexa.

The scenery on this November day was very different from the vivid fall colors of her first trip to Kingdom Lodge. Today, nearly all the trees were bare. Brown and shriveled leaves clung to a few forlorn pin oaks as if these trees couldn't face the coming winter without some attempt at armor. The cloudy afternoon accentuated the shadowy gloom of the forest. Alexa thought the gray tone was fitting for the mission she was on today.

"You're not seeing this area at its best," she said to Reese. "In the spring, summer, and fall, it's beautiful over here—just forest and farmland. The towns are few and far between, and very small. There are only a handful of traffic lights in the entire county. The place we're headed to, Kingdom Lodge, is lovely. It's a beautiful old lodge, built for hunting, fishing, and social events. Caleb's father is minister of a church in this area. It's privately owned, I think by the congregation. Caleb's family is part owner."

Alexa nearly missed the lodge. Catching the small sign out of the corner of her eye, she slammed on the brakes a few yards past the entrance. They hadn't seen any other cars on this stretch of road, so she backed up carefully and turned into the drive. When Alexa turned off the car, she said, "The lodge is just behind this hedge. I'm going to go in and find Caleb. Do you mind taking Scout for a walk while I talk to him? There's a beautiful lake in front of the lodge."

"You don't want me to go inside with you?"

"I think I should speak to him alone. But, if I need you for some reason, I'll find you or call on your cell." Alexa glanced quickly at her cell to verify reception.

"I'd rather be inside with you, but I understand that this is a private conversation. I won't wander too far."

As Alexa opened the car door, she heard gunfire in the distance. "Hear that? There's a shooting range out there to the right somewhere. Another good reason for you and Scout to keep close to the building."

Alexa moseyed along the lodge's wide porch. She felt like Daniel at the entrance of the lion's den. Then, she laughed.

There must be something in the air around here, she thought. Soon, I'm going to start speaking in Bible verses like Caleb's mother.

She paused a moment to look out over the lake. With the exception of a few Canadian geese, the wide span of water was empty. Everything was a shadowy gray, so misty that the dark mountain flowed seamlessly into the murky lake. For a moment Alexa fancied that the yawning expanse looked like a giant open mouth. Spooked, she stepped back from the railing.

"My, you are on edge, aren't you," she muttered. "Let's just get this over with." The disturbing atmosphere evaporated when Reese and Scout walked into view, headed for the lakeshore.

Turning away, Alexa walked to the front door. She drew a deep breath before reaching for the knob and pushing the heavy old iron and timber door inward. Pausing briefly inside the door to allow her eyes to adjust to the gloom, Alexa focused on the fire crackling in the huge stone fireplace in the center of the room. A scent of creosote hung in the air as if the chimney wasn't venting properly. Caleb rose from one of the deep chairs in front of the fire and walked a few steps in her direction.

"Thank you for coming, Alexa," he said, almost diffidently. "I know that it wasn't easy for you to agree to see me. Let's sit here. I was out most of the morning. The fire really takes off the chill. Weren't you going to bring a friend?" He reached out to touch Alexa, but she avoided him and walked to the chairs.

Caleb wore camouflage hunting pants and a brown waffle-weave Henley. A canvas camouflage coat hung over the back of his chair. She took in Caleb's dark good looks and his silvery eyes. On a primal level she was still attracted to this man, despite the way he had treated her. Perhaps that's really why she had agreed to drive all the way over here to Perry County to meet him. But, she knew that this attraction, no matter how strong, didn't outweigh the disillusionment and distrust she now felt for Caleb; nor had she changed her mind about breaking up.

She balanced on the edge of the chair facing his. "Hello, Caleb. My friend, Reese, is outside with Scout. I asked him to wait on the lawn since I thought we should have this discussion alone. I'm here because things ended things badly between us, and I didn't feel comfortable leaving things that way. But, I don't want to mislead you. I'm not looking for reconciliation."

"First of all, I want to apologize to you. I was way out of line with the things I said to you. Not as an excuse, but I would like to explain my reaction." Caleb leaned forward, clasping his hands together. "I was shocked to find out that you were part of the clinic and even more shocked that you never mentioned this in all the months we were dating. Abortion is something that my family and I are strongly opposed to. Learning that you were part of this awful thing just threw me for a loop."

"Look, Caleb. I'm not really sure why we never discussed my work at the clinic. To be honest, we didn't delve too deep in any of our conversations. We always kept things light. I wasn't hiding my volunteer work at the clinic from you. It's public knowledge. It just never came up. But, the clinic is about so much more than abortion. That facility provides family planning and general medical services to thousands of low-income women. Abortion is only one service that we provide to a handful of women in need."

"Alexa, I know that you are a very caring person. When I thought about it more, I wasn't surprised that you volunteer your time to help poor women. And, of course, I know that your upbringing was much more liberal than mine. Now that I hear you talk about the clinic, I can see how you overlook the abortion aspect because of the other services."

Alexa raised her hand and shook her head. "Stop right there. You are not understanding me, Caleb." She enunciated each word carefully as if speaking to a child. "I strongly support a woman's right to choose, including abortion rights. I am at the clinic because I believe in all of the services that it provides."

Caleb's expression became even more somber. "Alexa, I like you. Our relationship started out as casual dating. You're right; we had a lot of fun together. At first, I found our differences in politics and our approaches to life intriguing. I've never really known a woman as smart and independent as you. Then, I found myself developing real feelings for you. That's why I brought you here to Kingdom Lodge to meet my parents. I would like to think that we could move beyond this clinic issue."

"Even if we could get past our differences, I'm not interested in trying. Last week, you stepped over the line. I'm not just talking about your excessive anger and name-calling. I'm talking about the physical abuse. I won't go so far as to call it rape, but it certainly wasn't consensual sex." Alexa was starting to get pissed off all over again. She wanted to end this conversation. Coming here and trying to end things amicably had been a mistake.

"Caleb, we dated for a few months. We had a good time, and now it's over. Let's just leave it at that."

When Alexa put her hands on the arms to push out of the deep armchair, Caleb leapt to his feet and stood in front of her. "Don't go yet. Give me just a few more minutes. You came all this way. Just a few more minutes."

"All right." Alexa sank back into the seat. She'd give him five more minutes at most. Concerned that Caleb seemed to be getting worked up again, she wrapped her right hand around the cell phone in her pocket. She had already set Reese's number on speed dial.

Caleb sat back down slowly. Instead of continuing the conversation, he wrapped his hands behind his head and looked at the floor. Alexa sighed but let Caleb gather his thoughts. Finally, he looked up but didn't meet Alexa's eyes. As he looked past her, Alexa heard footsteps approaching behind her chair. Reese, coming to check on her? When she turned, she blanched to see that it was not Reese, but Reverend and Mrs. Browne.

"What's this?" she said to Caleb. Instead of answering, Caleb rose to his feet and pulled two chairs closer to Alexa.

"Hello, dear," Mrs. Browne said as she lowered herself into a chair.

Reverend Browne continued to stand, towering over her. When he nodded, Caleb sat back in his chair. The reverend spoke, "Hello, Alexa. Caleb told us of your disagreement and about your connection to those godless baby killers at the clinic. He asked us here to pray for you. It is not too late. God forgives those who repent and acknowledge the error of their ways. In John 8, Jesus told the woman who had been brought to him as a sinner, 'Then neither do I condemn you. Go now and leave your life of sin.'"

Without waiting for a response, the reverend raised both hands in the air. "Let us pray. God, our Father, we are here today to save the soul of this young woman, Alexa Williams. In her innocence, she has unknowingly strayed down the sinner's path, but her heart is pure. Our son has chosen to have this woman in his life, and we ask for Your guidance in saving this woman and washing her clean of her transgressions. Father, please show Alexa the way to Christian living and the redemption that only You can bestow. Blessed is the name of the Lord, Amen."

Stunned to see Caleb's parents appear, Alexa had been paralyzed. She had assumed that she and Caleb were alone. Now, it was clear that his parents had been here all along. Having the discussion with Caleb here had been a setup for this religious intervention by Reverend Browne.

When Reverend Browne drew his prayer to a close, Alexa bolted out of her seat. While Caleb and Mrs. Browne spoke their Amens, she stepped away from the Browne family circle by the fireplace. "I believe that you are acting with the best of intentions, but I don't share your beliefs. I am proud to be involved with the clinic. I have no plans to stop my work there. Caleb, we've said everything that needed to be said between us. Please don't contact me again." Alexa turned and raced to the door.

Spying Reese and Scout by the lake, Alexa called that she was ready to leave. Instead of waiting, she rushed toward the Land Rover. Just before she stepped through the hedges into the parking lot, Alexa glanced over her shoulder and saw Caleb watching her from the back window. Perhaps it was a reflection on the glass, but at this distance, Caleb's eyes had become the same lifeless gray as the afternoon sky.

Alexa shrank into the driver's seat of the Land Rover listening to distant gunfire. She jumped when Reese opened the back door for Scout. Seconds later, he climbed into the seat beside her. Alexa turned the ignition before Reese closed the door. The minute that his seatbelt struck its buckle, Alexa raced from the parking lot. She wanted to put Kingdom Lodge far behind them.

"How did things go? With the way you're driving, I'm thinking, not so good."

Alexa took the hint and slowed to the speed limit. She took a few minutes before replying. "The conversation with Caleb was difficult, but I made it clear that we're over. Then, it got really weird when his father and mother walked in and prayed for my salvation. Did I mention that his father is a minister of some fundamentalist congregation over here?"

"What? His parents were there? They prayed? Why?"

"Because I work at an abortion clinic, I'm a sinner. I'm not sure where they intended to go after the prayer, but I decided that I wasn't interested in finding out. I left. I can't believe I agreed to come here. What was I thinking?"

"Hey. Hey. Don't start second guessing yourself. You wanted to give this guy a chance to make his case. Who would have imagined that he would bring his parents along? How old is this guy anyway?"

"Old enough that he shouldn't need his parents to be around for a conversation with an ex-girlfriend. That little bombshell came out of left field."

They rode in silence for quite a while as Alexa dealt with her anger at Caleb and her fury with herself. She had driven over to Kingdom Lodge to put an end to Caleb's incessant calls, but it would have been better to just ignore him completely.

In an obvious effort to distract Alexa, Reese started a conversation. "Have I ever told you how much I like your wheels? Every time I ride in this Land Rover, it takes me back to Africa. Over there, all we drove were Land Rovers. They're ideal for the bush and will go through almost anything. We got stuck from time to time during the rainy season. The mud in remote parts of Africa can be unbelievable. Every time though, we managed to pull ourselves out of the muck by using the four-wheel drive and a winch. I know that some of the safari companies use Toyota Land Cruisers, which are pretty great vehicles. But, I'd always choose a Land Rover. I just love these babies. How did you get this one, anyway?"

Alexa made an effort to escape her bad mood. "This Land Rover has been in our family for years. My dad bought it from a client back in the nineties. He had represented this guy in a bankruptcy proceeding, and the man offered this car to Dad as part of his payment. Even then, the vehicle had a few hard years on it. But, the client had been flush when he bought the car. I think it was a special edition that he bought the first year Land Rover sold the Defender in the United States. It was one of only five hundred that were imported. Dad decided it would be great for us to use at the cabin, so they made a deal.

"I always loved this car as a kid. I needed a car when I moved out of the city. So, I asked Dad if I could have it. It was pretty beat up by that time, but I found a place outside Philadelphia that works on vintage Rovers. They fixed the engine like new, but I didn't want to sink a lot of money into the body. It's the perfect ride for Scout and me. Isn't it, buddy?" she asked the dog lying in the back.

"The gas mileage is pretty terrible, but I don't really do much long distance driving. And the white color is not the best for living in the country, but it certainly gets me back to the cabin in the winter. I really like the way the back door opens to the side. Most of the new SUVs have doors that lift up and down."

By the time they finished talking Land Rovers, they reached the cabin and Alexa had calmed down. She thanked Reese for riding with her to Kingdom Lodge. He seemed to sense that she wanted to be alone and made no effort to come into the house.

"I'll call you tomorrow," he said before he left. "I'm working all day, but I'll check in with you. Later this week, I'm heading home to my parents' house for Thanksgiving. Take it easy tonight." Turning to the mastiff, he patted the dog's huge head and instructed, "Scout, take care of her."

Chapter Twenty-Four

Alexa fumed about the debacle at Kingdom Lodge for most of the week. It was difficult to find words for Caleb's atrocious behavior. Bringing his parents to pray over Alexa like she was a lost soul who need to be saved. She felt like Caleb had violated her a second time on Saturday.

Truth be told, Alexa was angriest with herself. She was a fool. Why had she thought that Caleb deserved even a chance to apologize? Caleb's meltdown that night at the cabin had caught Alexa unawares, but she had walked willingly into the ambush at Kingdom Lodge.

"Seriously, what were you thinking, Alexa?"

Even Tuesday's after-yoga session at Om Café with Melissa and Haley hadn't helped. That conversation had only made Alexa feel worse. When Alexa told her friends everything that happened at the lodge, Haley said, "There is no doubt that this is one of the weirdest breakups in modern history. I can't believe he brought the parents. But, Alexa, you've always had this tendency to try to make everything OK when your relationships fall apart. That Jake guy in high school. That tool, Trent. Now, Caleb. If you don't watch out, all this make-nice impulse is going to get you into real trouble."

"Thanks. I come looking to you guys for support and I get dime-store psychoanalysis."

"What I can't believe," Melissa chimed in, "is that you drove the whole way over to East Bumfuck nowhere by yourself to break up with this loser. As bizarre as this whole thing sounds, I'm astounded that put yourself at risk like that. You're an attorney, for God's sake. I thought you were smarter than this, girl. Why didn't you ask one of us to go along?"

"I wasn't alone," Alexa said testily. "Reese Michaels was with me."

"Who?" Melissa asked.

Haley jumped in before Alexa could answer. "Melissa, you are so behind the times. That's what you get for missing two Tuesdays in a row. Reese Michaels is the gorgeous new park ranger that Alexa has lined up to take Caleb's place."

Despite Alexa's protestations that Reese was just a friend, Melissa wanted to know everything about this guy. Haley was only too happy to oblige. Alexa just listened to her two friends discuss Reese until Melissa asked, with a toss of her auburn curls, "Haley, describe exactly what you mean by gorgeous."

Alexa finally jumped back into the conversation. "Wait. I actually have a picture of him. I took one on my cell phone for him to send a friend in Kenya."

When Melissa saw the picture on Alexa's cell, she squealed, "I know this guy. Well, I don't really know him, but we met last summer on the deck at Outlaws. I was there with Francine one Friday after work, probably in late August. He was with a group of friends from Pine Grove Furnace State Park. Some of them were still wearing their uniforms. I remember this guy because Francine really, really wanted to hit on him. You know how brazen she is. She would try to pick up a priest at Mass if she thought she could get away with it.

"Anyway, poor Francine was just beside herself because she couldn't get near Reese. Some young blonde who looked about nineteen was sticking to him like glue. She had her arm around him every few seconds and stayed by his side all night.

"Francine tried to take a run at him when the blonde chickie went to the ladies' room. She dragged me along when she approached the group. She knew one of the lifeguards from Laurel Lake, so it gave her an excuse to say hello. We talked to the lifeguard for a little while until Francine found a way to rope Reese into the conversation.

It was just idle bar talk. We were never actually introduced, so I didn't get his name.

"Then the blonde Lolita emerged to monopolize your Reese. Soon after that, the entire group left the bar. Francine talked about the guy for weeks afterward—until she met Keith, who is now her squeeze du jour."

"What did she look like, the blonde?" Alexa asked.

Melissa looked at her friend in confusion. "I don't know; like any nineteen-year-old, with a tight ass and a decade's less wear and tear. She had her hair pulled up into a ponytail and was wearing one of those tank tops that bared her flat little stomach and a pair of shorts that bared just about everything else. At first glance, she looked slender enough to blow away like a feather. The more I studied her, I realized that she was actually one of those girls who looked fragile but could whip your ass in tennis or baseball or whatever." Melissa started laughing hilariously. "Clearly, I was just jealous of the bitch."

Alexa soon made her excuses and left Haley and Melissa to continue their chat. Her heart had gone cold when Melissa said she had seen Reese with a young blonde girl last summer. As she drove home Alexa turned this revelation over in her mind.

Was this just another coincidence? Or had Reese been with Elizabeth Nelson? After all, he was the one with the history of sexual assault, and Alexa had only his story that the accusation was false. Granted, she had confirmed that the charges were dropped, but there had been no specific details in the news reports.

Then, there was the other possible connection to Reese. Elizabeth's body had turned up in Michaux State Forest. Who knew those woods better than one of the park rangers? Maybe he had shown up at the scene that day to keep track of what the police were doing. It would be clever to insert himself into the investigation to make sure the police didn't hone in on him as the killer.

As Alexa's mind dissected the various possibilities, she realized that she had leapt to the worst possible conclusion based on very little evidence. There must be thousands of young blonde girls in Cumberland County, and the likelihood of this girl being Elizabeth Nelson was slim. However, she continued to fret about it. Her recent experience with Caleb had revealed just how dense she could be about a guy that she liked.

More alarming was the way that Alexa had felt when she heard about Reese and the blonde. It reminded her of the day Trent told her he was accepting an offer with the law firm in L.A. Alexa hadn't realized until the moment Melissa spoke, but she had fallen hard for Reese Michaels.

Chapter Twenty-Five

With all the turmoil in her romantic life, Alexa was really looking forward to the familiar routine of Thanksgiving dinner with her family. She and Scout arrived at her parents' house before nine o'clock on Thursday morning to help with the cooking.

As the family sat down for their midday feast, Alexa felt like she'd slipped into her favorite cardigan; cozy and warm. It was so comforting to spend the holiday with a good meal and her beloved family.

The conversation touched on Alexa's parents' planning for a new vacation, then moved to some renovations that Graham and Kate had begun. Finally, Kate circled to a topic that Alexa had hoped to avoid. "How are things with you and Caleb? Weren't you going to some family event with him a few weeks ago?"

"Caleb and I are over."

"Oh, no. I had high hopes for the two of you." Kate pouted.

Alexa's mother offered her opinion. "I'm sure that you know what's best. I don't think I ever met this Caleb fellow. Are you OK?"

"I'm fine. It was my decision to break up. I'd rather not go into the details."

"Leave the girl alone," her dad commanded. "Her love life is none of our business."

"Thanks, Dad."

The discussion came to an abrupt end when Courtney piped up, "Grandma, when can we have Aunt Alexa's pumpkin pie?"

After dinner, Alexa and Kate did the dishes while Graham and her parents retired to the living room to watch football. The kids were taking an after-dinner nap.

Alexa had just joined the group in front of the television when the doorbell rang. "Strange to have visitors on Thanksgiving Day," observed her mother. Graham jumped up to answer the door.

A few seconds later, Graham stuck his head into the living room and looked at Alexa. "Caleb is out here and wants to speak to you. Should I tell him to leave?"

Alexa was first startled and then furious. She put down her drink and said, "No. I'll speak to him." She stalked angrily to the foyer where Caleb was waiting.

He looked up and said, "I'm sorry to interrupt your family time, but I really wanted to apologize."

"Caleb, we have nothing further to talk about, and I'm not ready to accept your apology. We are over." Realizing that her entire family was listening from the living room, Alexa kept it brief. "Please leave."

Instead of leaving, Caleb grasped her arm. His eyes glistened silver with tears. "This means so much to me. My parents just don't understand why you left. I can't tell you how important it is that you come back to me."

"Caleb, I don't want to discuss this. I just want you to leave." Scout had been sleeping near the fireplace but bounded into the entrance hall, barking when he heard Alexa's tone of stress.

"Sit, Scout," she told the anxious dog. When Alexa looked up, Graham and Kate were standing under the archway.

Graham spoke to Caleb. "Hey man, I understand that breaking up can be hard, and I don't want to get into the middle of this. But, you've come to our parents' house in the middle of a holiday celebration and, clearly, you're stressing out my sister. I think you need to do as Alexa asks and just leave."

Kate added, "Caleb, Alexa has been through so much lately—the shooting at the clinic and finding that dead girl. Now's not a good time. Give her some breathing space."

Caleb kept his eyes downcast while they spoke, but at Kate's words he lifted his head abruptly. "What dead girl?"

Graham cut Kate off before she could respond. "This discussion is over. You need to leave, Browne." He took Caleb by the elbow and walked him back out the door.

Caleb stepped onto the front porch and turned to look at Alexa with a mix of bitterness and sadness. "This is not over. Coming back to me could save you. We need to talk."

Alexa stepped forward and said wearily, "Caleb. I'm finished talking. We are over. I don't believe that I need to be saved from what you see as my sins. It won't do you any good to pursue this further." She closed the door firmly in his face.

For the next half hour, the family fluttered around Alexa with concern. Scout hovered, galvanized into full protective mode by all the emotion he sensed in the room.

Graham apologized, "I should have never let him in the door, Lexie. I'm sorry."

Her mom said, "I realize that there's a lot that you haven't told us. But, this incident certainly diminishes my impression of that young man."

"It sounds like dumping Caleb Browne was a good idea," her father concurred.

Alexa managed to accept all the well-meaning support without divulging too many details. "Look, Caleb can be a nice guy. For a while, we had a lot of fun. But, then I found out how conservative he is. And, his entire family is really into the pro-life movement. When he found out that I volunteer at the clinic, it became a real problem."

"You said something about being saved?" her mother asked.

"Yeah. His father's a minister, and he wanted to save me from the error of my ways. That was the final straw."

After things had finally settled down, Alexa turned to her sister-in-law. "Kate, I hope you haven't told anyone else that I was the one who found that dead girl's body."

"Yes, honey." Graham's tone carried a hint of anger. "I thought I had emphasized how dangerous it could be if the criminals found out about Alexa's involvement."

Kate was totally taken aback. "Of course I didn't tell anyone, but I just assumed Caleb knew. After all, he's your boyfriend."

"He never really was my boyfriend, Kate, even though you wanted him to be. He was just a guy that I went out with sometimes. And, I didn't tell him about the dead girl. It shouldn't really hurt that he knows, but Graham is right. The police told me to keep my role in discovering the body quiet."

Alexa was thrilled when halftime ended and the football game drew everyone's attention away from Caleb's surprise visit. But, Caleb's intrusion had put a damper on the rest of the holiday. Alexa stayed until dark then gathered up her containers filled with leftovers and headed for home.

Walking into the dark cabin, Alexa felt an unease she couldn't explain. Scout acted restless, too. Alexa chalked up her disquiet to the confrontation with Caleb and figured that Scout was just reacting to her own mood.

Alexa leafed through a fashion magazine but couldn't concentrate on the pages. Every time a log cracked in the woodstove, Alexa jumped. Scout paced circles in the dining room, stopping to snuffle at the closed laundry room door and the front door.

Frustrated, Alexa threw the magazine onto the coffee table. "Scout, come here. You're making me nervous. Or maybe I'm making you nervous. We both need to chill."

When the mastiff came to sit by her chair, Alexa switched on the television and watched a mindless comedy until she couldn't take it any longer. Emotionally exhausted, she trudged upstairs to bed.

Chapter Twenty-Six

With the law office closed for a long Thanksgiving weekend, Alexa slept in on Friday. After a good night's rest, Alexa resolved to put Caleb Browne behind her.

Always looking for the silver lining, Alexa realized that she had learned something important. This dalliance with casual fun and hot sex had been a gigantic mistake. She needed to return to a simpler approach: find a man that she was truly interested in and just let the relationship unfold.

Alexa's improved mood plummeted when she walked outside. Broken glass carpeted the deck below the laundry room window. Jagged shards frosted the deck like ice, wintry in the morning sun. Alexa could find no natural explanation for the damage, like a fallen branch or tree limb. It was pretty clear that someone, maybe vandals, had shattered the big window.

Alexa ducked back inside to check for additional damage. She went straight to the laundry room, located beyond the dining room. Alexa breathed a sigh of relief when she found that the ancient screen on the inside of the big window was intact. The heavy metal mesh kept both the broken glass and the vandals outside the cabin. For once, Alexa appreciated her dad's tendency to pinch pennies. When he turned the old screened porch into a laundry room, her father hadn't replaced the sturdy old screen. He had just slapped a window in front of it.

Alexa marched around the cabin, checking all the other windows, but could find no other damage. However, there were deep gouges on the front doorframe where someone had tried to pry the heavy old wooden door open. She remembered her unease last night and Scout's restlessness.

We both must have sensed the presence of intruders, even though we missed the damage.

As Alexa swept up the shards of glass, Scout ambled up the steps. "Watch it, buddy," Alexa cried. She dropped the broom and rushed to grab the giant dog by the collar, guiding him away from the glass and into the cabin. After she finished collecting all the smashed pieces and dumped them into the trashcan, Alexa phoned her father.

"Damn," he said. "All these years and we've never had a break-in—even that year they had all those robberies at the summer cabins in the park. We're so far back from the main road, I never imagined that a burglar could find us. You're OK, right?"

"Yes, Dad. This must have happened before I got home last evening. It was dark when I got here, and my hands were full of leftovers. Even with the porch light on, I didn't notice the broken window or the scratches."

"You had the porch light on while you were gone? That's strange. Usually these vandals only target the cabins that look closed for the winter. I'll call the state police and the insurance company. Since it's the day after Thanksgiving, the insurance people probably aren't working, but I'll leave a message."

"OK, Dad. I'll put some of that heavy plastic over the window after the police take a look at it. Don't worry. This was probably just a random thing." She made a lame attempt at humor. "Kids all hopped up on turkey and pumpkin pie are out for a drive. They turn down the lane, see this cabin with no cars around, and decide to break in. When it didn't go easy, they took off."

"I hope you're right, sweetie. Your mom and I have plans with the Mathesons this afternoon, but I'll be out tomorrow to take a look. Maybe we should get you a security system."

After breakfast, Alexa dragged a big roll of plastic out of the storage area beneath the cabin and lugged it up onto the deck. She propped it up against the wall, then went to find a hammer and some nails. Next, she took a few pictures and emailed them to her dad.

The incident concerned Alexa. Sure, South Mountain saw its share of burglaries. Almost every winter, a few break-ins were reported at the seasonal cabins on the outskirts of the park and state forest. But, they were usually places that were closed for the winter. As her father had pointed out, someone trying to break into an occupied cabin was unusual, especially with a porch light burning. Even with no car in the driveway, it was pretty nervy to attempt a break-in here.

On the other hand, whoever tried to break in hadn't been very thorough. They would have had better luck with the big dining room and living room windows, but maybe they assumed those windows had the same sturdy screens as the laundry area. If the vandals had walked around the back of the house, they would have had a better chance of getting in through the bedroom windows that were almost level with the hill. Alexa figured it was too dark back there. Maybe they forgot a flashlight. Or maybe, an owl hooted and scared them away.

The state police didn't arrive until after one that afternoon. A failed break-in was clearly low on their list of priorities. A very young looking Trooper Graves inspected the door and window. He asked Alexa a few questions and then said, "I'll file a report on this. I know you'll need it for insurance purposes, and it's good to have the details on record. Frankly, I would be misleading you if I say that we'll catch the perpetrator. There really isn't much to go on. These old log walls and the cedar doorframe are too rough to show fingerprints. Luckily, the vandals never got into the house.

"I suspect this is a random crime of opportunity. Someone drove down your lane, saw an empty house, and decided to break in. When it became more difficult than they expected, they gave up.

"Call us if there is any more suspicious activity. And, of course, dial 911 if they would happen to come back while you are home."

The trooper helped Alexa tack up plastic to cover the gaping hole. Just as they finished, Scout gave out a high-pitched yelp. Alexa turned to see the mastiff holding his front paw high in the air; blood streamed from his leg onto the deck.

"Scout, what happened?" Alexa rushed over and saw that the dog had a gash down the back of his paw and lower leg. A pointed piece of glass, covered in blood, lay on the deck at his feet.

"What's the matter with him?" Trooper Graves leaned over to look at the dog's injury. "Can I help?"

"I thought I collected all the broken glass, but I must have missed a piece. He's cut his leg pretty badly. We need to get the bleeding stopped." Alexa ran into the house for the first aid kit. When she got back, the trooper helped her bandage Scout's leg, but the wound continued to bleed.

"I need to get him to the vet. Can you help me get him into the car?"

Alexa coaxed the limping dog down the steps to the Land Rover, but he was clearly in pain. The brawny young trooper helped lift Scout into the back of the Land Rover, where Alexa wrapped the mastiff in a blanket. Thanking Trooper Graves, Alexa jumped into the car. When she reached cell phone range, Alexa alerted the vet that Scout needed emergency treatment.

After medical attention from the veterinarian, Scout was in much better shape. Dr. Buck cleaned the deep gash on the dog's leg and closed it with eleven stitches. The mastiff was still groggy from the anesthesia.

Dr. Buck elected to keep Scout at the clinic over the weekend. "When the anesthesia wears off, I want to maintain mild sedatives and keep an eye on that bandage. He needs to keep the leg still for a few days so it can heal. Call me on Monday, and we'll decide if he can go home."

Alexa collapsed onto the couch when she walked through her door. Pulling an afghan to her chin, she stretched out for a nap. When she awoke, the room was dark and the house felt empty without Scout.

After a makeshift dinner of Thanksgiving leftovers, Alexa turned on the TV. She chose one of her favorites, *Pride and Prejudice,* in an attempt to restore her faith in love. But, she was just too distracted to focus on the movie. A jumble of thoughts intervened—Scout, the attempted break-in, Caleb and his parents, renewed suspicion that Reese was not what he had seemed.

Alexa lifted the phone to tell her parents about Scout, but remembered that they were out with the Mathesons. She had no sooner put the phone down when it rang. Reese was calling from the road.

"Hi. I'm on my way home. My family had a great Thanksgiving. How was yours?"

Alexa was happy to hear Reese's voice despite Melissa's news about the blonde girl at Outlaws. "We had a great Thanksgiving dinner. But, today was not so good. Someone tried to break into the cabin yesterday while I was at Mom and Dad's. I didn't find the broken window until this morning."

"Are you OK? Did they steal anything?"

"The vandals never got inside. But, Scout cut himself on a piece of glass. The cut was so deep that I had to take him to the vet for stitches. I think he'll be OK, but the vet kept him for the weekend."

"Where was the cut?"

"His leg. If the state trooper hadn't been here about the break-in, I don't think I could have gotten Scout into the car. I feel so guilty. I thought I had gotten all the glass cleaned up."

"Hey. Don't beat yourself up. Scout would have never stepped on glass if some jackass hadn't broken your window. Was it one of those big front windows? Glass probably flew all over the place."

"The laundry room window. It was a real mess."

"I have an early shift tomorrow, but I could help with any repairs later on."

"That's OK. Dad and I have it under control. I'll just see you for dinner, like we discussed." When they ended the call, Alexa felt much better.

Exhausted for the second night in a row, Alexa went to bed early. Before she crawled beneath the covers, she unlocked the gun closet in the upstairs spare bedroom and pulled out her dad's shotgun. She loaded shells into the double barrels of the old Fox twelve gauge and took the gun and a box of shells back to her bedroom. With the shotgun on the floor beside the bed, Alexa rolled over and fell into a deep sleep.

Alexa apologized to Reese when he arrived for dinner, "Sorry, but it's Chinese again. I didn't have time to cook today. I had a busy day. This morning, I helped Dad board up the laundry room window. In the afternoon, I visited Scout at the vet. "

"Fine with me. I love Chinese."

Reese ate most of the emperor's chicken and finished off the rest of Alexa's sesame chicken for dessert. Watching his enthusiasm for Chinese food, she felt better about serving takeout to her dinner guest.

Seeing Reese made Alexa happy. Despite her continuing doubts, it felt right to have him kicked back on the couch, drinking after-dinner coffee.

"It seems empty in this place without Scout," Reese remarked.

"I really do miss the big beast. He seems to be healing nicely, but it will be a while before he can come home."

After putting the last plate in the dishwasher, Alexa bounced over to Reese with two fortune cookies in her hand. "OK. Now is the time to learn what the future has in store. What's your fortune? Wait, I'll go first."

Her expression sobered when she read aloud, *"A thrilling time is in your immediate future.* This must have been meant for last week. Vandalism and Scout getting hurt are enough in the thrill department. I can't imagine that there's anything else to come."

Reese smiled wickedly as he read from his strip of paper, *"Happy life is just in front of you.* I wonder what that might mean ..." He reached for Alexa's wrist and gently pulled her down next to him on the couch. "Could this be the thrilling time that your message is talking about?" he murmured as he leaned over to kiss Alexa.

For several minutes, everything floated away as Alexa became lost in Reese's embrace. Kissing this man felt so right that she didn't want him to stop.

All too soon, he pulled away and declared, "I've wanted to kiss you since that day we sat up on Flat Rock and I saw how fearless and centered you were. I was so bummed when I found out about the boyfriend, but I could tell when you talked about the guy that things weren't really right between you. So, I bided my time, Alexa. Now that you've broken up with Caleb, I just couldn't wait any longer."

Alexa looked at Reese and smiled. "We met in a really terrible situation and have been getting to know each other pretty well. I have to admit, that I've been thinking about you as much more than a friend. I'm ready to see where this goes, but this whole thing with Caleb sort of knocked me off my bearings. So, I'm not ready to leap into a new relationship too quickly. We need to take it easy." Alexa laughed. "But not too easy," she said as she ran her hands through Reese's thick brown hair and pulled him to her for another kiss.

A little while later, Reese stood to leave. "I better get out of here before that whole going slow concept goes completely out the window. Plus, I'm working again tomorrow. My boss and I are going to try to track down some of those sites where these militia units train. On Sundays, the switchboard is bombarded with phone reports about automatic weapon fire on state lands, so we're continuing to try to catch them.

"Make sure you lock up tight tonight. The thought of burglars coming back makes me worry."

"I'll be fine, Reese. I'll make sure that everything is buttoned up tight. And if those guys come back, I've got Dad's shotgun locked and loaded. A shotgun blast fired over the head can be a powerful deterrent to petty crime." Alexa stood by Reese at the door and kissed him one more time. She had to stand on tiptoe to reach his mouth. "Call me tomorrow?"

"Absolutely."

Alexa laughed in a combination of delight and consternation as she heard Reese's Jeep disappear down the drive.

After all this self-doubt and agonizing about Caleb, you turn around and immediately get involved with Reese, she admonished. Not to mention ignoring the recent information that might suggest he murdered Elizabeth Nelson.

"What are you thinking?" she asked herself aloud.

But, in her heart, Alexa knew exactly what she was thinking. She had been attracted to Reese for weeks. This was not going to be a casual fling. This was going to be so much better.

Chapter Twenty-Seven

On Monday, Dr. Buck discharged Scout with instructions to limit the dog's activity for a week or so. In a quandary about how to best care for the big dog, Alexa called her parents for help. They agreed that Scout could recover at their house. They were home most of the day, and their kitchen door opened to ground level. The dog would have someone to nurse him and wouldn't have to deal with all the steps at Alexa's cabin.

Alexa stopped by to visit the dog on Monday and Tuesday evening after work. Her parents were spoiling Scout like crazy. With all the attention from Mom and Dad, the mastiff didn't seem to miss Alexa at all.

When Alexa rushed into the clinic on Wednesday, she was shocked to see Doc Crowe sitting in a chair behind the counter talking to Tanisha. Shedding her damp coat, Alexa made a beeline through the crowded waiting room straight to his chair.

"Doc, I didn't even know that you were out of the hospital. You can't be back to work already ..."

"He's not working, and this damn fool shouldn't even be here," grumbled Tanisha, shaking her cornrows in dismay. "I don't know why Alice drove him down here. They just discharged him yesterday."

"Tanisha. I am right here and can answer Alexa myself. I appreciate your concern, and I will take it easy." Doc turned to Alexa. "I just wanted to stop in for a few minutes to check on things. When Elise called to say that the police were here again this morning, I felt compelled to stop by. Alice reluctantly gave me an hour here, but I suspect she'll show up to claim me a lot sooner."

Doc looked like he should be home in bed. He was still quite pale and had lost a lot of weight. "Doc, you need to take care of yourself. I'm glad they let you out of the hospital, but I doubt your doctor said you were in good enough shape to come to work. How many times have I heard you complain about patients who don't follow the doctor's advice?"

"I won't overdo it, child. Don't worry about me."

"Why were the police here? Do they have a lead on who shot you?" Alexa asked.

"Unfortunately, that's not why they were here," Doc answered. "There was another threat in this morning's mail. It's different from the others."

Tanisha shoved a piece of paper across the desk, and Alexa read, 'LIFE FOR LIFE, EYE FOR EYE, TOOTH FOR TOOTH, HAND FOR HAND, FOOT FOR FOOT, BURNING FOR BURNING, WOUND FOR WOUND, STRIPE FOR STRIPE.'

"The police took the real note, but I copied down the words. Barb says that this is a passage from the Bible; Exodus, I think she said. This threat is just one more reason why Doc should not be here, but instead of staying away, what's he do? He comes rushing into the clinic."

"I just wish they would catch this guy," Alexa responded before she went to take care of the patient who was standing at the counter.

By mid-afternoon, quiet reigned in the waiting room with only a few women waiting for appointments. Alice had come to collect Doc, who seemed happy to be heading home to bed. The flow of patients had slowed to a trickle, and Alexa finally had a chance to catch her breath.

"I'm going to run down to the corner for some chai tea. Tanisha, do you want any? What should I get for Barb and Dr. Kearns?"

It took at least ten minutes to collect orders from the doctor, the nurses, the physician assistants, and Ryan, their heavyset security guard. Finally, with list in hand, Alexa stepped out onto the sidewalk. She paused on the doorstep to raise her hood against the drizzle. She had been in such a rush coming to clinic at noon that the protestors across the street had barely registered. Now she noticed that the crowd was much bigger than usual, which was surprising given the rainy day. There must have been twenty to thirty in the group chanting and marching in a haphazard circle with their signs.

Puzzled, Alexa stayed a little longer on the threshold, watching them. Most of these protestors seemed new. Alexa didn't recognize many faces, until one man standing at the far edge of the circle caught her eye. The tall man in black looked vaguely familiar. At that moment, he broke away from the crowd and strode to the edge of the pavement.

Alexa gasped when she registered that the man was Caleb's father, Reverend Browne. He had clearly recognized Alexa. Halting at the curb, he stood ramrod straight and glared at her with a thunderous expression. The huge man wore a long dark coat and a broad-brimmed black hat. The drizzle formed droplets on the wide brim and collected in his long gray beard. For a brief second, Alexa imagined that the minister glistened like a ghostly apparition. But the furor in his eyes was all too real.

After a few seconds, the other protestors noticed Reverend Browne's focus on Alexa. They crowded behind him, shaking their signs at Alexa and calling out their usual epithets. Amid this frenzy of righteousness, their leader remained implacable, his silver-gray gaze never leaving Alexa. His eyes smoldered as if he was condemning her to the seventh level of hell.

Reverend Browne's accusatory stare paralyzed Alexa for several long minutes. The security guard broke the spell when he opened the door and asked, "Is there a problem out here?"

"No. Everything is fine, Ryan. Thanks." Alexa tore herself away from Reverend Browne and continued on her way to the coffee shop.

The encounter with Caleb's father spooked Alexa. She had already figured out that these protestors were from Reverend Browne's congregation, but she had never seen the minister himself on the picket lines. His presence there had to be more than coincidence, and the malice in his eyes was disturbing.

Alexa tried to put herself in the Browne family's shoes. Caleb learns that the woman he brought home to meet Mama is involved with the abortion clinic. A huge blow to Caleb, who is desperate for Papa's approval.

When he tells his father, Papa decides that I can be saved. I'll bet the good reverend was already writing a triumphant sermon about leading one of the devil's handmaidens down the blessed path to redemption. Instead of letting them save me, I blow off the minister's conversion attempt and dump his only son. This man is used to having people obey his every command. I'll bet he showed up here today with this huge group just to show me his disapproval. It's more than creepy.

In the fifteen minutes it took Alexa to get the drinks and return to the clinic, the protestors vanished. Apparently, they had accomplished their goal for the day —chastise Alexa. She was glad to avoid another confrontation with Reverend Browne. As Alexa opened the clinic door, she glanced over her shoulder. Although the street was empty and silent, she felt like someone was watching.

Alexa had trouble concentrating on the special report she was writing for the board, so she had to stay late to finish. Tanisha and the rest of the staff left for the day. As she sat in the empty office, Alexa had to admit that she felt safer with the security guard there.

The night guy, Henry Bricker, had replaced Ryan at five o'clock. Henry looked like a slightly younger version of the day shift guard; same paunch, but his head was shaved, probably in an effort to look tough. After a brief conversation with the guard, Alexa had to upgrade her estimation of Henry. Apparently, he was a genuine tough guy, a former Marine with two tours in Iraq under his belt.

Alexa was just wrapping up her report when Emily Baxter sailed in through the back door. "Emily, I haven't seen you for a while. You don't usually work Wednesdays, right?"

"No. I had a church social last evening, so I switched nights. Doc Crowe doesn't mind which nights I work as long as I get all the billing done on time."

"How are the kids?"

"They keep me busy," Emily responded as she took off her heavy coat. "I get a little break when I come in here to work at night. Plus, it gives Glenn a chance to have the kids all to himself," she added with a wicked smile.

Emily was the medical coder and billing specialist for the clinic. The slender twenty-something's two children, a four-year old girl and a two-year old boy, needed her full attention during the day. Emily worked three evenings a week at the clinic after her husband, Glenn, came home from his factory job.

One day in the mall, Alexa had met Emily's two adorable children. They took after their attractive young mother with brown eyes and sandy-blonde hair. Alexa knew that extra cash was the only reason Emily left them three nights a week.

"Do you feel uncomfortable here on your own at night?" Alexa asked.

"I never worried until all this business with Doctor Crowe. I wasn't working the night he was shot, but it must have been terrible. Glenn is a little concerned, but Henry and I have become good friends." She directed a smile toward the security guard sitting in the waiting room. "I feel safe with him here. Besides, I'm just the bookkeeper. Who would want to harm me?"

"Well, I'll get out of your way. It's time for me to get home." Alexa lifted her coat off the hook, and laughed as she noticed the black buttons. "Oops. Wrong one." She put the wool tweed back and slipped on the other gray coat, the designer one with gray bone buttons and a mandarin collar.

"I guess we both like gray, although I could never afford something that soft. Is that cashmere?" Emily asked.

"Alpaca. I got this when I lived in New York City. I'm just sad that it's gotten cold enough to wear a heavy coat. Nice to see you, Emily."

Henry opened the locked front door for Alexa and stood on the pavement, watching her walk down the block. Alert to any hint of danger, she dashed the short distance to her car. The guard stepped back into the clinic when she reached the Land Rover door.

In one fluid motion, Alexa tossed her purse through the open door, aiming for the far seat, and clambered onto the running board. When a loud metallic clang reverberated down the empty street, she jumped and nearly slipped back onto the pavement. Holding her breath in the ensuing silence, Alexa scanned the neighborhood, searching for the source of the noise. Seeing nothing out of the ordinary, she began to breathe again and slid into the driver's seat.

As she pulled away from the curb, Alexa started to feel a little silly about her overreaction to a random night noise. Then she decided to give herself a pass. After all, the guy who shot Dr. Crowe was still out there somewhere.

Chapter Twenty-Eight

Reese stopped by after Alexa arrived home. This was the first time they had been together since Saturday night, but Alexa felt no awkwardness. Alexa couldn't wait to tell him about the encounter with Reverend Browne earlier that afternoon. "It was so creepy the way he just stood and glared at me. It was like that comic book guy with the laser vision."

"Cyclops in the *X-Men*. You are a woman after my own heart."

"Well, I grew up with a brother who was addicted to all things comic book. The only difference between Reverend Browne and Cyclops is that the X-Men are good guys. Even though he's a minister, I didn't sense goodness and light in that glare he sent my way this afternoon."

"There is something fundamentally weird about this guy," Reese observed. "No pun intended. He jumps into the middle of his son's personal relationship and tries to save you with prayer. Then, he shows up at the clinic to confront you in some way. I don't like it. Maybe he's just a harmless religious fanatic or a father who has an unhealthy involvement in his son's life, but he could be dangerous. Have the police considered that these protestors might have something to do with Doctor Crowe's shooting?"

"Wouldn't that be one of the first places the cops would look? I mean it's so obvious. They are parked across the street from the clinic chanting several days a week. I think the police surely must have investigated the church and decided that the protestors are a harmless pain in the ass. They have the proper permits; they seem to work within the rules."

"But what about all the guns?"

"What do you mean?"

"That lodge we went to is the church's lodge, right? The whole time Scout and I were waiting for you, there was gunfire."

"Yes. All the guys that I met there are hunters. Caleb told me that the lodge has a big shooting range for target practice. In fact, he and three of his friends went out and did some shooting on the day I was there for a picnic."

"Getting ready for deer season is one thing. Some of what I heard was automatic rifle fire. I think that it's unlikely that any of the good church members would be taking to the forests with AK-47s to hunt whitetail."

"I think I'm going to ask around about these people. Maybe the rangers over in the Perry County parks know something about them."

"It sounds to me like you're seeing militia behind every rock. I'm seeing the X-Men. You're looking for that guy from Waco, what was his name? David Koresh."

"Well, we have made some progress on the militia problems in this side of the valley. My boss and I didn't come across any actual militia on Sunday, but those telephone tips led us to two places that appear to be training sites. We found piles of bullet casings from high-powered weapons. We're working with the police on a plan to stake out both places on weekends as soon as deer season ends. Maybe we can catch some of these guys and clear them out of Michaux."

"It's hard to believe that someone would use the state forest for paramilitary training. I know that there are hundreds of acres of land in Michaux and some of it is pretty remote, but it seems like a risky move on their part."

"Actually, more like eighty-five thousand acres. There is an official shooting range in Michaux, over on the Franklin County side. It has been closed for a year or so because the Department of Conservation and Natural Resources wanted to assess the environmental impact. When we started getting complaints about gunfire in the state forest, we initially thought that some people were still using the site, despite all the warning signs that are posted.

"But, there were no signs of recent use at the old shooting range. So, we went looking for other sites nearby. We were surprised that the first place we found wasn't even that far off the main roads. There's a forest road only a mile or so past that snowmobile area where you found Elizabeth Nelson. This training site is a narrow branch road that once was used for logging. One of the things that helped us spot the turnoff was evidence of recent traffic on that old logging trail.

"Like it or not, I've gotten an entire education on the militia movement lately. Apparently, there was a real surge in the formation of these militias after the big incident at Waco, as you mentioned. I didn't realize that you were both a comic book and militia buff."

"Everybody knows about Waco and that other one, Ruby Ridge."

"Well a lot of this is new to me. Apparently, a whole subculture out there took those two FBI actions as evidence that the United States government was going to start taking away everyone's guns. So, their response to this perceived threat was to go out and buy guns like crazy."

"Makes perfect sense," Alexa said in a tone laden with irony. "You're worried about losing your guns, so you go out and stock up with more."

"Yes. But, these folks weren't just buying deer rifles and shotguns. They were out stockpiling assault weapons and forming militias to train with these weapons. Most of these people were far right extremists who worship at the altar of the gun, so they were already passionate about their right to bear arms. And, many of them were convinced that the FBI was going to start a door-to-door gun confiscation.

"Around the same time, a parallel movement latched onto this conspiracy theory about the New World Order. Supposedly, this New World Order was using the United

Nations to build a single world socialist government. These people were convinced that the government was building concentration camps for dissenters and that United Nations troops were camping in national parks in preparation for this final takeover.

"So, you mix the extreme right wing gun nuts with the extreme right wing conspiracy theory nuts and you've got a toxic brew that gave rise to all these militia groups. They popped up all over the country and were going strong until the Oklahoma City bombing. Then, public attention finally focused on these homegrown militias. By the late 1990s, arrests and dissension in the ranks had practically wiped out the militia movement.

"In recent years, some of the diehards are revitalizing the movement. There are groups in the South, the Midwest, and here in Pennsylvania. So, we think that this activity in Michaux may be connected with one of the new groups here in the state."

"It's hard for me to understand this extremist mentality." Alexa frowned. "Clearly, their experiences and beliefs are very different from mine. I wasn't really aware of the history behind this whole militia movement, although I have some knowledge of the militia role in the anti-abortion movement. Scott Roeder, the man who killed Dr. George Tiller, the Kansas abortion doctor, was a member of a militia and anti-government group of some sort. And there's a group called the Army of God that has a how-to manual that includes instructions for 65 ways to destroy abortion clinics. I guess it's not surprising that anti-abortion extremists find common ground with other right-wing fringe groups."

"A lot of the militia groups see themselves as Christian patriots." Reese agreed.

Alexa shivered. "It's sort of scary to think that a bunch of these crazies are shooting automatic weapons around here."

"Those sites we found are probably twenty miles or more from this cabin," Reese said, reassuringly. "But, it is frightening. We want them out of the state forest. And, I think the law enforcement people that we are working with want to shut them down altogether."

When Reese left a little while later, he kissed Alexa and said, "Maybe we can have a real date soon. I was thinking Saturday, but my shift could run as late as nine that night. Would Sunday work?"

"I think my calendar is clear that day." She smiled. "I'll have to stick close to home for a few days when I get Scout back out here to the cabin. But, based on his progress, I think he's got at least another week to be spoiled by Grandma and Grandpa. Sunday would be good. Do you want me to cook?"

"No, no, no. This being a date, I will take you out to dinner," he said with mock solemnity. "We can pick the restaurant later this week. No Chinese and no Florentine's. Let's try something different, maybe get wild and crazy and drive the whole way to Harrisburg. I'll call you to finalize the details, but I might not be able to get back over here until Sunday." With another quick kiss, Reese left the cabin.

Chapter Twenty-Nine

Thursday, November 22, 1934.

Little children, come unto me ...

Surprisingly, Winifred had laid out clothes for all three of the girls at the foot of the bed the sisters had shared last night. In a voice like honey, she said, "Your daddy wants you to dress in your Sunday best today. Norma, you help Cordelia. Dewilla, after you dress, I'll do up your hair real nice in those barrettes you like."

As the Noakes family walked to the car, the nice man who owned the trailer court came by. He greeted them in his booming voice, "Don't you girls look pretty today? You must be going somewhere special, I'd guess. Well, it certainly is a beautiful day for travel. It's cold, but that November sunshine sure feels good."

Daddy agreed, "Yes, sir. A nice day." Stowing their suitcases in the trunk, he told the man, "We've traveled a long way, and today is special. We're setting out on a new path."

He glanced at Winifred, who nodded and said, "That's right, Elmo. It's the path we must take."

Dewilla wondered what they were talking about, but she was really too tired to care. Norma hadn't even heard the conversation because she was putting fussy Cordelia into the car. Dewilla could see that Norma was struggling to lift the child. Both of her sisters seemed to have as little energy as she did. Yesterday, Norma explained that the reason they were tired and headachy all the time was because they weren't eating much.

As the car pulled out onto the narrow country road, Norma asked, "Daddy, are we going to get any breakfast today?"

"We'll see what we can find down the road here," he replied. "You girls just sit quiet. Try to keep our baby girl from fussing."

Dewilla knew what Daddy's words meant. No breakfast.

She tried to choke back her sobs so Daddy wouldn't get mad, but tears spilled down her face at the news. She didn't know how much longer she and her sisters could go without a real meal. Other than the little bit of beef stew last night, their only food yesterday had been some butter bread and a little scrapple. The meal had come from a farmer lady who had agreed to have Daddy do some chores.

"I don't have enough to feed five of you properly," she said. "With Thanksgiving coming up next week, I have a big meal to prepare for my family. But, I can spare a little for you. These girls look so peaked. I can see they need something to eat." Dewilla thought that the big slice of bread, still warm from baking, was one of the best she had ever tasted—almost as good as Mama's.

Now, her stomach was growling again, and the prospect of missing another breakfast made her cry. She studied Daddy and Winifred in the front seat and wondered why neither one of them ever complained about the hunger. Maybe Daddy was embarrassed about not having enough money to buy them food. Daddy had always been a proud man.

But, that didn't explain Winifred's silence. Since the day she had moved in, Cousin Winnie had complained all the time about the smallest things. Winifred whined about the weather, about her wardrobe, about her parents who wanted her to leave the Noakes family and come home. So, it was strange that she didn't complain about an empty stomach.

Last evening in bed, Norma had whispered something really disturbing to Dewilla. "I think that Daddy and Winifred are hoarding food for themselves. Daddy is so besotted with Winifred that he's keeping food back for her.

Don't you think it's strange that she never complains about being hungry?"

"Norma, Daddy would never do that."

"Don't be so sure, Dewilla. Daddy has changed ever since that woman came to live with us. I don't trust her, and I'm worried about him."

Today, Dewilla thought about Norma's remarks and remembered the torrid scene she had witnessed between Daddy and Winifred at the tourist court. More tears ran silently down her cheeks as she looked at Winifred, sitting like a well-fed princess in the front seat next to Daddy. What Norma said was true.

Daddy wasn't Norma's real Pa. Mama had been married before, and Norma was her child from that marriage. Dewilla thought of Norma as her sister, just the same as her full sister, Cordelia. But, Dewilla had to admit that Norma often could see Daddy in a clearer light. Maybe blood ties were like the trees in the forest. Blood could cast a deep shade and make it harder to see what was in Daddy's true heart.

Chapter Thirty

Alexa was ready to break for lunch on Thursday when Melinda knocked and popped her head through the doorway. "The police are here to talk to you."

Alexa looked up in surprise. Her first thought was that the state police had made a breakthrough on Elizabeth Nelson's murder and wanted to tell her about it. Or, perhaps there was a lead on the vandalism at the cabin. Melinda hadn't said exactly which policemen wanted to speak to her, and Alexa had met many different officers of the law in recent weeks. Nonetheless, she was bewildered when her old friend Officer Starke walked into the office. He and the older gentleman who accompanied him both had grim faces.

"Alexa, this is Detective Hiram Miller. There was an incident at the clinic last night and we'd like to ask you some questions."

"Incident? What happened?"

Detective Miller was the one who replied. "We'll talk about that in a minute. First, can you tell us when you left the clinic? We understand that you stayed later than usual yesterday?"

"Yes. I got behind on paperwork, so I stayed until it was finished. I'm not sure exactly what time I left ... probably close to six o'clock. The second shift guard had come on duty maybe an hour earlier. Also, Emily Baxter had just arrived. I think she usually starts at six on the evenings that she works. What is this about?"

The detective continued as if he had not heard her question. "Did you see anything or anyone on the street when you left? The security guard, Henry Bricker, said that you left through the front door."

"No. The street was quiet. The protestors had left a few hours earlier. I didn't see any pedestrians, and I don't

215

even think any cars went down the street between the time I left the clinic and when I reached my car. I've been there late before, and it's usually pretty quiet in that neighborhood in the evening. I heard one brief clang-y noise, but it sounded like random street noise, garbage cans or something like that."

"Do you usually park out front or in the staff parking lot?"

"It varies," replied Alexa, her concern rising with each question. "Sometimes, I'll duck down the alley and see if there are any empty spaces. As usual, I was running late yesterday, so I just grabbed a spot on the street."

"What were you wearing last night?"

"A gray pantsuit and an aqua blouse."

"Coat?"

Alexa gestured to her charcoal wool coat hanging on the corner coat rack. "That's the coat I wore yesterday. Look, Detective, what is going on? I don't feel comfortable answering more questions until I understand why you are asking them. Nothing out of the ordinary happened while I was at the clinic last evening. It sounds like you've already spoken to Henry, the security guard. He can confirm what I told you. And Emily was there part of the time as well. You can talk to her."

The detective replied in a heavy voice. "Unfortunately, we can't speak to Emily Baxter. That's why we are here. She was shot and killed in the clinic parking lot last night around nine."

Alexa gasped and slumped into her seat. "Killed? That can't be. Emily has two young children at home. She never antagonized anyone. Why would someone kill Emily?" She sat forward. "Shot like Doc Crowe? Is this the same person who tried to kill him ... the one who has been sending hate notes?"

Officer Starke, who had completely abandoned his condescending air of a few weeks ago, answered the question. "We have to run tests, of course. But there was a bullet recovered from the scene. It is the same caliber as the one fired at Doctor Crowe. We'll know more soon."

"How did it happen? Where was the security guard?"

"It happened in the same place as the attempt on Doctor Crowe's life—the clinic parking lot. The security guard walked Mrs. Baxter to her vehicle, as per procedure. However, he left as she was putting some papers into the back of her hatchback. He heard a loud crash in the front of the clinic, like glass breaking. Believing Mrs. Baxter to be secure, he went back through the clinic to investigate the noise. Someone had tossed a concrete block through the front window.

"Mr. Bricker called in to report the vandalism and then took a walk around the outside perimeter of the clinic building. When he reached the parking lot, he found Mrs. Baxter lying on the ground next to the open driver's side door. The shooter must have fired only minutes after the guard left. Mr. Bricker didn't even hear the shot. We believe that an accomplice created a diversion with the concrete block to draw the guard away. It worked."

With tears in her eyes, Alexa repeated her earlier question. "Why Emily? She wasn't involved in medical procedures at the clinic. All she did was submit the bills."

This time Detective Miller answered. "At this point, we're not sure why they killed Emily. We're not even sure she was the intended target. All we know is that no one who works at that clinic is safe until we catch this bastard. That includes you, Ms. Williams. Don't go near the clinic. It will be closed for several days at least. I can't emphasize this enough; you need to be very alert at all times. We thought we were dealing with a single anti-abortion extremist. Now, it appears he had help. Be on your guard."

Emily's murder had taken place too late to hit the morning's newspaper, so Alexa looked at coverage online. There were a few brief articles that mentioned the death, but few other details. The police had not even released Emily's name to the press.

Alexa called both Elise and Doc Crowe, but they had little more information. Both doctors were reeling from the news that one of their own, a young mother, had been killed at the clinic. The board had called an emergency meeting later that afternoon to discuss whether to close the clinic until the killer or killers were arrested. At this point, they were extremely concerned about the safety of the clinic staff and patients.

Alexa tried to immerse herself in work, but she kept thinking of Emily's children crying for their mother. She felt like she could have done something to prevent Emily's murder. If she had been more alert when she left the clinic, she might have seen the criminals lurking around. If she'd told the guard about that loud noise, he might have called the police. If she had only stayed a few more hours at the clinic, the presence of a third person might have forced the criminals to cancel their plan. Alexa knew that many of her thoughts were irrational, but she felt guilty that, other than the security guard, she was the last person to see Emily alive.

Reese called Alexa on Friday afternoon. "I just found out about this shooting at the clinic. I had an early shift on Friday and didn't read about Emily Baxter's murder until I came home this afternoon. I called you as soon as I saw the article. Are you OK?"

"As OK as I can be. Emily's family must be devastated. How do two small children really understand that their mommy won't ever be coming home? These bastards who shot her and Doc make me so angry. Who's next on their list?"

"Hey, I think you need someone to talk to about this. I can tell that everything is starting to get to you—which is not surprising. Why don't you come up to my place for dinner? Nothing fancy. I'll just run over to the general store and get some sandwiches. You shouldn't be alone."

Alexa didn't really feel like sitting by herself in the empty cabin and brooding about this latest tragedy, so she accepted Reese's offer. "I'll just stop by the cabin to change into jeans. Will six o'clock work?"

"Whenever you get here is good. See you soon."

Alexa followed Reese's directions to his house. He lived a few miles east of the state park in an old farmhouse that he shared with another park ranger. Although it was the first time Alexa had been to the place, she found it easily. She pulled the Land Rover into an empty space next to Reese's beat-up Jeep and a gleaming silver Porsche 911 that probably belonged to the roommate.

Reese popped out of the front door and walked out onto the porch to greet Alexa. "Hi. I'm glad you decided to come." When she stepped up onto the porch, Reese pulled her into his arms. "I know these last two days must have been pretty rough." As they walked to the door, Reese whispered, "I didn't realize that Jim was going to be here tonight. He's usually out on Friday nights. I hope you don't mind."

"No. It will be nice to meet him."

When they reached the kitchen, Reese introduced her to his tall, burly roommate, Jim Kline. Jim looked like a lumberjack in his plaid flannel shirt and jeans. He wasn't exactly what Alexa had expected. Reese had described his fellow ranger as a bit of a ladies' man and party guy. "Is that your Porsche? Nice car." Alexa remarked.

Interest in his car was apparently the way to Jim's heart. As the three of them sat down to turkey sandwiches and store-bought potato salad, they spent quite a while talking about the finer points of German engineering.

Alexa found Jim to be a pretty funny guy. He was a font of amusing stories about the park and his friends, which kept both Reese and Alexa laughing during the simple meal. As the three of them dove into the brownies, Jim launched into a new topic.

"Alexa, you are such a lovely lady. Do you have any friends who are as beautiful and charming as you—and currently unattached?"

Alexa laughed at his shameless flattery while Reese joked, "If you do have any unattached friends, you should keep them as far away as possible from this guy."

"Most of my friends are either married or in a committed relationship," Alexa replied. "But I would be happy to introduce you to my friend, Melissa."

Jim whooped. "I knew you would have a friend." Then, his eyes narrowed in suspicion, "What does she look like? She's not a beast, is she?"

"I think she is very nice looking," Alexa said, honestly. Somehow, Jim had such a disarming air that Alexa hadn't been put off by his sexist question. "But, I've found that sometimes guys look at these things differently. Reese, I think you may have met Melissa."

"I thought the friend that I met was named Haley and she's married?"

"Yes. You did meet Haley when we were at Florentine's. However, Haley and I were talking about you one night after yoga class. Melissa mentioned that she met you one night this past summer at Outlaws. Jim, you may have been there, too. Melissa said that a whole group of people from the park were having a party on the outside deck."

Reese continued to look puzzled, clearly unable to place Melissa. However, Jim let out another hoot and cried, "She must have been at Outlaws the night we had the going away party for Natalie. No wonder you can't remember Melissa. Natalie was all over you like white on rice. She headed off any other woman who got near you."

Reese looked embarrassed. "Of course, that was the night. I do remember talking to two women for a brief time. One of them looked like a hippie with spectacular red hair. I don't remember the other one much ... was she a big woman with a lot of wild jewelry? But, you're right, Jim. I couldn't get away from Natalie. I finally had to leave the party."

Jim jumped back in to the conversation, directing his attention to Alexa. "Natalie was this pretty little blonde intern who worked in the park office this summer. The party was actually a farewell party for her and a few other interns. Natalie sure did have a thing for Reese. It provided the rest of the rangers with a lot of entertainment, watching Reese try to dodge that young thing."

Reese groaned and said to Alexa, "She was a nice kid, but she couldn't have been more than nineteen. She developed a huge crush on me early in the summer. No matter how much I tried to discourage her, she remained hopeful. I sure hope she doesn't come back this summer. Or that she finds a boyfriend in college."

Alexa laughed at the story and secretly breathed a sigh of relief. She had never truly believed that the young blonde Melissa had seen with Reese was Elizabeth Nelson. Still, there had been a nagging doubt. Hearing these two talk about the besotted young intern confirmed Alexa's initial instinct. Reese was one of the good guys.

"Maybe we can get together sometime, go out for drinks or something, and I'll introduce you to Melissa. Just let me know," Alexa said. "She's got a quirky sense of humor. You two might just get along fine."

When Jim wandered into the living room to watch a hockey game, Reese and Alexa discussed Emily Baxter's murder. It was good to have someone to talk to about the tragedy.

"You need to be very careful," Reese told Alexa. "Whoever is behind this violence is a force to be reckoned with. Clearly, he is targeting people who work at the clinic. You are at risk and need to be very cautious. Not just when you're at the clinic. You don't know what these people are capable of doing."

Chapter Thirty-One

Saturday afternoon, Alexa spent a few hours at her mom and dad's with Scout. She couldn't believe how much she missed her big mutt. After an early dinner, much of it spent discussing Emily Baxter's murder, she tore herself away to drive home in the gathering dark.

On the road, Alexa's mind wandered. Emily's death continued to hit Alexa hard. She didn't understand how anyone could callously kill a young mother, no matter how deep their hatred of abortion. It didn't make any sense that people who felt it was wrong to kill an unborn child had no problem killing an adult. But, Alexa knew that zealotry was rarely rational.

She feared that the gunman was going to try to kill everyone who worked at the clinic. They all needed to be vigilant and stay on the lookout for all possible threats.

Alexa's thoughts turned to Elizabeth Nelson's death. She resolved to call Trooper Taylor on Monday to see if the police had made progress on the young girl's homicide. She was still committed to acting as the girl's advocate and pushing the police to solve her murder.

Nearly two months had passed since Elizabeth had been killed. Alexa regretted that she'd lost track of the investigation, but she had been preoccupied with everything else that was happening at home and at the clinic. She knew that her involvement wouldn't produce any clues or solve the case, but Alexa believed that her continued interest might help spur the police to greater efforts to solve it.

Alexa's mind continued to drift. With all the other things going on, she hadn't really analyzed Wednesday's confrontation with Reverend Browne. But, as she considered it now, she realized the whole incident had been very disturbing. Reverend Browne had stared at

Alexa like a cobra trying to mesmerize a bird just before it struck. To Alexa, the minister seemed more malevolent than benevolent; clearly he was unlike any man of the cloth that she had ever encountered.

She was so glad that she had ended things with Caleb. Both her former lover and his peculiar family were much further over the edge than she had ever imagined.

"Speak of the devil." Alexa realized that she was approaching Caleb's sporting goods store and let out a bitter laugh. Alexa braked as she noticed a vehicle ahead with its driver's door hanging open into her lane. A man was standing in the street, talking through the open door to someone in the darkened vehicle.

The huge neon Browne's Sporting Goods Store sign bathed the man in a kaleidoscope of reds and blues. Alexa winced when she recognized Caleb. In an effort to avoid another emotional encounter, she slouched down in the seat, hoping that Caleb wouldn't spot her.

In that instant, Alexa registered that the vehicle was a light-colored van with a roof rack. When she passed, Caleb appeared to be engrossed in conversation with a man in the driver's seat. A baseball cap threw the man's face into shadow. He sat sideways, his body angled toward Caleb. Alexa gasped when she glimpsed the mottled green and brown pattern of his pant leg in the neon glow. Camouflage.

The van. The baseball hat. Camouflage clothes.

Alexa's heart lurched. It took all her willpower to resist flooring the Land Rover, but she didn't want to draw their attention.

A torrent of thoughts streamed through Alexa's mind. The van and its driver looked like the ones she had seen the day she found Elizabeth Nelson's body. Could the man in the van be the same one who sped past her on that mountain road? Even more alarming, could Caleb somehow be involved with these people?

"No," Alexa moaned as she headed for home.

Caleb has certainly turned out to be a different man than I thought he was. But, he can't have anything to do with the murder of that young girl. Perhaps the man was just one of his clients. Caleb specialized mainly in hunting supplies like rifles and bows. The store carried rows and rows of camouflage for every type of hunt and season.

Alexa equivocated. It was dark, and the area's only source of light was the glow from Caleb's big ass neon sign. If called upon to testify in court, she couldn't confirm with complete certainty that this was either the van or the driver she had seen weeks ago in Michaux Forest.

As hard as Alexa tried to explain away what she had just seen, the sick feeling in the pit of her stomach undermined any attempt to stay rational. The panic that gripped her when she saw Caleb talking to the man in the light-colored van just wouldn't go away. She didn't think that Caleb had noticed her passing; he had been very wrapped up in conversation, facing toward the van. However, Alexa probably had the only ancient Land Rover in the area, and Caleb knew the vehicle well.

As she reached the outskirts of town, dismay hit Alexa like a ton of bricks.

Caleb knows I found Elizabeth's body. Kate let it slip on Thanksgiving. He could tell the van guy that I was there. And, if that guy is the killer and remembers passing me on the road, he could put two and two together and conclude that I could identify him and his friend.

After a few miles, Alexa calmed down and decided to report that she may have seen the van again. She berated herself that, instead of panicking, she should have picked up her cell and called Trooper Taylor right away. She just didn't seem to learn from experience.

Alexa kept one hand on the steering wheel and used the other to rummage through her purse for her cell phone. She had reached a deserted back road that cut through several miles of farm fields so she felt it was safe to make a call. She pulled up the number for Trooper Taylor. Before she could dial, she noticed headlights approaching rapidly from behind. Alexa put the phone on the seat and slowed a bit to allow the oncoming vehicle to pass on the narrow road.

As the vehicle drew nearer, Alexa realized from the position of the lights that it was one of those huge pick-up trucks that were a favorite of farmers in the area. The bright headlights seemed to illuminate the Land Rover's entire interior. "Turn down your lights and back off," Alexa yelled. This truck was a pain in the ass and traveling much too close for safety. She slowed a bit more, hoping that the monster vehicle would just pass her.

Her anger turned abruptly to fear when she felt the Land Rover lurch forward. "What the hell?" Alexa shouted as she realized that the truck had hit her rear bumper. As she struggled to keep her car on the road, the big truck fell behind slightly then rammed her again. Alexa's heart was pounding as the Land Rover leapt forward and she wrestled the steering wheel for control.

Just as quickly as it came, the truck backed off and took a left onto a small road. In a few seconds, the truck's taillights disappeared into the distance. Almost at the same moment, Alexa saw the lights of a car that had just crested the hill ahead, coming toward her.

"Thank you, thank you," Alexa breathed a sigh of relief. The driver of the truck must have seen the car coming and had been scared away by the thought of a witness. The oncoming car passed by without slowing. It was likely that those in the passing car hadn't seen anything of the incident with the giant pick-up.

Alexa pulled to the side of the road and sat until her legs stopped shaking. Her skin was clammy with nervous perspiration, her breathing ragged.

When she caught her breath, Alexa fished a flashlight out of the glove compartment. Glancing all around to make sure the truck had not returned, she steeled herself to step out and check the damage. There was surprisingly little damage, at least that she could see in the dark. This Land Rover was built for rough terrain and African safaris, so it was up to some hard treatment. But her beloved vehicle had seen years of use and would need to be checked out fully in the daylight.

Alexa climbed back in the Land Rover and started for home. She wanted to call the police, but she was too shaky to drive and try to dial the phone at the same time. Plus, she was less than five minutes from where cell phone coverage became spotty. Since it was just a few minutes more until she could reach her cabin, Alexa decided to get home as quickly as she could and make the call from there.

When she pulled in front of the cabin, Alexa looked around carefully. At this point, she was starting to think that maybe the vandalism at the cabin was not random and it was connected to the truck ramming her on the road. Her window had been broken just like the one at the clinic the night of Emily's murder. Had Alexa become the next target on the list for the anti-abortion nut who had shot Dr. Crowe?

But, it seemed more than coincidence that she saw Caleb and the man in the light van less than twenty minutes before her Land Rover was rammed from behind on a dark country road. She had not been able see anything about the truck through the glare of the headlights, other than that it was big. Caleb had a huge double cab Ford F-150 with a grille on the front, and he certainly knew the direction that she would take on her way home.

Alexa shuddered as she locked the door behind her, threw her purse and cell phone on the counter, and ran to the phone to dial 911. When she described what had happened, she asked the 911 operator, "Please inform State Police Corporal George Branche and Trooper John Taylor about this. I'm afraid the people who hit me tonight may be tied with a murder case they are investigating." The operator asked if Alexa needed an ambulance. When she declined, the calm voice on the other end of the line advised Alexa to lock herself in the house and wait for the state police to arrive.

Alexa shrugged off her down jacket and went back to throw the deadbolt on the door. Then, she picked up the phone to call Trooper Taylor directly. She was so relieved when he answered the call. She filled him in on what had happened this evening, first seeing the man in the light-colored van at Caleb's store and then being rammed by the pick-up truck on her way home.

The trooper told her that he would be driving out to her house within the hour. He wanted to speak to her further and promised to work with the patrol troopers, who were already dispatched in response to her 911 call. "When we get there, I'll also tell you what I can about a new lead we have on Elizabeth Nelson's case. We may have a breakthrough."

Her final call was to Reese. Reaching out to him was something that Alexa did almost without thought. As she listened to the phone ring, she realized that this evening's events had dispelled any lingering suspicion about Reese's involvement in Elizabeth's Nelson's death.

Just hearing Reese's voice helped calm Alexa. He was very concerned when she told him about what had happened and promised to come to the cabin as soon as his shift ended. Alexa also mentioned that the trooper had told her that they might have a lead on Elizabeth's murder.

"Yes. I just heard about that earlier today. Apparently, a woman who knew Elizabeth just found out about her death. I can't remember her name ... I think it was the name of a state, like Carolina—no, maybe Georgia. Anyway, this woman left the area to visit a friend and ended up finding a new job there. She just returned home to visit her parents last night. They must have mentioned the murder and the victim's name. When they told her that the authorities were looking for information about Elizabeth, she called the police. This Carolina or Georgia woman used to hang out with Elizabeth socially, and she has given the police the name of Elizabeth's boyfriend.

"But we can worry about that later. Just stay inside until the police arrive. I hope they can figure out who was driving that truck."

"Me, too. I don't think I'll feel totally safe until they track the bastard down. Go ahead and finish your shift. I'll be fine; I've got two state cops on their way here. I'll see you after you're done with work." By the time she ended the conversation, Alexa had regained some of her equilibrium. She was still scared, but beneath the fear was a burgeoning anger at the jerks who had tried to run her off the road. Could Caleb really be involved in all this?

Chapter Thirty-Two

Tapping her foot, Alexa stood at the kitchen counter, uncertain what to do until the police arrived. She knew it could take some time for a state trooper to reach the cabin. Finally, the chill of the cabin broke through her indecision. She was freezing. Alexa threw a few logs in the stove and ran up to her bedroom for a warm sweater.

Alexa pulled an ancient wool sweater over her head and then switched off the light. At the threshold of her room, she paused. Was that a vehicle coming down the lane? "Wow; that was fast," she exclaimed. Almost instantly, she registered the deep rumble of the motor. A big truck, not a police car.

Oh, no, she thought. They followed me home.

Shaking, she forced herself to tiptoe across the dark bedroom to the window. Keeping her body against the wall, she edged the heavy drape aside, peering out with a single eye. The vehicle sat below. The chrome bars of its oversized grille gleamed like massive teeth in the glow of the porch light. Alexa cried out softly when the doors of the dual-cab pick-up opened and four men climbed out. They made no effort at concealment, walking boldly toward the cabin.

One of the men was Caleb. All four men wore dark camouflage and carried nasty looking guns in their hands like the ones soldiers carried in war movies. Although baseball caps shadowed their faces, she knew the other three men had to be Caleb's best friends: Joel, Daniel, and Gabriel. Just then, the tallest one turned so the light hit his face—the face that Alexa had likened to an Irish angel. Gabriel.

Alexa's chill melted into a burning knot of implacable rage. "I've had enough of Caleb Browne and his asshole friends," she spat. She knew these guys were deadly, but she wouldn't let them get the best of her.

Alexa scurried to the bedside phone and dialed 911 for the second time that night. She couldn't get the words out fast enough. "This is Alexa Williams. I live at 1915 Hunter's Hill Lane, Newville. Four men are trying to break into my house. I think they are the same ones who tried to run me off the road earlier. They have guns. I need help."

Before the dispatcher could respond, a huge crash sounded downstairs. They had shattered the living room window. Unlike the laundry room, the other two big front windows had modern screens. It wouldn't take these men long to break that last flimsy barrier.

Abruptly, the noise stopped, and one of the men yelled. "We know you're in there, bitch. We know what you've seen. I hope you are ready for judgment tonight."

Then another voice cackled, "That abortion lover ain't ready for the Lord's judgment. She's going to burn in the fires of hell."

Alexa moved toward the window again but stopped in her tracks when she heard his voice. Never in a million years could she have imagined hearing that familiar voice in a situation like this.

Caleb shouted, "Alexa. It would be better if you just open the door and come out. Maybe we can come to an understanding. Hell, you're a lawyer. You know how to cut a deal. Think about it. If you don't come out in two minutes, this situation is going to get ugly."

In a lower tone, Caleb warned his buddies, "Watch out for the dog. I told you how big this fucking animal is. I don't understand why he's not barking. He's very protective, and he could do a lot of damage. Joel, you need to take the dog out the minute you get a bead on him."

Alexa remained silent. No way would she walk downstairs to "cut a deal" with those maniacs. Such horseshit. Her best chance of surviving this night was to get out of the cabin before they found her.

The police might be on their way, but she couldn't gamble on them showing up in time to save her. Caleb and his friends could kill her in an instant, and the cops would arrive to find her body. Another young woman, dead in the forest.

"Bastards," Alexa muttered at their plan to shoot Scout. But, hell, she thought. If these assholes were prepared to kill me, why not my dog? Caleb should have realized that Scout wasn't home. With all this noise, the dog would be going nuts. But if these guys were too clueless to figure out that Scout wasn't around, great. That would work to her advantage and make the men more cautious when they entered the cabin.

She darted across the dark room to her closet and drew out an indigo fleece jacket. She fished a black watch cap from the jacket pocket and pulled it over her honey hair. Grabbing a flashlight and some shotgun shells from the nightstand, Alexa hoisted the loaded shotgun from beneath the bed. Zipping the extra shells into her pocket, Alexa briefly considered trying to scare the men away with a shotgun blast but quickly passed on the idea. Her shotgun was no match for the arsenal these guys were packing.

Alexa crept down the unlit hallway to a back bedroom. Holding her breath, she unlocked the window. She hoped like hell that all four men were still out front. Raising the window might make noise and bring them to the back of the cabin. Her fear of being heard was partially allayed when a voice shouted, "You had your chance, bitch. We're coming in." A chorus of profane shouts rose from the front deck.

A ripping noise downstairs signaled the end of the living room screen. Spurred into action, Alexa raised the window. Ignoring the slight screech, she slid over the sill and dropped to the ground in one smooth motion. Although the bedroom was on an upper level, the cabin was built into the hillside, making Alexa's drop less than five feet.

She paused to listen after she hit the ground. All the commotion was still around front. Gathering her courage, Alexa fled up the hill.

She took a left the minute her feet found the trail. She knew that all her options entailed risk. Should she head off the trail and just try to disappear into the woods? She abandoned that plan and decided to stay on the trail to reach the main road. She hoped that she would meet the police or could flag down a passing car.

Alexa sprinted down the bumpy path. When she tripped over a root, she nearly dropped the shotgun. She needed to slow down. With almost a mile until the main road, it would be better to slow her pace and avoid a fall.

After a minute or two, Alexa heard shouting and cursing coming from back at the cabin. "Shit." She'd had no choice but to leave the window open; she couldn't close it from the ground below. But the gaping window was like a neon arrow, pointing to Alexa's escape route.

Panic made Alexa clumsy. Desperate to cover more ground, she lengthened her stride but bumped the shotgun with her knee. Fumbling to hold onto the gun, Alexa stopped again to listen. Her heart lurched when she heard distant steps behind. She thought longingly of the cell phone sitting on the kitchen counter but pushed the thought aside. There was no reception anyway.

Alexa started moving again. She could hear the footsteps drawing closer and closer. It sounded like just one person. The group must have split up.

Alexa had relied on her blue jeans and indigo jacket to help her blend into the night. However, the full moon was only a day or two away. The moonlight illuminated the path in front of her. But, it made Alexa a sitting duck if Caleb's posse spotted her on this trail.

When she heard the roar of a truck engine, Alexa faltered. The truck was headed her way, and the guy behind her was gaining ground. She had to give up on heading for the main road and change directions. And, she had to do it now—before the truck got there.

Without hesitation, Alexa left the trail and flew down the steep slope. Abandoning any effort at stealth, she dashed across the gravel lane, making for the pines. Headlights bounced off the trees to her left. The truck was just seconds away.

Alexa made it just in time. As she entered the deep shadows of the pine forest, the night exploded in sound. Her pursuer signaled the pick-up truck driver with a sharp whistle. The vehicle screeched to a halt. A wild burst of gunfire filled the air.

A series of soft thuds punched the big tree next to Alexa's shoulder and she dropped to the ground in terror. Small branches and shards of pine bark peppered the ground, blanketing the forest with the scent of fresh cut evergreens. She could feel the kiss of soft pine needles on her cheek as she closed her eyes and gasped for air. Each time a piece of debris ricocheted into Alexa, she flinched, fearing the worst.

The shots stopped. Leaping to her feet, Alexa scooped up the shotgun and ran for her life. The carpet of pine needles muffled her footsteps and the towering conifers blocked most of the moonlight.

On the move, Alexa thought about her next step. The truck had cut off her access to the main road. Running aimlessly through the woods didn't sound like much of a plan. She needed to find a place to hide. In an instant, Alexa knew where to head. From the moment she had stepped into the pines, instinct had been guiding her toward the perfect place to take cover.

On high alert, Alexa stole through the pines, placing each step carefully. The forest had fallen oddly silent as if the owls and other small nocturnal creatures sensed an encroaching menace. Even the constant autumn breeze had fallen still. In the unnerving hush, Alexa picked up a whisper of voices behind her; the trigger-happy guy on the trail and his pal in the truck. They sounded a fair distance away, but she worried about the other two. They could be anywhere out here.

Alexa continued on her course. She had spent so much time in this cathedral of pines that she had little trouble finding her way, even in the black of night.

When she reached the far edge of the grove, she halted behind a big tree. The trunk of the huge virgin pine could hide three of Alexa. Comforted by the tarry smell of pine sap, Alexa closed her eyes and leaned her cheek against the rough bark. The few seconds of respite helped slow her racing heart. She took several deep breaths and felt calmer.

Alexa became conscious of a pain in her left shoulder. One of those falling branches must have really wacked me, she thought. She rested the shotgun against the big pine and touched the sore spot. It was soaked. Had she been shot? Alexa freaked out for a minute then explored the shoulder carefully with her right hand. Yes, it was wet and it hurt, but it didn't seem to be bleeding profusely. Only a small area of her fleece jacket was damp.

Alexa struggled to quell her despair. Calm yourself, Alexa, she commanded. She knew that blind fear could make her stupid.

After a few more deep breaths, Alexa realized that she had no more time to waste. She had to ignore her shoulder and move on. Still, she hesitated, reluctant to leave the shelter of the towering pines. Ahead yawned a wide clearing that she must cross to reach her destination.

Finally, Alexa pushed herself away from the giant tree. When she stepped toward the broad expanse of low grass, she froze. In the looming darkness she heard a crackling on the left. She stood perfectly still, heart accelerating. Her apprehension increased as the rustling movements drew closer.

In the moonlight, Alexa made out several low shapes moving through the dry grass. She stifled a laugh. It was only small herd of deer. Her relief turned to consternation when the deer bolted. Their white tails flickered like fireflies in the moonlight as they fled.

Alexa melted into the protection of the tree line until she could determine what had spooked the deer. The sound of voices ahead confirmed Alexa's fears. The other two men were on the prowl.

With each second, Alexa felt more and more trapped. Until she could pinpoint the position of the men in the meadow, it would be a fatal mistake to cross into the open. However, Alexa couldn't wait much longer to move forward. The two men behind her would eventually find her trail through the pines.

As Alexa debated whether to follow the deer, she spied movement across the meadow. Two men walked slowly along the gravel road that led to Our Lady of the Forest chapel. Alexa couldn't make out their faces, but the moon cast enough light for her to follow their progress. They were heading away from the chapel, toward the main road.

In the still night, Alexa could catch snippets of conversation floating across the meadow. Making little effort to keep his voice down, the taller one complained, "Where can that bitch be? I can't believe she got away from us. She must be running blind out here in the dark. Maybe Caleb and Gabe got her with those gunshots, but they didn't signal the all clear. So, she must still be on the loose."

"Yeah. I'm starting to get damned nervous," the smaller man agreed. "This was supposed to be a simple operation. Move in, take her out, and clear the area. Now, weapons have been discharged; that attracts attention. And, we're still bogged down in this search. But, she's seen us, so we've got to finish what we started."

Despite her fright, Alexa found the conversation amusing. These two sexist jerks, probably Daniel and Joel, couldn't fathom a woman who could navigate these woods on her own. But, their blind arrogance actually helped Alexa. They were searching for a timid little flower, stumbling hysterically through the darkness in blind panic. She had to prove them wrong.

Daniel and Joel's voices faded as they moved farther away. When they disappeared into the darkness at the far end of the meadow, she decided to move. She was running out of time.

Alexa held her breath, tightened her grasp on the shotgun, and dashed across the field to Our Lady of the Forest chapel. Rapidly making her way around the back, she found the springhouse, and behind it, the entrance to the Underground Railroad station. Alexa brushed aside the rhododendron branches overhanging the door. The rattle of the dry winter leaves echoed loud as a drumbeat, broadcasting her location.

She hesitated for a few seconds, dreading a rush of footsteps. Nothing. So, Alexa dropped to her knees and pulled aside the rusty iron plate. Hesitantly, she thrust the flashlight into the yawning hole and turned it on. Finding the top rung of the ladder, she forced herself to step into the cavern. She climbed cautiously down the ladder, searching out each rung with her toe. She left the shotgun and climbed back up the ladder to seal the opening. Back on the dirt floor, Alexa shielded the flashlight as she took a quick survey of the room.

Making her way to a corner of the cavern, Alexa sat down and doused the light. In the inky blackness of the cave, Alexa felt like screaming and crying, but she did neither. Instead, she listened intently and readied the shotgun.

The earthen and stone cavern was totally silent and smelled a little dank.

Like a tomb, she thought morosely.

Although this relic from the Underground Railroad made a good place to hide, the single entrance meant that she was completely trapped if Caleb and his buddies found her.

As the minutes ticked by, Alexa felt her panic subside. She doubted that Caleb or his Perry County friends knew about way station. Few locals were even aware of the cavern. Alexa thought she was safe but couldn't be sure.

Alexa switched the flashlight back on to examine her shoulder. Although it throbbed, the wound had stopped bleeding. Deciding that her best move was to let it alone, Alexa clicked off the light and wearily settled back against the wall.

Just as Alexa began to believe that she had escaped her pursuers, her heart sank. She heard voices outside. Muffled by the ground above her head, the conversation seemed to emanate from the direction of the church. One voice sounded like Caleb's. She imagined that she could identify three other distinct voices as well. The four men must have met. Now, they all stood just yards away from Alexa's hiding place.

She picked up the shotgun, ready to fire if Caleb and his friends found the cavern. Alexa tried to slow her breathing.

Loud banging noises erupted from the church. Were the men trying to break into the sanctuary? When a burst of gunfire rang out, Alexa nearly lost it.

The shooting stopped and the voices grew louder. The men were fighting among themselves. Alexa heard one voice, perhaps Caleb, say, "What are you doing? My God, this is the Lord's house."

Someone else, maybe Joel, screamed back, "Time is slipping away and we need to find that bitch, no matter where she is."

A third voice intervened. "She's not in the church anyway. Let's keep looking."

Alexa tensed as the voices approached the entrance of the cavern. The four men were still squabbling about their next move. When she heard the dry rustle of the bush above, Alexa nearly jumped out of her skin. She held her breath for what seemed like hours, but the voices slowly moved away. Somebody must have brushed the big rhododendron in passing, but they had not found her.

Soon, silence returned.

Chapter Thirty-Three

Alexa sat shivering in the darkness chilled by the clammy sweat-soaked sweater under her fleece. She tried to ignore the discomfort, hoping that body heat should eventually dry her clothes. Fighting to stay calm, Alexa tried to keep the fear at bay by putting all the pieces together in her mind like a mental puzzle. She approached the exercise like she would prepare for a legal case. When she was finished, she didn't like the picture that the pieces formed, but Alexa was pretty sure she had figured it out.

The three men with Caleb tonight were almost certainly his best friends, Gabriel, Joel, and Daniel. Elizabeth Nelson was the Beth that had been mentioned that day at Kingdom Lodge. What was it that Leah had said? Something like Gabriel broke up with Beth because he found out that she wasn't a nice Christian girl? And, the other woman there that day, the one that Alexa liked, was named Georgia. She was there with Daniel. Georgia had said that Gabriel and Beth had been a beautiful couple. Alexa thought that this statement could easily apply to the tall, striking Gabriel with his copper hair and the slender Elizabeth with her blue eyes and white-blonde curls.

Of course, whether Beth was a nice Christian girl probably didn't matter while Gabriel was sleeping with her. It only became an issue when she got pregnant. Dr. Crowe had said that Elizabeth had decided to terminate her pregnancy partly because she had grown afraid of the father. Alexa speculated that Gabriel had finally exposed Beth to his church environment and his true character, and that scared her away. Or maybe he brought one of his AK-47s to dinner one night.

239

From what Alexa had learned about Elizabeth Nelson, the girl was a computer geek and a bit of an introvert. Nonetheless, she liked the party scene in the Northwest and had not been deeply religious. Something had happened to make her break things off with Gabriel. From what Doc Crowe and her parents said, Elizabeth must have been scared and was preparing to leave town to get away from her ex-boyfriend.

Alexa thought that she might never know the details of the night that Gabriel killed Beth. He probably found out about the abortion and was furious. Clearly, the abortion issue was a major brick in the foundation of the Church of the Blessed Lamb. Gabriel, like Caleb, had drunk that Kool-Aid from birth. So, the fact that his girlfriend had aborted his child must have pushed the volatile Gabriel over the edge. She marveled at the paradox of Gabriel—a man with the face of an angel but the heart of a murderer. Alexa barely knew the man, but she felt like a Philistine to even consider that a man so beautiful could be evil.

It was pure chance that Alexa had been driving down the road that day to see Gabriel, and, probably, Daniel or Joel speeding past in that van. She shuddered to think that they had probably dumped Elizabeth's body in the woods only a few minutes before she stopped at the pullout with Scout. She hated to think what might have happened if she had arrived at the clearing while they were carrying Elizabeth's body into the forest.

It was also pure chance that she was dating Caleb at the time this all happened. But, that had turned into bad luck for Alexa. Her relationship with Caleb would probably have broken apart anyway when they finally realized that the two of them were fundamentally incompatible.

Yet, if I hadn't been involved with Caleb, he would have never learned from Kate that I found Elizabeth Nelson's body. And then, when I drove past tonight, Caleb must have instantly recognized my Land Rover.

Not your typical end to a romance, Alexa thought wryly. Now my former lover is running around the woods with his friends trying to kill me because I can identify one of said friends as a murderer.

As Alexa ran with her thoughts, she recalled what one of the men had shouted at the cabin, that she would go to hell because she was part of the abortion clinic. She thought it reasonable to conclude that Dr. Crowe's shooting, Emily Baxter's murder, and the other threats at the clinic were probably all connected to Gabriel as well. The first series of notes sent to Doc had said, "You will be the third to die." That must have been Gabriel targeting the doctor because he had done the procedure to terminate Elizabeth's pregnancy. Gabriel must have thought of his unborn baby as the first to die; he killed the second, Elizabeth; and Doc was to have been the third. Instead, they killed a young innocent mother, Emily Baxter, who had only the most tangential connection to Elizabeth's abortion.

Alexa asked herself: Who knows when Gabriel and his friends will stop? They are clearly prepared to add me to the list tonight. What havoc has been created here because of one unplanned pregnancy? Wrong. It wasn't the pregnancy. Blame it on this extreme set of beliefs espoused by Reverend Browne and his flock. Why else would Joel, Daniel, and Caleb get involved in helping Gabriel cover up a murder, no matter how good a friend?

Alexa's thoughts turned to the night in the clinic when she had spoken to Emily just hours before the young mother was killed. Such a shame that her two babies would grow up without their mother—not to mention the loss that her husband must feel for his wife. Alexa fastened on a remark that Detective Miller had made, something like, "She may not have been the target." She remembered the way Emily's sandy-blonde hair had lifted as she took off her dark coat upon entering the clinic. What if Detective Miller was right about the shooter's intended target? What if the target had actually been Alexa? She and Emily both had worn dark coats; both had dark blonde hair. That's why the detective had asked Alexa what coat she had been wearing. Maybe Caleb and his friends had killed Emily by mistake when their true target had been Alexa. Alexa was filled with despair to think that, in some way, she may have been responsible for Emily's death. Silent tears ran down her cheeks as Alexa was overcome with guilt about Emily's death.

The time went by slowly. Alexa's clothes had nearly dried and she stopped shaking. At some point, Alexa realized that hours must have passed since she had climbed down the ladder, but she still could not gather up enough courage to leave the cavern. She pictured clambering out of the old way station into the waiting arms of Caleb, Gabriel, and their friends. Perhaps she had used up her fragile store of bravery in that headlong dash away from the cabin, ending up in this place that had offered refuge to so many before her. She was exhausted both physically and emotionally and could not bring herself to abandon the relative safety of the cavern.

During the lengthening hours, Alexa thought about the Babes in the Woods, who had been killed so close to where she was hiding now. She shivered as she pictured her own dead body lying in that spot where Dewilla and her two sisters had been found so many years ago.

Alexa imagined she felt the presence of all those slaves who had originally found refuge in this dark cavern. She thought of the mothers, fathers, children, and even elderly slaves who had passed through here a century and a half ago. She imagined the terror they had felt when the Confederate troops had been standing above the cavern with Father Roberts. Alexa had gotten a taste of that terror tonight but could barely conceive of the raw courage it must have taken for those slaves to flee the South and head toward freedom, hunted every step of the way.

Alexa dozed off, despite her fear and the cold that had seeped through her bones from the damp cavern. When she awoke, she was surprised that she had slept. Then Alexa noticed that the texture of the light had changed. Even though she was underground, there were a few small pinholes built into the cavern that provided a muted light. The pitch dark had lightened to a murky gray, indicating that dawn must have arrived.

Alexa debated about what to do. She realized that it had been hours since the police had arrived at the cabin to find her missing. Reese had also promised to come over when he finished his shift. By now, the police and Reese surely would be looking for her. Caleb and his friends would certainly have vanished the minute that the police came on the scene. But, still, last night's experience made her wary.

She was mentally preparing herself to climb up the ladder and step out of the cavern when she heard footsteps above her. When the bush above the entrance rustled, she grabbed the shotgun poised to pull the trigger, and stood to face the ladder. Alexa's heart pounded as the metal grate shifted above her. Everything changed in an instant when she heard Reese's voice calling, "Alexa are you down there?"

"Yes. Thank God you're here." Alexa eased her finger off the trigger and engaged the safety before she dropped the shotgun to the ground. She ran across the earthen room while Reese made his way down the ladder. He folded her into his arms.

"I have been worried sick about you. We've been looking for you for hours. We were afraid that you had been hurt or worse. Then, I remembered about this place. Alexa, I am so glad that you're safe." Then, Reese stepped back and held Alexa at arm's length to look at her. "Are you OK?"

"Yes," Alexa found herself crying. "I'm OK, but it was close. I'm pretty sure that bastard, Caleb, and his friends were going to kill me."

"Let's get you out of here and then we can sort things out."

Chapter Thirty-Four

Sunday evening, Alexa sat in her parents' living room with Scout at her feet and breathed a sigh of relief. Starting with Alexa's rescue at dawn from the underground cavern, the day had been long and trying.

Reese, her dad, and Graham had all taken part in the search party that had been organized to look for her during the night. Reese and Graham had been together when they found her in the cavern. After alerting the police by walkie-talkie that Alexa had been located unharmed, they had taken her back to the cabin. Her father was waiting outside and folded his daughter into his arms, relieved to see that she had not been hurt or worse.

Wrapped in the safety of her father's embrace, Alexa gave into her emotions and wept uncontrollably. She was tired beyond words. She finally collected herself and stepped out of her dad's arms. After one look at the trashed cabin, now a crime scene, she began to cry again.

Medics on the scene checked Alexa out quickly and bandaged her shoulder. But, her dad insisted that he take her to the emergency room for a thorough examination before any police questioning. When Norris Williams climbed onto his high attorney-at-law horse and insisted on something, he usually got his way. This time was no exception.

The ER physician treated Alexa for mild hypothermia and shock. He confirmed that the injury on Alexa's left shoulder was a bullet wound, although it required only minor attention.

"You're lucky," he commented. "The bullet only grazed the skin. A few inches to the left, it would have hit bone and muscle. That would have been serious damage."

After stitching the gash on her shoulder, the doctor gave her a tetanus shot. Alexa had to remain in the emergency room for several hours while they pumped intravenous liquids and antibiotics into her. There was probably a sedative of some sort, too, she guessed, because she began feeling pretty woozy. Lying on the narrow emergency room bed under a pile of warm blankets, Alexa drifted off to sleep. By that time, her mother had arrived and sat watch by her bedside.

The doctor discharged Alexa a little after noon, suggesting that she take several days off work. "I think your body is going to feel worse tomorrow than it does today. And, you've had quite an experience. Take some time to recover."

After a stop for a burger and milkshake at O'Hara's, Alexa's parents drove her to the state police headquarters. Alexa spent several hours answering questions and going over everything that had happened. Graham was by her side, as both her attorney and her brother. For once, Alexa welcomed his support.

Caleb, Gabriel, Daniel, and Joel had all been arrested and were in the Cumberland County jail. Apparently, it had not been long after Alexa fled out the back window of her cabin that a state trooper arrived on the scene. Her favorite policeman, Trooper Taylor, pulled up in front of the cabin only minutes later. Neither police vehicle had used their sirens since both thought that their visits were simply follow-ups to the earlier incident with the truck. However, when the police found the front door of the cabin hanging wide open and the living room window smashed in, they immediately went into action, calling for additional backup.

The four friends had still been in the woods looking for her. They had no idea that the state police had arrived at Alexa's cabin. Although it had taken some time searching in the dark forest, the burst of gunfire at the church had helped point the police in the right direction. The state troopers found Gabriel and Caleb in the pines. They arrested Joel and Daniel a few minutes later when they emerged from the forest near Caleb's truck. Apparently, the four men had not anticipated that Alexa would call 911 or that the police would get there so quickly if she did. What they hadn't known, of course, was that the police were already on the way.

Working from the information provided by Daniel's former girlfriend, Georgia, the police had determined that they had sufficient evidence to charge Gabriel with murder and Daniel as an accessory. At this point, the only charges Caleb and Joel faced were in conjunction with ramming Alexa's car and destroying her house. However, the police were still sorting through additional charges related to Alexa's shooting. They thought that Caleb and Joel might also have been involved in covering up Elizabeth's murder.

The police were working to determine if the four men were also connected to the violence at the clinic, including Emily Baxter's death. It was likely just a matter of time until they brought additional charges in those matters as well.

Now, Alexa was at her parents' home, trying to regroup. The family had been fussing over her for hours. Her mother had made an enormous dinner of round steak and mashed potatoes and gravy, one of Alexa's favorite childhood meals. Graham and Kate were there as well but had left the kids at home with a babysitter. They didn't want to worry about editing the evening's conversation or explaining the trauma that their beloved Aunt Alexa had endured. Her parents had also asked Reese to join them for the meal.

"Alexa, we are just so thankful that you are OK," her mother said for the umpteenth time. "When the police called to say you were missing, we were out of our minds with worry."

"I picked up Graham and we raced out to the cabin. By the time we got there, the police had taken Caleb and the other three into custody. But, no one knew where you were. Those four thugs wouldn't say anything to the police and were asking for lawyers. Graham and I were frantic."

"Yeah," Reese chimed in. "I got there not long after Trooper Taylor. We heard the automatic rifle fire out in the woods a few minutes later. I was so worried that you might have been shot. The state troopers, who had been first on the scene, headed out in the direction of the gunfire, and I went with them."

"Thank God Graham and I weren't there yet. I don't know how we would have coped, hearing those gunshots. But, it was bad enough to arrive and find that you were still missing. We imagined that you could have injured yourself out there in that dark forest."

"Or worse," Graham chimed in. "She could have been lying out in the woods somewhere, bleeding from a gunshot wound. It was pretty scary, midget," he said to his sister.

"It wasn't too great from my point of view either," Alexa observed drily. "I've had better evenings."

"You were so brave, darling," her mother said. "I must say that it was wonderful how many of our friends joined the search. When your dad called and told us the situation, Kate and I got on the phone and called the Pattersons, and Kate's brother, Jimmy, and Pat O'Donnell. Pat must have been the one to call some of the other people from the law firm. I understand that Melinda and her husband came out. Also, wasn't Brian Stewart there with his girlfriend, Norris?"

"Yes, he was. It turns out that he's dating that intern we had in the office last summer. I should give him a lecture about that. The relationship clearly violates our non-fraternization policy. After I thank him for joining the search party, of course."

"Intern?" Alexa chuckled. "He's dating Jessica, the pretty blonde student from the law school?" That must have been why Brian was nervous about his girlfriend, she thought. The girl was not jailbait as Melinda and

Tiffany had speculated. But the firm did have a strict policy about office dating. Alexa wondered when they had started this little romance.

"Give him a break, Dad. It can't violate the policy because she doesn't work in the firm anymore. I'm amazed that Brian actually came out to look for me, given our working relationship."

After dinner they moved into the living room with Scout on Alexa's heels. The dog had shadowed her all evening, limping after his mistress on his bandaged paw. "We're quite the pair, aren't we?" Alexa said, hugging the big beast. "Caleb's crew shattered the glass window that injured you. Now, look what they've done to me."

The conversation soon lagged. It was clear that the entire family was worn out. Reese, her father, and Graham had spent the entire night as part of the search party looking for Alexa. Meanwhile her mother and Kate had waited at home by the phone, desperate for news.

Although none of them spoke the words aloud, Alexa knew that everyone had feared that they would not find her alive.

The outpouring of love from the Williams clan warmed Alexa's heart and eased the terror that she had experienced the night before. The evening dragged on, however, and she was glad when Graham and Kate left to relieve their babysitter. Soon after, Mom and Dad went upstairs to bed. Even though they were very active, she could tell that the lack of sleep combined with the strain of the last twenty-four hours had taken their toll on her parents.

Finally, Alexa was alone with Reese. They had not really had any time together since he had pulled her from the cavern. Reese rose from the chair by the fireplace and walked over to Alexa, who was snuggled under an afghan in the corner of her parents' huge leather couch. He sat down beside Alexa and gathered her in his arms, saying,

"You must be absolutely exhausted. Why don't you go to bed?"

Instead of going to bed, Alexa settled into Reese's arms and moved over to give him more room on the couch. With their heads together as they lay on the big sofa, Alexa and Reese carried on a conversation in low tones.

"I'll sleep better knowing you're here," Alexa said warmly. Her parents had invited Reese to bunk down in Graham's old room, recognizing that he had been awake all night as part of the search team. "I am tired, but mostly I feel relieved. This reminds me of how I feel when I've completed a really complicated and lengthy legal case. I feel a sense of accomplishment but am so glad that it's over.

"In this case, I'm so glad that Elizabeth Nelson's killer finally has been found and arrested. It also looks like the police are now on track to make arrests in Emily Baxter's murder and Doc's shooting. Who knew it would be the same group of suspects? I don't know if I'll ever get over the fact that Emily was probably killed because she was mistaken for me." A tear slid down Alexa's cheek as she thought again about the young mother whose life had ended so senselessly.

Reese didn't say a word but held Alexa a little tighter until she recovered her composure.

Alexa continued, "Another thing. You have no idea how glad I am that Caleb Browne is out of my life. My biggest regret is that I ever got involved with him. I thought he was a nice guy, even though we didn't have a whole lot in common. We had fun for a few months. Now I find that I really never knew him at all."

"Look, Alexa, don't be so hard on yourself. Caleb lived two separate lives. To most people he was the respected business owner who lived a fairly unremarkable life. Only his best friends and his church knew that he was actually a dangerous religious fanatic crusading against abortion."

"I actually think he tried to break away from all of that, but his father's pull was just too strong," Alexa replied.

She propped herself on her elbow and turned toward Reese. With a smile, she said. "There's one more thing that makes me glad. Do you want to hear about it?"

"Sure," he answered with a goofy grin. "Let's get all this glad stuff out on the table."

"I'm so glad that I met you. The circumstances in which we met were awful, and these two months that we've known each other have been pretty tumultuous. But, in some ways, I feel that all the turmoil has actually brought us closer together. Who else would have thought to look in the Underground Railroad site for me?"

Alexa took Reese's hand and looked into his clear blue eyes, "We still need to take it slow. We still need to get to know each other better. But, I am so grateful to have you in my life."

Chapter Thirty-Five

Thursday, November 22, 1934.

Babes in the Woods

Dewilla hated this new road. Tall charcoal trees pressed in on both sides of the car and blocked any glimpse of the sky. The big trees loomed like evil giants and grabbed at the puny vehicle with twisted claws. The Pontiac's tires rolled over the rough gravel with angry pops. The Noakes were alone in this bleak wilderness. They passed no houses, no cars; nothing but endless trees.

Daddy had turned onto this narrow road early this morning. With each mile, the dark forest pushed farther into the car until it became a silent passenger. Daddy and Winifred hadn't spoken for hours. Norma drifted in and out of sleep. Even Cordelia had stopped fretting, too worn out to even cry. Instead, she curled against Dewilla with her thumb jammed into her mouth. Mama would have given her the devil for sucking her thumb, but Dewilla was just happy that Cordelia could find some comfort.

For a few promising moments, the landscape changed to lacy evergreen trees with long needles that glistened with sunlight. Dewilla wasn't sure exactly what these trees were, but they reminded her of the tall evergreens in Utah and California. She smiled when they drove through a stand of mammoth old evergreens. The huge sentinels encircled the car with their enormous branches, turning the road into a warm green tunnel.

Then the Pontiac reached the top of the mountain. Dewilla's heart sank when she saw another never-ending mass of gray giants on the far side. A thick mist rose from the dark forest. As they descended into the ominous fog,

Dewilla imagined that she saw forbidding faces peering from the dripping trunks.

Daddy broke the silence when he said to Winifred, "This looks like as good a place as any." He pulled the car to the side of the road. "Girls, we're going to stop here for a rest. You can go to the bathroom and we'll have a drink. Get your coats on and bundle up tight."

They piled out and Daddy fished an old wool blanket out of the trunk and spread it on the ground. When she walked toward the blanket, Dewilla faltered as a wave of dizziness swept through her. She felt so weak.

The girls took turns going behind the bushes. Winifred went first and returned to sit stiffly on the blanket. Soon, all three girls took seats beside their cousin. Daddy passed around a canteen with water and they each took a sip. Dewilla thought that it was around noon, but she knew there would be no picnic lunch today.

Tendrils of cold fog slipped beneath Dewilla's wool coat and slithered down her spine. She pulled her soft fur collar tight against the chill. But her legs, bare above thin white anklets, were exposed to the November air. Cold seeped through the thin soles of her patent leather Mary Janes. Dewilla wrinkled her nose at the sulphurous odor of damp and decaying leaves.

Daddy paced back and forth. When the girls had finished taking turns with the canteen, Daddy did something very strange. He pulled Dewilla and Cordelia up from the blanket and into his arms. Daddy hugged them so long that his rough coat scratched Dewilla's face. Daddy called them his little darlings. When he released them, he looked so sad.

"Girls, I am so sorry that I couldn't provide for you like I should. Norma, perhaps I should have let you go to your family after Mary died. But, I loved you too much to let you go. I love you all. It hurts me to see you suffer for my sins." When Daddy fell silent, Winifred stood and put her arm around his shoulder.

"Be strong, Elmo Noakes. You know what must be done," Winifred said in a stern voice, speaking to Daddy like he was a wayward child.

Dewilla was confused. Daddy never talked like this. Mostly, he told the sisters what to do, quizzed them on their lessons, and punished them when they were fractious. Before Mama died, Daddy had been a bit of a cut-up, laughing and joking sometimes. But lately, Daddy was always solemn and stern, except when he was making doe eyes at Winifred. The only time Dewilla had seen Daddy emotional like this was when Mama went to Heaven.

Dewilla sat back down on the blanket and looked at Norma for an explanation, but Norma seemed tense and had a very worried look on her face. The same awful feeling of dread that she had experienced at the roadside spring seized Dewilla. Something wasn't right with Daddy, and Winifred was as pale as a ghost.

Dewilla said a silent prayer to Mama in Heaven, "Please, come and save us from this hunger and cold." It seemed as if misery had stalked the Noakes since the day they left California.

Daddy shuffled over to Norma and held out his hand. Daddy looked as gray and tall as the trees. "Norma, child, walk a ways with me. I want to speak to you about something in particular."

Norma rose reluctantly, and with a fearful glance at Dewilla, followed Daddy over a ridge into the deep forest. A gust of icy wind blew down the mountain, and the giant gray trees erupted into a horrible frenzy of clattering branches.

Winifred started talking loudly, and said, "Why don't the three of us read some Bible passages. I miss going to church on Sundays with traveling and all. Why don't I read you the Twenty-Third Psalm?"

Winifred lifted Cordelia onto her lap and wrapped her in an ugly green blanket with purple trim. She read from a small Bible, "The Lord is my Shepherd." This was one of

Dewilla's favorite Bible passages. Hearing Winifred recite the familiar verses helped ease Dewilla's dread.

Winifred began a new psalm, but Dewilla couldn't concentrate on the words. Daddy and Norma weren't back yet. She thought she heard crashing in the distance and Norma shouting, "No!" At that moment, Winifred raised her little girl voice like a preacher on the pulpit, "A time to weep and a time to dance."

Dewilla couldn't be sure if she had heard Norma or just the wind. She hoped that Norma wasn't fighting with Daddy. Daddy didn't like sass or backtalk.

Winifred's voice grew thick with tears and she began to falter. She broke off abruptly when Daddy staggered out of the dark forest alone.

Shoulders hunched like an old man's, his expression was a frightening mix of anger and sorrow.

"Where's Norma?" Dewilla asked with alarm. She jumped to her feet. "I thought I heard her shout."

"No, you didn't hear anything. We found a pretty little stream back in the woods and she wanted me to bring you to see it." Daddy looked long and hard at Winifred and gave a slow nod. Then, with a heavy sigh, he reached for Dewilla's hand.

When Dewilla looked up at Daddy, she saw evil in his eyes. This was not her Daddy; this was some monster inhabiting his body. The gray trees had claimed him.

"No," she screamed. "I won't go with you. What did you do with Norma?" Before Daddy could react, Dewilla twisted from his grasp and raced into the woods toward Norma.

"Norma, Norma, where are you?" she called as she sprinted through the dark trees with Daddy hard on her heels.

When she flew down the other side of the hill, Dewilla came to an abrupt halt. Norma was lying on the ground, still as death. There were marks around her face and neck. She looked like a broken doll.

In the instant that Dewilla realized that her sister was dead, she felt Daddy's big hands on her shoulders. Dewilla was terrified, tears streaming down her face. Daddy turned her around to face him. He reached forward to gently brush the tears from her cheeks and said, "Dewilla, I didn't want it to be this way. I'm sorry."

When Daddy's big hands circled her neck, Dewilla let out a single sob. Then she closed her eyes and flew to Mama and the angels.

Chapter Thirty-Six

Alexa would stay in her old room at Mom and Dad's house until they could repair the cabin. For the next few mornings, Alexa was barely able to climb out of bed. The emergency room doctor had been right about the way her body would react to her ordeal. Alexa thought she was in good shape. However, she had abused every single muscle in her body with the drop out of the cabin window and desperate dash through the woods. Her shoulder throbbed where the bullet had nicked it. Bruises covered her entire body.

She took the entire week off work. Brian continued to surprise her with his compassion and had quickly agreed to complete some of her outstanding work.

Alexa's story caught the attention of the national media, which descended upon Carlisle in full force. For several days, reports about the "Abortion Clinic Killers" dominated the 24-hour news cycle. Corporal Branche appeared on all the news shows. Reporters and their camera crews invaded the clinic and pursued Doc Crowe all over town.

Although the press camped outside her mom and dad's house for days, Alexa avoided them. She gave a brief statement to the assembled reporters on Tuesday afternoon, her dad by her side. Shortly after, Alexa agreed to a single interview with Rachel Maddow. She was relieved when a breaking political story drew the media to Washington, D.C.

The state police stopped by on Friday to update Alexa on their investigation. Corporal Branche's face wrinkled in concern as he asked, "How are you coping with all this, Alexa?"

"I'm trying to get back to normal, but it's been hard. My aches and bruises are healing, but I'm not sleeping very well. I'm still having nightmares about being chased through the woods."

"Things will get better with time, but you've been through a traumatic experience. I wish I could tell you that it's all over. But, it's going to be months before you can leave Caleb Browne and his friends totally behind you. You will almost certainly be called to testify in some of the criminal trials."

Trooper Taylor chimed in. "We've charged Gabriel with Elizabeth Nelson's murder and Daniel and Joel as accessories. Daniel drove the van when he and Gabriel dumped Elizabeth Nelson's body in Michaux State Forest. We're still trying to determine if Caleb had a role in Elizabeth's death.

"We've also charged Joel in the death of Emily Baxter as well as the shooting of Doc Crowe."

"Joel? Not Gabriel?" Alexa asked in surprise.

"No. We learned that Joel was a marksman in the army. We matched his high-powered rifle to a bullet embedded in Emily's car and another removed from Doc during surgery."

"How sad," Alexa commented. "His wife, Leah, will be raising their new baby without a father."

"Of course, they've also been charged with several counts related to the night they rammed your car and attacked you at your home. It will be a long time before these guys see the outside of a jail, if ever."

That evening, Reese arrived with more news. "I told you that I heard automatic rifle fire that day at Kingdom Lodge. My boss just found out that the place is linked to our militia investigations. The murder cases led police over to the place, where they found evidence that Kingdom Lodge was hosting militia training for right wing extremists. Apparently, some members of Reverend Browne's congregation were involved."

The following weekend, the Williams family threw themselves into getting the cabin back in shape. Her father had gotten a professional cleaning crew to vacuum the shattered glass and a contractor to repair the damage to the door. On Saturday, the family and some of their friends finished the job. Alexa's parents invited Graham and Kate, their kids, Reese, people from the law firm, and Haley and Melissa. Reese brought his roommate, Jim, and Alexa made good on her promise by introducing him to Melissa.

After a few hours of work, the afternoon devolved into a party. Alexa perched on a stool at the kitchen counter and smiled at the animated group of family and friends who filled her home. She knew that her parents had engineered this event to help dispel the demons that had entered her beloved cabin with Caleb and his posse. The trick worked. She couldn't wait to move back here with Scout. But it would still be nearly a month until the special order for the big window arrived and the place became habitable.

Two weeks later, on a blustery Saturday in mid-December, Alexa drove out to the cabin to pick up some clothes for the workweek. Scout was getting around fine now, but she decided to leave him at her parents' because she needed room in the back of the Land Rover to pile her suits.

Alexa felt like her life was getting back to normal, and she was anxious to immerse herself in the routine by moving back into her own home. It would also be easier to spend time with Reese without her parents looking over her shoulder. She and Reese had been growing steadily closer since the night he found her in the cavern. They had finally had that official first date last night. As their relationship deepened, she couldn't believe that she had ever doubted Reese or suspected him of killing Elizabeth Nelson.

Alexa was somber as she arrived at the cabin. Seeing the huge board covering the front window didn't help her frame of mind. Although she had participated in the family work party, today was the first time she had been back to the cabin on her own. Her solemn mood reflected her dismay at all the bad things that had happened here.

However, the minute Alexa stepped over the threshold, her mood lifted. She loved this place and wasn't going to let Caleb Browne and his fanatical friends ruin it for her.

Alexa made two trips back and forth to take shoes and a basket of clothes to the car. On her second trip, she retrieved the shotgun from the Land Rover. The gun had been traveling with her since leaving the Underground Railroad cavern. That morning, her father had stowed the old twelve-gauge in the trunk of his car before he drove Alexa to the hospital. Later, she had transferred it to the bedroom at her parents' house. Today, she had decided to get the gun out of the way and bring it back to the cabin.

With the Land Rover nearly loaded, Alexa wandered into the chilly living room. A shaft of sunlight streaming through the only intact window fell on the couch where she sat, but the board over the living room window shrouded the rest of the room in darkness. Alone in the cabin for the first time since the night she had been forced to flee in terror, Alexa had to admit to some reticence about returning. She really wanted to come back home to this place she loved so much. But, that night had cast a shadow on her safe haven, creating an ambivalence like this play of light and dark in front of her.

Intellectually, she knew she was safe. Caleb and his friends were in jail. They couldn't come after her again. Still, the aftermath of that night had left Alexa feeling vulnerable. The day she had found Elizabeth Nelson's body in the woods had been the first in a series of violent events that had hurt and killed people she knew well. Then, Alexa had become a target and barely escaped with her life.

She remembered that long-ago thought that finding Elizabeth's body had opened a tear in the fabric of her universe. Now, Alexa's universe was in tatters, and she wondered if her life could ever be the same. She realized that it wasn't moving back home that scared her, it was the hard-earned knowledge that the world was a more dangerous place than she had ever imagined.

Shaking off this gloomy detour into introspection, Alexa rose to finish gathering her things. Returning to the dining room, she fished the plastic baggie with shotgun shells out of a box of books she'd brought from her parents' house. She loaded the gun and propped it against the couch, intending to run it up to her bedroom when she did her final run to get her suits on hangers.

Remembering that she needed a heavy coat for walking Scout at night, Alexa headed to the pantry where she kept an old down jacket. When she emerged from the pantry with the jacket, she jumped at a loud knock on the door. She hadn't heard a car pull up in front of the house, but from the pantry she usually couldn't even hear the TV in the next room.

Alexa smiled and hurried to the door, dropping the coat on a chair. Maybe Reese had come to surprise her. Alexa threw open the door but was taken aback when she saw Reverend Browne standing on the threshold.

"I don't think this is a good idea," Alexa said and tried to close the door. But the reverend blocked the heavy door with his powerful arm and forced his way into the room. He launched into a tirade, his face livid; his beard quivering with indignation.

"I have waited for this day of reckoning when I could deal with you face to face, you heathen slut. You seduced my only boy. You polluted him with your touch, you unclean daughter of Satan. You are a whore and a baby killer." The reverend was dressed in his usual black with clerical collar, the familiar black brimmed hat planted squarely on his head. In a towering rage, the minister's entire body trembled with anger.

"You have ruined Caleb's life, and you must pay. You are just like those other sluts; my own daughter who became a harlot and a baby killer and that blonde jezebel who flouted the Lord's will by murdering Gabriel's child."

As he ranted, Alexa searched for a way to defuse this situation. When he paused for breath, Alexa spoke with determination. "Reverend Browne, I understand why you are upset with me, but I really don't want to discuss this. Please leave."

Despite her calm tone, Alexa was on the edge of panic. Reverend Browne clearly was not in a mood for rational conversation. She calculated her chances of escaping through the front door. The back door was double-locked and would take too long to open. So, the front door was her best option for avoiding further confrontation. Alexa stepped back, trying to draw the big man farther into the room so she could slip out the door behind him. Unresponsive to her efforts, Caleb's father stood firm near the threshold.

Alexa blanched when the minister drew himself fully erect. His huge silhouette extinguished the light from the open doorway. Yet, his silver eyes glittered with cold fire.

"Leave?" he scoffed. "I don't believe you understand." Then the reverend bellowed. "For I am the servant of God —an avenger who carries out God's wrath on the wrongdoer. I am the Commander of the Army of Judah.

"I dispatched those four boys on a mission to send you to Hell, but they were weak. Caleb was weak, just like the day that Rebecca had to be punished for her sins. Gabriel, named for God's own archangel, was weak when it came to what had to be done with that little blonde. And, Joel failed when his bullet did not hit the heart of that filthy doctor whose hands are steeped in the blood of innocent lambs.

"I am here to do what those boys could not. I will always do what is necessary to serve the Lord, our God."

Reverend Browne's voice took on a maniacal pitch as he shouted, "Vengeance is mine, I will repay, sayeth the Lord." He stormed toward Alexa.

Listening to this diatribe, a chill ran down Alexa's spine. She understood that this was not just an over-the-top, angry parent standing before her. This man was almost certainly certifiable, and she was in serious danger. As the minister moved toward her, Alexa darted toward the living room. If she could make it upstairs, she could call 911 or use the back window as an escape route.

The old man moved like lightning as he leapt across the floor, trying to cut off Alexa's retreat. She sprinted to the far side of the dining room, but in seconds, he had swallowed the gap between them. Alexa wrenched away as she felt Reverend Browne's massive hands dig into her shoulder. She gagged when she caught a whiff of lime aftershave mixed with acrid sweat. Panicked by the man's rapid advance, she tipped a wooden chair into his path.

Alexa fled into the living room, desperate to reach the stairs. Undeterred by her attempt to trip him up, the enraged minister dogged her every step. When his calloused finger grazed her cheek, terror galvanized her into summoning a burst of speed.

Alexa turned when Mrs. Browne appeared in the open doorway into the cabin, screaming, "Jebediah, no! You must stop. Please don't do this again." She halted on the threshold, anguish written across her face.

Caught up in his frenzy of anger and hate, the reverend glanced at his wife for no more than a second. Then, the imposing man continued to chase Alexa.

Alexa had paused behind a high-backed wing chair when she heard Mrs. Browne enter the room, hoping that his wife's intervention would halt the reverend's rampage. Things began to move in slow motion as Alexa saw the look of despair on Caleb's mother's face when her husband ignored her plea. During the moment of distraction, Alexa spied the shotgun leaning against the chair in front of her. She grabbed the gun from the floor, and in a smooth motion released the safety.

In that instant, Alexa's fear exploded into blazing anger. She was so very tired of these people who had wreaked havoc on her life because of their perverse view of Christianity and their anti-abortion cult. This madman standing in front of her was the worst of all. He was responsible for twisting so many minds.

Aiming the shotgun at Reverend Browne's chest, she said calmly, "Reverend, one more time, I am asking you and Mrs. Browne to leave. I am sick to death of you, and if you try to harm me, I will not hesitate to shoot."

Seeing the gun in Alexa's hands brought Reverend Browne up short. For a moment, he halted just a few yards away from Alexa's position behind the leather wing chair. Alexa tensed when the minister reached into his coat pocket, thinking he was going for a handgun. Instead, he brought out a small Bible and touched the book to his heart before returning it to his pocket.

Then, everything seemed to happen at once. Alexa braced the shotgun, ready to fire.

The incensed minister took two great strides across the floor, clearly intent on killing Alexa with his bare hands. Reaching the armchair, he catapulted toward her and roared, "Blessed is mine, sayeth the Lord."

Mrs. Browne let out another earth-shattering scream, "Nooooo ..."

Alexa pulled the trigger.

Chapter Thirty-Seven

After Alexa pulled the trigger, Joanna Browne ran to her fallen husband, cradling the reverend in her arms. The shotgun blast had hit the minister in the chest as he leapt toward Alexa. He was dead by the time his wife reached his side.

Alexa couldn't bring herself to touch the man who had tried to kill her. She could barely look at him. There was blood everywhere. She had never seen so much blood.

In a daze, Alexa moved to the phone and dialed 911. Pulling on a coat, she stumbled outside with the shotgun and a box of shells.

Sick to her stomach, Alexa huddled in the corner of the deck in a patch of sun. Inside, Caleb's mother lamented and prayed over her dead husband. Alexa cradled the shotgun in her arms for protection. She didn't fear Mrs. Browne but worried that others from the congregation might be nearby.

When the police and an ambulance arrived, two state troopers approached her slowly with their guns drawn. "Drop the shotgun," they commanded.

Alexa rose with difficulty, shaking from the cold. She left the shotgun lying on the deck. She had trouble putting her words together. "Shot him. Going to kill me."

"Miss. Who did you shoot?"

"Reverend Browne. I'm pretty sure that he's dead. He's in there on the floor with his wife. She had nothing to do with the attack ... she tried to stop it."

While the police secured the house, the paramedics confirmed that Reverend Browne was dead. One of the paramedics led Alexa to the ambulance and wrapped her in a space-age blanket for warmth.

"We need to treat you for shock."

A few minutes later, the police led Mrs. Browne from the cabin and down the steps toward their vehicle. As she passed Alexa sitting in the back of the ambulance, Mrs. Browne slowed. This distraught woman barely resembled the elegant woman Alexa had first met. Her hair was tangled and the entire front of her dress was soaked in her husband's blood.

"I am so sorry, child. I am so sorry about everything. I should have spoken up with Rebecca, but I was raised to obey my husband. I didn't listen to the Lord himself. Deuteronomy 31:6 says 'be strong and courageous. Do not be afraid or terrified because of them, for the Lord your God goes with you; he will never leave you nor forsake you.'

"I see now that if I had more courage, so many lives could have been saved. I knew from that first day I met you that you were a different type of woman, one with courage and a mind of her own. You would have been so good for Caleb, but I couldn't save him from his father's influence.

"I loved Jebediah, but he could be a hard man in his service to the Lord. You did what you had to do, and I understand." She smiled wanly. "The Book says 'Let all bitterness and wrath and anger and clamor and slander be put away from you, along with all malice. And be kind to one another, tenderhearted, forgiving each other, just as God in Christ also has forgiven you;' Ephesians 4:31-32. I will hold that thought in my heart when I think of you, child."

Alexa hardly knew what to say. She knew that this woman came from another generation and had led a very different and more constrained life than her own. But, how could she obey her husband to the point that she stood by while he killed their only daughter and pushed their only son down a path that ended in prison? Joanna Browne struck her as an intelligent woman. She must have seen the inherent hypocrisy of a pro-life doctrine that employed murder to advance its message. How could she condone her husband's zealotry?

Even more astounding was the fact that this complicated woman could find compassion in her heart for Alexa after all that had happened. Finally, Alexa found the words to respond. "Mrs. Browne, I am sorry for all you have lost."

Soon, the cabin was again surrounded by police cars and taped off as a crime scene. Alexa was relieved when Trooper Taylor arrived. Sitting alone in the ambulance, she began to recover from the shock of taking Reverend Browne's life. She started to worry that she could be facing criminal charges. The police had only her word about this confrontation with Reverend Browne. Although Mrs. Browne seemed to be in a penitent mood, Alexa was far from certain that she would corroborate the story of the woman who killed her husband and ruined her only son.

While Alexa had made it clear that she killed Caleb's father in self-defense, the original troopers on the scene were strangers. These officers only saw a young woman who had killed a minister, rarely a profession that they linked with the violent behavior Alexa was describing. The policemen had, however, allowed her to call her father. He and Graham arrived only moments after Trooper Taylor.

Alexa had a difficult few days until she was completely cleared of any wrongdoing. The police questioned her for hours. Even worse, the national media had flocked back to Carlisle to cover the latest installment in the sensational "Abortion Clinic Killers" case. Alexa had to evade the press every time she left her parents' house.

Strangely enough, Joanna Browne had confirmed Alexa's story. Her husband's death opened up the floodgates, and the minister's wife told the police a long and twisted tale of violence and religion gone awry. The death of the patriarch of the Church of the Blessed Lamb impacted Caleb and his friends as well. They thought

Reverend Browne was invincible and had followed him without question. When he died, Caleb and two of the other young men crumbled, and a larger story emerged.

Alexa learned the details when Corporal Branche and Trooper Taylor visited one evening. When they arrived at the scheduled time, she ushered them into her parents' living room where Reese was waiting.

"Ranger Michaels." The corporal shook Reese's hand. He turned to Alexa, "With everything that you have been through, we thought you deserved to know the entire story. Through interviews with Mrs. Browne and the men in custody, we've been able to piece together most of it."

Trooper Taylor smiled. "There is some good news. It's possible that you won't have to testify in any court proceedings. It looks like most of these guys are going to plead out. And, they've all been talking." The trooper began the story.

"It was Reverend Browne, not Gabriel, who killed Elizabeth Nelson. And, she was not the only young woman that the fanatical preacher murdered. It started with his daughter, Rebecca, who had chafed against her strict religious upbringing and rebelled by running with a wild crowd of teens. When she got pregnant, Rebecca went to Maryland for an abortion rather than face her father with her pregnancy.

"Somehow, the reverend learned of Rebecca's abortion. In a rage at his daughter's sin and disobedience, he killed her in front of his wife and son. The family buried Rebecca's body in a field and invented a story about Rebecca moving away to get married."

Alexa thought of all the fond stories that Caleb had told about his sister. How horrible that he had watched his father murder Rebecca.

"The minister killed at least two other young women in the Church of the Blessed Lamb when similar transgressions came to light. The congregation's fanatic hatred of abortion and cult-like reverence for their spiritual leader provided him with cover for his actions.

"A few years ago, Reverend Browne took his campaign against the evils of the godless, modern world one step further. He linked up with a southern militia movement that had been trying to expand northward. This group, called the Army of Judah, was readying for the Armageddon that they believe is coming in a battle between the righteous true Christian believers and the godless society currently in control of the U.S. government.

"The reverend assembled a branch of the militia and recruited Caleb and his three best friends to join. Because of his experience in the army, Joel became one of Reverend Browne's key lieutenants. Caleb took on the role of quartermaster and used his sporting goods business to arm the troops. He also used his so-called business trips to maintain contact with the southern branch of the Army of the Judah."

"All those trips to Atlanta. I never suspected." Alexa whispered.

"Why would you?" Reese took her hand.

Corporal Branche turned to Elizabeth Nelson's murder. "One of Elizabeth's friends from Portland surfaced when the national news broke the Abortion Killers story. You may have seen her interviews on several cable networks." His scorn was palpable. "From phone conversations and emails from Elizabeth, she was able to fill in some missing pieces.

"When Elizabeth Nelson met Gabriel at a bar in Mechanicsburg, she knew nothing about his secret life. She fell in love with a beautiful man who created elegant furniture and made her laugh.

"After a while, Elizabeth had noticed some disturbing things about Gabriel. He started to reveal a life view that was much more conservative than she had realized. Even more concerning, Gabriel erupted into angry outbursts that hinted at an undercurrent of violence. As she got to know Gabriel better, Elizabeth first became disenchanted, and then frightened.

"When she learned that she was pregnant, Elizabeth decided to end her relationship with Gabriel. A few days before Elizabeth came into the clinic for the abortion procedure, she broke up with Gabriel and told him she was leaving Carlisle. Then, her boss at Technostorm convinced her to stay in the area until she completed her current project."

"So, what she told Doc Crowe was true." Alexa said.

"Yes. Gabriel confessed the rest. He was distraught about Elizabeth's move back to Portland. One day in early October, an acquaintance mentioned that she was still in the area. Gabriel went to Beth's place, determined to win her back.

"Elizabeth's mistake was to let him into her apartment. While there, Gabriel spotted some papers with instructions concerning her abortion procedure at the women's clinic."

In an animated voice, Trooper Taylor took up the narrative. "Gabriel went ballistic. When she admitted to the abortion, he struck Elizabeth, knocking her out. Gabriel panicked. He carried her to his pick-up and drove to Kingdom Lodge. He called his best friends for advice, and soon Reverend Browne became involved. The minister told Gabriel that Elizabeth had pay for her sins, but Gabriel refused.

"Elizabeth awoke during the heated debate among the five men. Still groggy, she tried to flee, but was no match for Reverend Browne. The minister strangled Elizabeth before Gabriel could intervene. He instructed Gabriel and Daniel to take her body as far away as possible and get rid of it. As dawn was breaking, the two of them left Perry County to dispose of her corpse. They chose the Michaux Forest because their militia had passed that way a few weeks earlier."

"Elizabeth's murder precipitated the chain of subsequent events," Corporal Branche spoke in a pedantic tone. "Reverend Browne's hatred of the Cumberland Clinic rose to a new level. He told the militia that God had spoken to him and decreed that the abortion doctors must be eliminated. He ordered Caleb and Daniel to send the threatening notes. He assigned Joel, the sharpshooter, the task of killing Doctor Crowe."

His voice softened and he gave Alexa a look of sympathy. "When Caleb learned that you worked at the clinic, he was mortified. Reverend Browne was enraged to find that his only son had been involved with a 'baby killer'. To save you, Caleb came up with the plan to convert you to their cause. When you spurned salvation and walked out of the lodge, Reverend Browne went on a rampage. He commanded Caleb, Gabriel, Daniel, and Joel to add you to the clinic hit list."

Alexa jammed a balled fist against her mouth. Caleb had tried to save her.

Trooper Taylor apologized. "We know that this is hard for you to hear."

"No, go ahead. I want to hear it all."

"Joel made the first attempt to carry out Reverend Browne's order. In the poor light of the clinic parking lot, he mistook Emily Baxter for you. In a panic, Caleb came to warn you on Thanksgiving Day, but he says that your family threw him out. Unbeknownst to Caleb, his father had already sent Daniel and Gabriel to your cabin, where they planned to wait inside and grab you when you came home. An ancient window screen foiled their plan, and they left.

"When your family turned Caleb away on Thanksgiving, that humiliation was the final straw. He decided that you deserved whatever happened."

Alexa stifled a cry of distress. "Is there more?" Reese put his arm around her.

"One last thing." The trooper gazed steadily at Alexa as he finished. "The night that you passed Caleb and his friends in the van at his sporting goods store—it was a spur of the moment decision to launch an all-out assault. When they couldn't run your car off the road, they backed off and then decided to confront you at the cabin."

Alexa closed her parents' front door behind Trooper Taylor and Corporal Branche. She came back into the living room and plopped down on the couch next to Reese. Scout snoozed on an armchair near the fireplace.

Alexa exclaimed, "With each new piece of information that comes out, this story gets stranger. In one way, I feel sorry for Caleb. His father fed him that twisted version of religion for his entire life."

"It's hard to believe that one man could spawn such a culture of hatred and violence," agreed Reese. "But, I wouldn't let Caleb off so easily. He and his buddies nearly killed you."

"You're right. There's no excuse for what they did. But, I got off easy. Nothing will bring back Elizabeth and Emily or the other girls who were killed."

The lights from the corner Christmas tree cast a soft glow. Alexa leaned back against Reese and sighed. Then she grinned and said, "Now that this madness is over, we may find that we have nothing in common anymore."

"I'll take that chance," Reese replied. Then, he kissed her.

Epilogue

Elizabeth Nelson's parents took her body home to Oregon for burial, but Alexa decided to have a private memorial for the girl she had found lying dead under the mountain laurel. She chose the Babes' memorial as the place to remember Elizabeth. She also wanted to honor Emily Baxter, who had been the most innocent victim in all this violence.

Although she'd never known Elizabeth, Alexa felt an inexplicable kinship with the woman. Alexa would always bear the burden of knowing that Emily Baxter had died in her place. Alexa decided to walk to the Babes' sign in a personal pilgrimage.

This last day of December was clear and cold, even though there had been a dusting of snow in the early morning. With Scout by her side, Alexa walked through the cathedral of pines. The pine needles were dry beneath her feet since the arching expanse of tall trees prevented all but the heaviest snow from reaching the forest floor. As they walked, the English mastiff drew closer to Alexa's side.

"It is so nice to have you home with me, buddy," she said patting Scout's head. "I'm glad you're back in top shape." The dog's wound had healed completely.

As she made her way through the sighing pines, Alexa reflected on the weeks since she had shot Reverend Browne. She had experienced many sleepless nights, but she didn't regret pulling the trigger. She had done what was necessary to survive. She hated killing another human being—even in self-defense—and hoped that she would never be put in such a situation again. But Reverend Browne would not have hesitated to strangle her just as he had those other women. Alexa was at peace with what she had done.

She brought her attention back to the present. She and Scout had reached the Babes in the Woods memorial. The marker was decorated with flags and ribbons from people, who nearly a century later, still honored the three girls who had been murdered by their father.

Alexa leaned forward to place a bouquet of white roses on the snowy ground at the foot of the marker. Scout whined and lay down with his nose touching the flowers. Alexa spoke aloud in the quiet forest, "Rest in peace, Elizabeth. Rest in peace, Emily." After a moment, she added, "Rest in peace, Dewilla, Cordelia, and Norma."

The waning afternoon light filtered softly through the pines turning the snow-covered ground luminous. It was a beautiful winter afternoon, one that Elizabeth and Emily would never see.

A tear rolled down her cheek as Alexa contemplated the murder of the two young women. Everything she had heard about Elizabeth Nelson spoke of a young woman full of life and promise. Emily Baxter was a wonderful mother whose young family would never see her again. Alexa had been lucky to escape from Reverend Browne's reign of violence and vowed to honor these two women by living the best life she possibly could.

In many ways, this little ceremony was a way to mourn her own loss. In the space of a few weeks, Alexa had twice escaped death, the second time by killing Reverend Browne. As part of this horrific experience, she had overcome some difficult challenges. Alexa felt as if she had been knocked down by evil and stood back up a different person, hopefully wiser but certainly less trusting of the world. She acknowledged, with some regret, that the old Alexa was gone. She would never be quite the same again.

When the sun kissed the tops of the giant pines, Alexa knew the light would soon fade. She drew her private observance to a close by speaking the words engraved on the Babes' gravestone. She had memorized them when she was ten.

"Babes in the Woods.
Sleep tender blossoms folded so close
In slumber which broken shall be
By His gentle voice whispering low
Little Children Come Unto Me"

Placing her hand on Scout's collar, Alexa wiped away her tears. She leaned over to hug the mastiff and then straightened her shoulders. "Come on, buddy. Let's go home and get ready for the New Year. Reese is waiting for us."

As Alexa entered the cathedral of trees, a gust of wind whipped the pine boughs, sending puffs of snow floating into the clear air. A last ray of sun illuminated the spiraling crystals as they danced like dervishes over the white roses scattered on the ground.

Afterword

This is a work of fiction and my characters are drawn from my imagination. Any resemblance to actual people is purely coincidental.

Some of my historical references are based in fact. The Babes in the Woods were found dead in Cumberland County, PA. This region was also a key route for the Underground Railroad. The Confederates reached Carlisle and Chambersburg during the Civil War. However, everything that takes place in a historical context in this work is fictionalized.

The words from the Babes' gravestone can be found in Westminster Cemetery near Carlisle, PA. The headstone was erected by the local American Legion and others from the community, many months after the children were laid to rest. Some newspaper accounts indicate that the words are taken from a poem by Jean Lawrence of Sacramento, CA, written while police were trying to identify the bodies of the three dead girls found in the forest.

Some of the places in this novel are also real. However, many of the specific places exist only on the pages of this book. The Cumberland Clinic is not an actual medical facility. However, many brave men and women across the nation risk danger every day to perform legal abortions to women in need.

Acknowledgments

I want to thank my early reviewers for their help and advice on this manuscript: the Knowltons, the Kuehns, and Kelly Wachtman. And, of course, the crew at Sunbury Press. I also want to thank Trooper Jessica Williams of Troop H, Carlisle Barracks, for help in clarifying some state police responsibilities and procedures.

About the Author

Sherry Knowlton (nee Rothenberger) was born and raised in Chambersburg, PA, where she developed a lifelong passion for books. She was that kid who would sneak a flashlight to bed at night so she could read beneath the covers. All the local librarians knew her by name.

Sherry launched her writing career with a mimeographed elementary school newsletter and went on to write and edit for her high school and college newspapers. Since then, Sherry's creative and technical writing has run the gamut from poetry, essays, and short stories to environmental newsletters, policy papers, regulations, and grant proposals. **Dead of Autumn** is her first novel.

Sherry spent much of her early career in state government, working primarily with social and human services programs, including services for abused children, rape crisis, domestic violence, and family planning. In the 1990s, she served as the Deputy Secretary for Medical Assistance in the Commonwealth of Pennsylvania. The latter part of Sherry's career has focused on the field of Medicaid managed care. Now retired from executive positions in the health insurance industry, Sherry runs her own health care consulting business.

Sherry has a B.A. in English and psychology from Dickinson College in Carlisle, PA.

Sherry and her husband, Mike, began their journey together in the days of peace and music when they traversed the country in a hippie van. Running out of money several months into the trip, Sherry waitressed the night shift at a cowboy hangout in Jackson Hole, Wyoming and Mike washed dishes in a bakery. Undeterred, they embraced the travel experience and continue to explore far-flung places around the globe. Sherry and Mike have one son, Josh, a craft brewer in upstate New York.

Sherry lives in the mountains of South Central Pennsylvania, only a short distance from the Babes in the Woods memorial.